the
DISHONEST MISS TAKE

the
DISHONEST
MISS TAKE

a novel

Faye Murphy

bhc press

Livonia, Michigan

The Dishonest Miss Take
Copyright © 2024 Faye Murphy

All rights reserved. No part of this publication may be reproduced, distributed, or transmitted in any form or by any means, including photocopying, recording, or other electronic or mechanical methods, without the prior written permission of the publisher, except in the case of brief quotations embodied in critical reviews and certain other noncommercial uses permitted by copyright law. For permission requests, please write to the publisher.

This book is a work of fiction. The characters, incidents, and dialogue are drawn from the author's imagination and are not to be construed as real. Any resemblance to actual events or persons, living or dead, is entirely coincidental.

Published by BHC Press

Library of Congress Control Number: 2023946088

ISBN: 978-1-64397-394-4 (Hardcover)
ISBN: 978-1-64397-395-1 (Softcover)
ISBN: 978-1-64397-396-8 (Ebook)

For information, write:
BHC Press
885 Penniman #5505
Plymouth, MI 48170

Visit the publisher:
www.bhcpress.com

for George

the DISHONEST MISS TAKE

Chapter 1

"How was the trip? Minus the false imprisonment, of course."

"Long," I replied, giving my answer to the hideous peony wallpaper. Dan said it added character. I said it encouraged vandalism.

I dumped my bag where it was most likely to trip someone up and tracked down the source of the voice. Dan was in the kitchen, frantically poking the coal fire inside the stove, trying to get it hot enough to burn whatever he was cooking for the boarders that day. I leant against the doorframe and admired how the glow from the paraffin lamp lit up the beads of sweat on his forehead. As usual, Dan stood on the edge of his sanity, and as usual, I stood behind him, hands out, waiting to push.

"Got any jobs for me?" I asked.

Dan wiped his hand across his forehead, leaving a large smear of coal I decided not to point out. "A few hours ago, you were in jail."

"And now I'm ready to reenter society as a respectable citizen. Help me slot back into place as a well-oiled cog in the machine."

"You know I don't actually work for you, right?"

I raised an eyebrow. Dan was my secretary in all but wage.

He sighed. "I don't have any jobs for you."

"I don't believe that. I was gone a month; surely someone has picked up an ailment."

He stirred the pot hopefully, as though he could resurrect the vegetables. "They don't want you."

"Because of the arrest? I was acquitted."

He picked up a copy of the parish news and threw it towards me. It fell open at the regular gossip column by Maureen Butterswatch, the busiest busybody in Dippenwick. "The Apple Never Falls Far from the Tree: Charges Against Miss Take Dropped Under Mysterious Circumstances," the heading read. I scanned the rest of the article and then tossed it into Dan's pot. He spluttered indignantly as he fished it out with a spoon.

If it had been anyone else, they would have called it a tragic accident, as though people often accidentally stabbed themselves multiple times. But I was there, suspiciously sinking my career to new depths in exchange for vast amounts of money. I should have known it would end badly. No wealth was worth Lord Balthasar Forgo's conversation. His fascinating name was ruined by a character so dull, his biographer would be better off leaving it at the title page. He had the amazing ability to inspire complete apathy in any listener. As soon as he opened his mouth to embark upon yet another wearisome speech on the merits of cartography, my eyes would start to droop. Surely any would-be murderers would be sapped of strength the moment they entered his presence. The police disagreed. After all, I was a notorious ex-villain, known by the unfortunate alias "Miss Take." Who knew what my depraved mind was capable of?

"I guess I'll have to look beyond Dippenwick then. That's a real shame. I had good clients here."

Dan pulled a face. "I don't think popping over to the next hamlet will help you get away from that story. It got picked up by *The Times*."

Typical. The first well-written article Maureen managed, and it was slagging me off.

"Now might be a good time to emigrate," Dan said seriously.

As though that was an option. "International cooperation is not exactly at an all-time high, but I expect they would scrounge up some diplomacy if it came to extraditing me: the infamous Clara Blakely. Besides, England is my home, even if it is rotten to the core."

Dan sampled his stew and gagged. "What are you going to do then?"

"First, I'm going to arrange a little accident for Maureen. I don't think she'll be so dismissive of my services when her leg is broken."

Dan sighed wearily.

"Then, I'm going to track down the assassin who killed Forgo and get them to confess to the press, thereby clearing my name."

"Forgo was killed by an assassin?"

"I was as surprised as you."

I had not expected to be led to the jail's front desk to find a figure clad entirely in black leather perched on the windowsill. A mask covered their nose and mouth, and the rest of their face was shrouded in the shadow of an oversized hood. A flash of lightning had lit up the room. I blinked and the figure was gone, the rain blowing through the open window the only sign they were ever there at all.

An assassin from the Finishing School, that's what the constable said. Apparently, they had taken responsibility for Forgo's murder. They'd showed him the murder weapon. He'd examined it in great detail when it was pressed against his Adam's apple. I had never heard of an assassin claiming responsibility for a murder before, but neither had I ever heard of an assassin working in Dorset. It was enough to make me doubt their credentials, but they had jumped out of a window. Who else did that?

Dan was watching me with the misplaced concern he had wasted so much of his time with over the course of our friendship. "And your great plan is to find this clearly competent killer and sweet-talk them into a confession?"

"Something like that."

He picked up a pile of linen from the ironing board, fumbled his way into the hall, tripped over my bag, and set off up the rickety stairs. I followed him, stepping over everything he dropped.

"Has it occurred to you that this might blow over in a year or two?" he asked as he knocked on Mrs Winow's door.

We waited as she frantically tried to hide the cat she knew was not permitted in the property.

"I can't afford to spend the next year or two with no clients," I said. "I need to spend it with lots of well-paying clients so I can settle my debts and look forward to an early retirement. Plus, I know how these things can stick. These last four years I have been nothing short of angelic. But thanks to the gossip columns, my reputation remains in tatters."

"Fine. I know a lost cause when I see one. You never have valued my opinion before, why would you start now?"

"Of course I value your opinion. Do you think I stay for your delightful personality?"

"Speaking of delightful personalities, Arthur Todd paid a visit. He wants you to drop round the Brigade at your earliest opportunity."

I should have stayed in jail. The Hero Brigade was the worst, and the worst of the Brigade was the Community Squadron. It was where I had to carry out my ten-thousand hours of community service in a uniform that made me look like I was late to perform at a burlesque. It was also full of the most insufferable bastards, and of these bastards, Arthur Todd was the worst.

Engraved above the entrance to the hulking clubhouse, that somehow reminded me of Arthur's face, was: Protection Is Our Function. I was supposed to be happy that I had a "function," a use to which society could put me. It could have been worse. "Function" was the term that had caught on, but other names I had heard directed at people like me included "freak," "monster," "devil"; stuff like that. My personal favourite was "Thames baby." It made it sound like my parents had dunked me in the river as a newborn. If there was any evidence that near-drowning increased your chance of getting a function, they would have. They were good at many things, but consideration for my wellbeing was not one of them.

I took a moment to gather my thoughts and hair. Putting it in a bun always threw Arthur. He was scared of necks. The lump in question was in his office, growing out of his seat like a nasty spot of mould. The utilitarian room was gloomy, mostly because there was only one window and Arthur blocked it when he stood up. He made a show of pulling my chair out for me, turning the simple task of sitting down into a three-act farce. I gifted him one of the dazzling smiles I handed out like free samples.

"Now, Miss Blakely. I won't beat around the bush, so to speak."

I waited patiently.

He opened his mouth, then closed it again. He swallowed. "Did I offer you tea? Would you like tea?"

"No, thank you," I replied sweetly.

He was staring at my neck like it might transform into a snake and strangle him. There was only so much entertainment one could draw from a man floundering out of his depth. I let my eyes drift to the portrait behind his desk. Only people with heads larger than their hats had portraits of themselves on display in their own rooms. It showed Arthur gesturing to the Crystal Palace with his cane, that great waste of wealth constructed as part of the Great Exhibition of the Works of Functionables of All Nations. That had been ten years ago. Why, then, did Arthur look twenty years younger in the painting? The last decade must have been rough on him.

"Right," he stammered. "To business. This business with the… How shall we put it?"

"Prison?"

"Yes, that. It is a rather bad business. You understand?"

"I was falsely accused. It was a matter of wrong time, wrong place. The police were very apologetic."

"But this article printed in *The Times* said the circumstances of your release were…well, suspicious."

"I guarantee the reporter was mistaken." I leant forward and internalised a flinch when his eyes dipped south. "You know me, sir. Violence disgusts me. All I want is to help people however I can."

"I know, Miss Blakely. But you must think about how this looks. People may not want someone in your…circumstances roaming the streets at night under the guise of protecting them."

Would they kick me off the Squad? I sent a silent prayer to whatever god had a light workload that day that they would kick me off the Squad.

"Please, sir," I said, "don't take me off the Squad. It means so much to me."

"I may not have a choice."

I glanced down at my hands, sure I would start giggling if I looked at his pitiful face for a second longer.

"I don't want to make things difficult for you," I said meekly. "If you must, you must."

"I won't do anything yet."

Damn.

"I'll keep you on patrol for now, see if we get any backlash."

I focused on his receding hairline to cheer myself up. "Thank you, sir. I'm being called to business in London soon."

He frowned. "I hear Dirt Man's attacks have become more frequent. You should be careful."

Be careful? What was the alternative? Recklessly run around London calling Dirt Man a "lily-livered ratbag" and waiting to get brutally murdered by the latest evil stalking the streets? I quite enjoyed breathing, and I was inclined to keep doing it.

"I'll let London headquarters know you are coming and explain the situation. I doubt they will give you any trouble after my report on your character."

Poor, naïve Arthur. All it had taken was a few sniffles and a promise of repentance for him to believe that, deep down, I was a good person. It was pathetic.

He stood and sauntered to the window overlooking Dippenwick's main street, or in other words, only street. It was a village renowned for absolutely nothing. My temporary residency in it was the closest it would ever get to fame. Arthur clasped his hands in front of his stomach and rocked backwards on his heels. I prepared myself for what I knew was coming.

"I have previously made you aware of my affections," he began.

It was a strong start, better than his last proposal. I wondered if he had been practicing on some other poor, luckless girl. "And I am so thankful for your kindness to me."

"I hope you won't think I am overstepping my place if I say that a woman of your—and I mean no disrespect—age and meagre earnings should consider settling down with a family."

His teeth were more brown than yellow in some places. They were bound to fall out soon.

"I am sure I would be able to convince the court to shorten your sentence should you decide to follow your womanly calling."

"That is most kind of you," I replied. "You are so unlike other men. Many would be embittered by my rejection of their advances, but you bear it with such fortitude, never continuing to pursue or harass me in any way."

He cleared his throat awkwardly. "Well, it is the gentlemanly thing to do."

"I know that one day you will find a very special wife, one who is not married to her work as I am. I should take my leave." I stood, smoothing down the folds of my ridiculous skirt. Whoever was setting this trend needed to sit down with an architect. If they got any wider, England would need to rethink its infrastructure.

Arthur hurried to the door to open it for me. Clearly, a door handle was too technical for me to manage.

"And Arthur..."

He blushed at the use of his first name.

"I do not mean to pry, but I can feel some discomfort emanating from your heart. You might want to get it checked."

He paled.

"Until next time," I said with a smile.

There was no problem with his heart, but if he worried enough, he might cause one.

Chapter 2

The Finishing School could be seen from Buckingham Palace, probably to keep the latest royal in check. For over a century, it had been the most prestigious school of assassins in the country. I couldn't even name any alumni; that's how good they were.

I walked through the tall, spiked gates, bordered by stone lions chewing on skulls, to the large and imposing building. Its walls were a dirty grey, stained by the factories that insisted on seeing the city as a fish that needed smoking. People dressed in black traipsed in and out of the huge double doors, carrying books, lunchboxes, and swords. They paid me no mind, even though I had to be the brightest colour on campus. As I reached the door, I adjusted my travelling cloak and put on a smile. I had charmed my way through more threatening situations than this.

The door swept closed behind me, plunging me into darkness. I could feel the grandness of the hall, even if I could not see it. After my eyes had finally adjusted, I located the receptionist and tiptoed across the tiled floor as quietly as I could, but it still sounded like I was stomping in hobnail boots. The woman was tiny and completely swamped by a large woollen cloak. It may have been the end of summer for the rest of the country, but under this roof, life was eternally frigid. She scratched away at a piece of parchment with an expensive raven-feathered quill. Everyone knew the school was behind the times, but would a fountain pen be such a terrible betrayal of the aesthetic?

I cleared my throat. She glanced up at me and then went back to writing.

"May I help you?" She made it sound like I was far beyond help.

"I'm looking for an assassin."

"If you want to hire one, you need to go through the proper channels. Sit in a public house looking moody, or loudly proclaim your problems in a narrow alleyway in the dead of night. An assassin will approach you."

"I don't want anyone murdered. I want to talk to an assassin. A specific one, mind you. They're not really my type."

She looked at me again, squinting either in suspicion or because she was trying to see me.

"Honey, avenging a loved one who has been killed by an assassin won't bring them back. Going after the assassin is like blaming the taxman for the rise in taxes. You want my advice? Move on with your life and try not to make any enemies." She went back to her scribbling.

"I am not after revenge."

"That's what they all say."

"It was my employer who was killed. It's a relief, trust me."

"If you want to show your appreciation, you can make a donation to the school."

Talking to her was like sanding a brick with my thumbnail. "Is there any way you could arrange a meeting between me and this assassin? It is terribly important."

"Even if I wanted to help, the records are sealed. I have no way of knowing who's out killing whom."

"Is there someone else who can help me?"

"Even Her Royal Majesty doesn't have access to those records."

This was a waste of my time. I would have been better off sprawling myself across her desk and confessing my problems to the rafters. I thanked her, which she ignored, and clomped back the way I had come. After fumbling around in the dark, I found the brass handle and threw open the door, almost knocking over someone balancing a mace on top of a pile of textbooks. I held the door for them, then walked out into the daylight.

Even though I had barely been inside a few minutes, it felt like I was emerging from hibernation. Seagulls wheeled and dived in a sky of white clouds, the cobbled courtyard sparkled from last night's rain, and none of this mattered because I was no step closer to getting my life back. I could feel the building mocking me for thinking I could ever navigate its excessively complicated administration.

I really wished I could whine to Dan about the slipping standards in customer service, but getting the next stagecoach back to Dippenwick felt like giving up, and I was not in a giving up sort of mood. There remained one avenue left open to me. It was what Dan would call a "terrible idea," but what did I have to lose? My career was on its last legs now, anyway, and my golden years were behind me. I was nearly twenty: practically a pensioner.

I stalked away from the school, refusing to look back at its smug façade, and headed for Westminster, which was always a popular pressure point for the heavy hand of the law. It wasn't long before I found a policeman beating someone up. I lingered until he had finished, then waved him over.

"You want to report an offence?" he asked gruffly.

"Yes. I killed Sir Forgo." I nodded to the cuffs dangling from his belt and held out my hands politely.

London cells were not as nice as the ones in rural police stations. I even had to share. He introduced himself as William but said that since he could not read his birth certificate, I should not hold him to that. He asked me what I was in for, so I told him they thought I had killed a noble. He was so impressed, I had to backtrack and clarify that I barely had the wrist strength to shake someone's hand, let alone run their heart through with a dagger.

William explained that he was in for trespassing, or as he called it, "demonstrating against the oppressive ownership laws that separate the people from the land." This was not his first time in jail.

"It's the only platform available for a fella like me. Got to get my voice heard somehow."

I nodded sympathetically, wishing his voice was currently being heard by someone else.

"These landowner types are buying up everything around here. Just last year, they closed Mundmere Common. That's common land, that is. They have no right to close it. They say it's for conservation, but when I demand to see the evidence explaining how the commoners are damaging the wildlife, they have nothing to give me. What they don't get is that these green spaces they don't like us walking in are important for our mental health. Just you wait: in a few years, they'll have mass melancholia on their hands."

To think, I could have been on a boat to America if I had listened to Dan. It could have capsized and still have been more fun than this conversation.

"Have you had any luck with the court yet?" I asked politely.

He drew in breath, ready for his next recital. Then, he let the breath back out, his eyes fixed on a point over my shoulder.

"You wanted my attention. You have it."

I jumped at the unexpected voice. A figure was standing on the other side of the bars, loitering in shadow. In the gloom, I could just make out an oversized hood and black mask. The smell of leather was unmistakable.

"You're the assassin? The one who killed Forgo?" I asked.

"Actually, according to your arrest record, you killed Forgo." Her voice was rough, dry, and quite clearly pissed off.

"I truly am sorry," I said with a dash of sincerity, "but thank you for coming on such short notice."

She shrugged. "I was in the area."

I noticed something red dripping from her gloved hands. I assumed the blood was not hers.

"Do you have a thing for prison decor?" she asked.

I shook my head.

"A death wish, perhaps?"

"No."

"Then why are you so keen to take the fall for a murder you did not commit?"

"Look, I'll be straight with you. I know you were just doing your job murdering Forgo and I was just doing mine when I got wrapped up in it. Despite what you told the police, the press think I did it, and that's terrible for someone in my profession. I was hoping you could talk to them, sort this whole thing out."

"No."

"You wouldn't even have to give your name. I'm sure your…presence would be convincing enough."

"I owe you nothing. The only reason you aren't swinging from a noose right now is because I need Forgo's death officially recorded as the work of an assassin."

"Why?" I asked, genuinely curious.

"It's a small technicality that's really none of your concern."

I reminded myself that bars wouldn't protect me from retaliation if I punched her in the face.

"Could you at least tell me who ordered the hit so I can ask them to go public?" I pleaded.

"That would be a breach of client confidentiality."

"People order assassinations all the time. It's no big deal."

"Privacy is integral to maintaining any level of freedom in this state. Everyone should have the right to kill and be killed."

"But accountability is important too," William put in. "It's only through holding those in power to account that we can have the freedom you talk about."

I gave William a smile, thankful that someone had my back, even if they wanted to use it as somewhere to plant a flag. But he wasn't the one I was interested in talking to at the moment. I turned back to the assassin, ignoring him.

"Just tell them he cheated on his wife," the assassin said. "That's usually why these things happen."

"He didn't have a wife. She died of the plague years back."

"Maybe his kids wanted his inheritance."

"Plague got them too."

"How bad was the hygiene in that castle? Who's set to inherit?"

"Some second cousin twice removed who has as much ambition as a tadpole in a puddle."

"Forgo didn't have a brother?"

"No."

"Sister?"

"No."

"Friend?"

"No. Except for his extensive map collection, he barely had a life at all."

She hummed thoughtfully. "It's a true mystery. Are we done, then?"

"No." I folded my arms. "You're going to have to kill me because I'm not going to stop saying I killed Forgo."

"You would rather die than suffer a small unproven smear on your name?"

"Gossip can have disastrous effects for someone in my situation."

"And what situation would that be?"

It did not sound like she was mocking me. Could it be possible she had no idea who I was? Maybe assassins did not have access to the various rags that liked to denounce me whenever they remembered my unfortunate existence.

"Due to a misled youth and some terrible parenting, I am currently paying a rather large fine," I said. "Without my clients, I will end up in debtors' prison."

It was not a lie. My function gave me limited options when it came to a career. I relied on clients with deep pockets and low pain tolerances. They were, by default, weak and frightened, and would not want to employ someone they thought might stab them in their sleep. If I lost what was left of my good name, I lost everything.

She was quiet. She might have been studying me. It was hard to tell with the hood.

"You have a function," she said finally.

I nodded. "I'm a pain reliever."

She lapsed back into silence. I waited patiently.

"A colleague I work with has sprained his wrist. If you take his pain until it's healed, I'll pass your name around the network. There's a certain degree of risk in our line of work, so I can guarantee a steady stream of clients, and our pay is good enough for you to charge a high rate."

I doubted they would pay me as much as I was earning before, but if this was what I had to do to keep the dialogue open, so be it. Bargains were easier to strike without bars.

"Deal," I said.

"Let's go then."

She turned and was lost immediately to shadow.

"Aren't you forgetting something?" I called to the darkness.

"What?" the darkness called back.

"I'm in a cell."

Stepping back into the light, she pulled two slim slips of metal from her pocket and slotted them into the lock. It clicked open.

"Will they mind if I just walk out of here?" I asked.

"I told the police you would be leaving today."

Of course she did, but they probably thought she meant in a body bag.

"Were you raised in a barn?" William yelled as I followed her out. "Shut the door!"

I turned back. "Actually, I was raised in a mansion. Good luck with the revolution."

I closed the door with a little more force than was needed. My niceness reserves were running low.

Unfortunately, it became evident I would not be restocking any time soon. The assassin took me around the corner to a public house called the Cup of Lead Poisoning. It was clearly a popular spot with students. A woman had her head buried in a tome twice the size of her, and a group of young musicians were heckling an older man on stage about his rhyming couplets. There were plenty of assassins too. I made sure I stayed right behind mine so I did not lose her in the crowd.

She led me to a table in the corner where another assassin was sitting.

"Busy," he said without looking up.

"I need a word," my assassin replied.

"Can't you see I'm drowning my pain?" he said. "I made the mistake of using a throwing star earlier. I'm in agony."

"This is… What was your name again?" my assassin asked impatiently.

"Clara Blakely," I answered courteously.

My assassin said bluntly, "She's a pain reliever."

The new assassin looked up at me with sudden interest. He was not wearing a mask, presumably because he was drinking. His hair was shoulder length and greasy. A scar ran from just below his eye to the top of his mouth.

"Not *the* Clara Blakely, daughter of Marie and Wyatt Blakely?" he asked.

"Guilty," I said with a small smile.

Perhaps they wore masks so no one could see their jaws drop. It was not especially frightening to see him so completely starstruck. He gestured quickly to a chair. I perched carefully. Maybe it was just my paranoia, but I felt vaguely uncomfortable sharing a table with two assassins.

"Should the name Blakely mean anything to me?" my assassin asked.

"I forget you were raised under a rock," he replied. "The Blakelys were the Faceless Family, the most notorious criminals in London. Dirt Man may have the edge on victims, but the Blakelys did villainy properly."

"You're a criminal?" she asked me sceptically.

"My parents were the criminals, and their fame was short lived," I said cautiously. You never knew how people would react. One time, I had been pelted with fruit.

The man shook his head in awe. "I can't believe I'm sitting with Clara Blakely. I had your parents' wanted poster on my wall as a kid."

The barman approached with two tankards.

"I'll put it on your tab," he told my assassin. How he could recognise her was beyond me.

She pushed one towards her friend and one to me. It seemed suspicious she was not drinking. It was a very public place to be killed, but perhaps students stuck together when it came to crime.

"It's not poisoned," she said.

That was exactly what someone who had poisoned my drink would say.

The other assassin laughed. "Don't worry. If there was a contract on you, she wouldn't have brought you here to meet me. I might steal the reward for myself."

That was good to know. I took a drink, mainly because I was distracted, not because I had decided it was safe. If it was poisoned, it was with expensive stuff. The ale was so watered-down, you would not be able to hide piss in it.

"How exactly does your function work?" the new assassin asked.

Did he expect me to accomplish what scientists had failed to do for sixty years and explain functions? After decades of prodding us in the name of science, all they knew was the people who could walk through walls, animals that could shoot fire from their paws, and plants that could fly had been somehow mutated by all the new and exciting chemicals they were pumping into land, water, and air.

Even this vague conclusion was enough to bring Britain to its scabby little knees back in the day. People left the cities if they could; went on strike if they couldn't. Factories closed, stockpiles of chemicals no one would touch started to rot, and functionables were treated like the plague. It was John Blythwood who levered the metaphorical train of progress back onto the tracks. These creatures, he said, were not abominations with corrupted souls. They were improvements. Their godlike abilities were proof that industrialisation was part of God's plan. As essential cogs in the machine, they would allow us to work faster, longer, and better. It was Blythwood who coined the term "function." No one seemed to mind he owned fifteen factories that were on the brink of collapse.

"I take pain, not injuries," I explained. Imagine the fortune I could have amassed if I was a healer. "Your wrist will still have to heal naturally, but it will be a more pleasant experience. Of course, there are risks involved. Having an injury without pain can lead to further injury."

He frowned. "You get my pain? You're going to walk around feeling like you have a sprained wrist until it heals?"

"Precisely," I said.

He gave a low whistle.

When I started out, I downplayed the pain I felt, fearing the guilt would drive clients away. However, on this rare occasion, honesty did pay. The more I suffered, the higher I could put my price.

"What's your rate?" he asked.

"Five pounds a week, and I will need regular contact if you wish to remain pain free," I told him.

"Pretty steep, but I guess you deserve it," he said.

He slid a pile of coins towards me. I reached out with my function. I could feel every discomfort on his body: fading bruises, a bit of chaffing, and the constant nag of a sprained wrist. I drew the latter pain to me.

He carefully rotated his wrist. "Wow."

I placed my now stinging one on the table. I had suffered much worse.

"May I ask what happened?" I asked. Show an interest, let them tell their dull story.

"I landed funny after jumping from a window," he said as he continued to prod gently at his wrist.

"Why do you always use windows?" I asked.

He chuckled. "It's one of The Rules."

"The Rules?" I repeated.

He counted them off on his fingers. "Always work at night, don't use doors if it can be avoided, wear a hood even though it obstructs your peripheral vision and leather even though it squeaks in the rain."

"What would you have us wear?" the Forgo assassin asked. "Glittery unitards like the Hero Brigade?"

"It would certainly make the job more exciting," he replied.

I could almost feel her rolling her eyes.

"Got to go," she said, standing.

He shook his head. "Always working."

"You know me," she replied.

"You'll get rickets if you don't drop the mask once in a while," he called after her.

She gave him two fingers as she wound her way through the crowd.

"She's jealous she doesn't have a facial scar like me," he said. "Four years in the school and the most she got was a small bump on her knee from a poorly placed table." He held out his hand. "I'm Quentin Shadow, by the way."

I looked at it with a raised eyebrow. He remembered his sprain and lowered it guiltily.

"Shadow. Is that self-chosen?"

"No. Why?"

"No reason," I said quickly. "Are you allowed to tell me your name?"

"Did Morgan tell you it was forbidden?"

"Who's Morgan?"

He grinned. "The assassin who just left. The whole anonymity thing is so old-fashioned. Nowadays, there's much more networking involved. It's all who you know and meet and greets. We can't very well do that with no names."

Morgan. It was a shame I did not have a face to put to that name. "She did strike me as a little…" rude, aggressive, "traditional."

"She's just antisocial. She could kill a man with naught but a feather, but she won't be the greatest assassin of our generation, because she struggles to connect with people. She comes across as a bit hostile."

I never would have guessed. "Isn't 'hostile' the school's motto?"

"No, it's *Mors Tua Vita Mea*, but I'll admit it can seem a bit unfriendly. The board suffers with inclusivity problems. We're in the first year they let functionables apply."

I was surprised. I had thought the school was against functions, or as they saw it, cheating.

"Of course, I'm hardly likely to list my function under special skills," he continued.

"You have a function?"

"I see dead people."

I stared at him. "Come again?"

"Well, 'people' is a bit misleading. I see the spiritual echo of any living thing that has recently died."

I waited for him to crack a smile, slap me on the back, and tell me he was pulling my leg. He did not.

"Let me get this straight," I said eventually. "You developed the ability to see ghosts and yet decided to embark upon a career where you kill people for money."

He nodded. "The ghosts are never very happy to see me."

"You must have some awkward interactions."

"Yes, although I should clarify, I can only see them. I can't hear them, and they can't hear me, so our conversation is pretty limited. I carry this on me." He pulled a piece of paper from his pocket, which said, ***I'm sorry I killed you,*** followed by a sad face. "But you would be surprised how low literacy levels are, even amongst the upper classes. There's this new thing called 'sign language' which is speaking with your hands. It's great, but I have yet to kill someone who knows it."

This conversation was becoming more like a fever dream with every passing second. I wondered if someone really had slipped something into my drink.

"It will probably be easiest if I come find you for our next appointment," Quentin said, as though he had not just destabilised my views on the afterlife. "I'm a bit all over the place these days. Where are you staying?"

"I don't know. It looked like I was going to spend the night in jail."

"That's always an option, but the bathroom facilities are limited. I would offer you accommodation at the school, but the freshers would probably use you as target practice. I know a hotel nearby. What are your feelings on lice?"

"They build character."

"Great. I'll talk to the manager. I should be able to get you a reduced rate because I helped get his son into further education."

"The Finishing School?" I asked.

"Yeah."

"He must be so proud."

Chapter
3

I was woken by someone calling out on the street. It was hard to tell whether they were being mugged or selling newspapers.

I rolled over and screamed.

"Die quietly, would you!" the person in the next room shouted.

"Sorry," I yelled back once my shock at finding a figure perched on my windowsill had subsided. "Which one are you?"

"Charming," a voice I now knew belonged to Morgan replied.

"It's not my fault you all have the same tailor. What can I do for you?"

She hopped off the sill into the room. I scrambled out of bed, mostly concerned that if she was there to kill me, I was going to die in my Community Squadron uniform. I had been sent on patrol the night before and had been so exhausted that I had fallen right into bed the moment I was back. In Dippenwick, all you had to deal with was the odd cat in a tree. In London, there was usually theft, brawls, and at least one explosion.

"I saw you on patrol last night," Morgan said. "I didn't know you were in the Brigade."

"Community Squadron."

"I can see that."

The paid Brigade got custom uniforms, secret identities, and nicknames like Mr Indestructible and Miss Fortitude. We got a number and a blue unitard that showed all manner of sweat patches. It was made from this special synthetic material manufactured by BW Incorporated: founded by the famous John Blythwood, who never missed an opportunity to reap the financial rewards of his philanthropy. Quick drying, durable, and easily washable, it was also scratchy and lumpy.

Morgan crossed her arms. I could feel a judgemental stare emanating from somewhere inside the hood.

"Which side are you on?"

"Pardon?"

"Your parents were villains, you're no stranger to crime yourself, and now you're on the Hero Brigade?"

"I see you've done your research." I kicked myself for giving her attitude. In my defence, I hated mornings and I hated this line of questioning.

My parents had been born functionables at a time when the persecution was milder and the jobs more varied. They were proof that a function really could change your life. Both had gone from having nothing—no education, no prospects—to having a house and well-paying—if not particularly stable—jobs. John Blythwood himself would have used them as models of his theory if they had not decided to dedicate their rare skills to crime.

My mother was strong. Strong enough to pick up the house and move it if I missed curfew by ten minutes. She liked robbing banks. My father preferred robbing stagecoaches, but he was not opposed to the odd bank now and again. He was fast, especially when running away from my mother. They came to an arrangement which resulted in their marriage. As functions seemed to be inherited, they figured if they had a child, that child could be the most successful villain of the century. Safe to say, I was not quite what they were expecting. I'm of no use on a battlefield. Taking someone's pain and channelling it to someone else requires someone already being injured. Most of the time, that someone was me.

The end was inevitable. My parents had never got along. There was always more arguing than plotting at our pre-heist meetings. But when the hammer came down, it turned out I was the final nail in the coffin of their relationship. The one thing keeping them together was the hope that I would amount to greatness. When I didn't, it all fell apart. Their attempts to sabotage each other backfired, the press got involved, and prison reared its ugly head. I only avoided accompanying them to the hard labour camp because I provided copious amounts of damning evidence on them. In return for my cooperation, I got all my earthly belongings confiscated, a hefty fine, and fifteen years on the Community Squadron.

Plastering on a look of regret, I focused on keeping all traces of resentment out of my voice. "I was born into the villain life. I was too young to know any better when I did those things, but I've changed. I've picked my side now."

It was true, but it was not heroes or villains I chose. I picked capitalism.

I could have sworn Morgan twitched, but without the facial cues, I was finding her impossible to read. She turned back to the window. I assumed that was the end of our strange conversation.

"Breakfast?" she asked suddenly.

"What?"

"Can I buy you breakfast?"

"Can I ask why?"

She shrugged.

"Fine," I conceded. "But I'm taking the stairs."

It was hard to tell if Morgan was embarrassed by me or if she was just a fast walker. She led me to her choice of establishment, with me trailing half a street behind. I was not at all surprised when our destination was a frantic, noisy place with enough tobacco smoke for Morgan to disappear into.

"The stewed figs are good," she said.

"Sounds lovely." Sounded like boiled mush to me.

The waiter arrived, and Morgan ordered two plates of stewed figs and two coffees.

"And don't forget milk," she added, using a tone that suggested if he forgot the milk, she would break his face.

He withdrew with a whimper.

"I don't know why I said it like that," she confessed once he was out of hearing. "I really don't have strong opinions on milk."

She seemed so sad, I had to bite back a laugh.

"I suppose you're used to having to speak forcefully in your line of work," I replied comfortingly.

"Not really. We mainly work amongst the aristocracy, and they're all inbred and soft spoken. Sometimes, they haggle over price, but then they remember you're a trained killer."

I wished they paid the same respect to me.

"Why were you called Miss Take?" she asked suddenly.

I wondered if the table was too wide for me to reach across and stab her with my fork. "I suppose because they assumed, correctly, that I was unmarried and took things that didn't belong to me. I don't think whoever came up with the nickname was trying to be clever."

If I ever found the person responsible for it, their death would be too gruesome even for the gossip columns. My father was nicknamed Mr Swift, my mother Mrs Sturdy. Life wasn't fair.

"Why do you work as a pain reliever if you hate it?" Morgan asked.

"Who said I hate it?"

"You enjoy being in pain for a living?"

"I like to help where I can," I lied.

"As long as you're helping the rich," she said drily.

"The rich do run our country." Like a fairground on fire. "Besides, I like to think my community service evens it out."

The waiter arrived with our food. He put the milk down reverently. I thanked him while Morgan stayed silent. I was starting to guess it was more out of awkwardness than disdain for everyone and everything. With one hand, she reached up and pulled off her mask, but the combination of hood and smoke still obscured her face.

"Why did you become an assassin?" I asked, postponing the moment when I would have to eat the sluglike concoction.

She shrugged. "Because of my parents, I suppose."

"Were they assassins too?"

"No, they were assassinated. It made a big impression on me. An assassin can touch so many lives; not just the people they kill, but all those who are left behind. I guess I just wanted to make a difference."

She impaled a fig on her fork and chewed it thoughtfully. I did the same with a little more decorum.

"These are lovely," I lied.

If the objective was to have their seeds dispersed by animals, figs had done a poor job at market research. They looked weird and tasted bland at best. Morgan seemed to enjoy them though, the psychopath.

She shoved the rest of the fig into her mouth, nearly choking on it.

"What's it like on the Community Squadron?" she asked once she had stopped coughing.

"Considering a career change?"

"Hardly. I don't look good in rubber."

"It's like any other voluntary organisation: a little chaotic, but it has good intentions." Good intentions, lazy overseers, self-righteous volunteers who only did it for the chance to lecture people and occasionally beat them up, and unlike the paid Brigade, no one got a media thrashing when they were a little too handsy in the prevention of crime.

"What's it like in the Finishing School?" I asked.

"Considering a career change?"

"I don't look good in leather," I shot back.

"It's not too different from the other assassin schools, except it's got the prestige. It's basically seven years of tuition fees for a seal."

"The one with the man being impaled by lots of knives?"

"See, even you know it."

It was distinctive but not very imaginative.

"Seven years? You could become a physician in that time," I said.

"Our profession does have parallels with the medical industry. If either of us messes up, there's usually maiming involved."

"I suppose your parents must have been wealthy to leave you with enough to pay for your tuition."

"I let my sister have the fortune," she said dismissively. "I got a scholarship at the school. They didn't notice I had arrived for the interview, which was apparently a good sign."

I tried to imagine giving a fortune away. It was a struggle.

Morgan took a long gulp of coffee. She had barely touched the milk.

"What does your sister do now?" I asked.

"She's a mildly successful novelist. She wrote *My Deranged Murdering Sister*. Completely fictional of course."

"Of course." I sipped my coffee.

"Doesn't your wrist hurt?" Morgan asked suspiciously.

I looked down at the hand holding the teacup.

"It's not real pain, so using it won't make it worse," I explained. "You get used to carrying on."

If I lay in a swoon every time I hurt, I would never get anything done.

"If you can channel pain, why don't you pass it on to someone else?"

"That would hardly be ethical." Or legal. If I was caught doing it, I would get another day in court; something I was keen to avoid. I did occasionally pass it on to strangers, but only when I knew I could make a quick getaway if the accusations started flying or if I was sure they could never believe I would be so devious. I decided to risk it now. She had brought it up, after all. I edged the headache that had been building steadily throughout our breakfast onto her.

"Quentin told me about his function," I said by way of distraction.

"He sees dead people."

"He wasn't messing with me, then. I'm still struggling to understand his life choices."

"I think it makes sense. He gets a little more control if he's the one killing them."

"Do they follow him around?"

"Sometimes. Sometimes they just lurk at the scene of their death."

If Quentin or any of his weird assassin friends ever killed me, I was going to follow him around incessantly. I would cling to life for as long as possible just to annoy him. That sign language he mentioned sounded like a good thing to learn. I only needed to know curse words.

Morgan grabbed her mask and stood abruptly. "I should go. I've got a headache."

I wrinkled my brow in concern. "Would you like me to take it from you? I'm very good at headaches."

"No, it's fine. Breakfast is on me."

Was that how she ended all conversations, or had I made some terrible faux pas? At least there were no awkward goodbyes.

"And Clara…"

I turned in my chair. Morgan was standing in the doorway. She was not tall, but she still commanded a remarkable sense of presence. She was not someone you would want to glimpse over your shoulder in a darkened alley.

"My name's Morgan," she said and vanished into the street.

I watched the door swing shut, a smile playing on my lips. This was a significant development. It did not matter that I already knew her name. She had offered it to me, something I doubted she did often. Maybe she liked me after all.

With the prospects of a better deal hovering cautiously on the horizon, I decided it was time to write to Dan explaining that I would be staying in London for a while. After visiting the post office, I would return to Brigade Headquarters. My schedule might be filling up in the future. I needed to get ahead on my hours while I had the chance.

If you wanted something done, you went to the police station to be ignored, you did not even bother with the Hero Brigade. Their headquarters was in Mayfair, which told you everything you needed to know about how they saw themselves. The waiting room was as lacking as their complaints box. They had less authority than the police and less training, but boy did they tip the scales on panache. It was another form of John Blythwood's pro-function propaganda, trying to get people to see functionables as saviours and protectors, not monsters.

This was why the crowd in the foyer of the Brigade Headquarters was so suspicious. It could not possibly be people looking for help. I saw a bulk of muscle at the centre of the fawning mob and struggled to contain a sneer. Bedecked in red, white, and blue with a Union Jack hanging limply at his back was Mr Indestructible. He was the most self-righteous, pig-headed, patronising, vain moron I had ever had the misfortune of meeting. He was, of course, the darling of the Brigade. They advertised him as the epitome of Britishness, which I guessed meant he was polite enough to give you the time of day before punching you in the face. Aptly named, he was impenetrable to knives, guns, and bombs, and those were just the things we knew about. Personally, I would have liked to have had the opportunity to conduct a more thorough test. We didn't really get on.

He had headed the task force assembled to capture me and my parents. It was just the kind of high-profile case the Brigade liked. To say my parents were master thieves would give them far more credit than they deserved. There was nothing clever or subtle about them. The wreckage caused by their confrontations with the Brigade was far more costly than anything they stole. But they were conspicuous. They wore matching costumes and claimed responsibility for every major theft, even if it wasn't theirs. If they could have forced an orchestra to follow behind them playing a crescendo, they would have.

Their reckless flamboyance made it all the more embarrassing that Mr Indestructible failed to catch them for fifteen years. In the end, I had been the person who brought my parents in. Mr Indestructible had never forgiven me for showing the world just how incompetent he was. It was probably because of his disastrous experience with the Faceless Family that he opted to stay as far away from the Dirt Man case as possible. He wasn't going to make the same mistake twice.

I gave the crowd the widest berth I could manage and tracked down the volunteer coordinator, who was trying his best to avoid the volunteers.

"Clara Blakely, checking in."

He noted the time on his clipboard. The day was rushing towards night now. I had stopped in earlier but been told to come back later. The daytime patrols typically involved less fighting and more bribes, which meant they were often bagsied by the heroes proper.

"You can go on patrol with Miss Thomas." He beckoned someone over. "Miss Thomas, you'll be working with Miss Blakely tonight."

Miss Thomas was about my age, with a uniform starched and ironed to within an inch of its life and a face that had undergone the same treatment. Great, an actual volunteer. The only thing worse than the people who were forced to be here were the people who weren't.

"I don't want to work with her," Miss Thomas said. At least she was honest.

"It's either Miss Blakely, or no patrol," the coordinator said.

The answer should have been obvious, but Miss Thomas clearly had far too much dedication for her own good. She scowled and nodded, refusing to make eye contact with me.

"Cover Whitechapel," the coordinator said.

Great, a slum district. The last thing those people wanted was to be judged by two so-called heroes with enough time on their hands to do unpaid work. It would be a miracle if we got through the night without being beaten up and left in an alley somewhere.

Miss Thomas stalked ahead through the dense, sooty fog. I followed behind, carrying the lantern that would alert any wrongdoers of our approach.

We left Mayfair's affluence behind, where the streets were emptying as everyone sensible settled down to wait out the night. A group of men laughed loudly as they passed us, heading for Covent Garden. They were probably planning to frequent one of the area's many brothels. From the direction of the Thames, a foghorn sounded. It was never truly quiet in London, even on a warm, damp night like this one, when the wind was ripe for consumption. I was already starting to itch under the collar of my uniform.

I knew I should try and break the awkward silence between me and Miss Thomas. If we ran into trouble, she would be the person I would have to rely on to cover me. The way things stood at the moment, she was more likely to stab my back than watch it.

"I'm telekinetic, since you didn't ask what my function was," Miss Thomas said haughtily.

She had given me a perfect opportunity to bridge the gap between us, but it was hard to find the motivation to forge ahead when I already missed the blissful silence.

"Specifically, I can manipulate the movements of silk."

What an utterly pointless function. "What an interesting function. That must be useful."

"You're a pain reliever. I know all about you."

I bet she knew me better than I knew myself.

"Personally, I'm against the Brigade taking on criminals as volunteers. It damages the reputation of those of us who give our time willingly to help."

"It's very noble of you to give up your time."

"Well, yes, I suppose so, but I want to move up to the Hero Brigade proper. I heard starting at community level helps you at the interview stage. It shows I can work well in a team."

She could put "God's Intern" as past experience and it wouldn't change her underwhelming function. "Do you want to be a hero full-time then?"

"Temporarily, yes."

"Not long-term?"

She slowed her pace enough to let me walk beside her. What a privilege it was to have her deign to talk to my face.

"The Hero Brigade will help with my marriage prospects."

And there went the last shred of respect I had for her.

"You get to meet so many chivalrous men. Did you see Mr Indestructible in the foyer? He's so dreamy."

I made a humming noise, afraid if I opened my mouth I would gag. I was willing to bet his mask wasn't to protect his secret identity, but to protect my eyes.

"Do you think he's single? We can live in hope, can't we? Well, I can, no offence."

"None taken." If Mr Indestructible ever proposed to me, I would take the ring and jam it down his throat.

We had made it to Whitechapel. I knew because the smell of horse manure was now overwhelmed by that of human faeces. As we were now officially on patrol, we were supposed to be on the lookout for trouble. It was hoped that our mere presence would act as a deterrent, but most of the time it was a stimulant. We gave them something to aim at.

"I can't wait to go to the Brigade Ball. Did you see what Miss Fortitude wore last year?"

I hummed an affirmative. I hadn't, but I didn't want to encourage her to describe it. Miss Fortitude was the most powerful functionable in the Brigade, and yet all anyone seemed to care about was what she was wearing. She could vanish and reappear in a different place. They called it teleportation. I called it terrifying. She could even take people with her, and it was supposed to be quite an experience. I had travelled with my father at full speed many a time, and on every single trip, I threw up. I hated to think what Miss Fortitude could do to my stomach.

"It was gorgeous. I wonder what she looks like without her mask. I bet she's beautiful. I saw someone selling flowers the other day, and I think it could have been her."

"Really?" Miss Fortitude was one of the last defenders of a secret identity in a world of egotistical show-offs, and I doubted she went to the trouble so she could spend her downtime selling bouquets.

"Don't you think it's funny how people with functions are better looking than normal people?"

I had never heard anything more ridiculous in my life. Did she blindfold herself when visiting the Brigade Headquarters? It was like a house of horrors in there.

"I mean, compare Miss Fortitude to, say, her patron, Lady Blythwood. Blythwood looks like a horse."

I could see Miss Thomas had conducted a thorough study.

"Do you think Mr Indestructible is courting Miss Fortitude?"

"I'm afraid I don't know." And neither did I care. The two of them could go at it in the middle of Brigade Headquarters and I wouldn't mind one bit so long as I could get round them to log my hours.

"I hope they aren't even though they would make a good couple."

I had wondered why the Brigade would team distrustful, volatile Clara Blakely with someone so young and keen. Now I felt it was likely that even compassionate people were irritated by Miss Thomas. We were supposed to be working, yet the mindless drivel continued. The world had to have a severe shortage of receptive listeners if Miss Thomas thought she had found one in me.

I was so busy trying to ignore her that I did not realise she had stopped talking until she was gone from my side. I looked around and found her stalking up to a woman standing under a large lantern. I didn't know whether to be happy or nervous that Miss Thomas had found someone else to talk to.

"What is your business?" Miss Thomas snapped.

The Brigade needed to spend less time teaching people how to run in capes and come up with cringy catchphrases and more time on de-escalation.

"Oh sweetie," the woman mocked. "Would you like me to show you?"

I caught Miss Thomas's arm. "Thank you for your kind offer, but we best be on our way. You have a good evening."

I pulled Miss Thomas away.

"We should have arrested her. She was a lady of the night!"

"A prostitute? Her?" I shook my head. "She was a social worker, surely."

Miss Thomas stopped pulling. "You think?"

"Why else would she be in such a disreputable part of town, offering to show two God-fearing people such as ourselves her work?"

Miss Thomas furrowed her brow in thought. A novel experience for her, I was sure.

"Look! Brigands!"

Ah yes, a classic joke. The shout had come from a group of young men hanging around the kind of house that probably had twenty to a room.

"Go back to where you came from, freaks. You belong in a cage!"

They were harmless so long as they weren't antagonised.

"And you belong behind bars!" Miss Thomas shouted back. She was trying to get me killed.

"Come along, Miss Thomas. We better let them enjoy their evening." For the second time in less than a hundred yards, I found myself dragging her away.

"They were rude!"

"That isn't an offence."

"Yes, it is."

It was in the sense that anything we decided was an offence was an offence.

"Do you really want to waste your time arresting them? There could be a much more serious crime happening just around the corner."

There was a sudden clatter from a street up ahead. "Don't let it get away!"

"See, what did I—"

Miss Thomas was already running. I cursed and raced after her. If she was leading me into an ambush, I was going to have some serious words with her superior. I turned the corner and bumped right into her. She had stopped to stare at three men forcing a large dog into a cage. It was the mound of snapping teeth that had her frozen in horror, but I was more worried by the men. There was still time to slip back around the corner out of sight. No one would have to know.

"Stop!" Miss Thomas shouted.

The men looked up.

"By order of the Hero Brigade, I command you to set down your weapons and step away from the dog."

Miss Thomas looked very happy at her little speech. So happy, in fact, that she failed to notice it did not have its intended effect. The men were only armed with clubs, but it was more than we had. We were supposed to rely on our functions, which meant Miss Thomas was essentially unarmed.

One of the men took a step towards us. I pulled the pain from the dog and passed it onto him. He cried out and clutched at the phantom bruises that had appeared all over his body. Served him right for the casual animal cruelty.

"I suggest," I said calmly, "that you listen to my colleague."

The men hesitated. Even with the lantern, it was unlikely they had recognised me. All they saw was a functionable and a man I hadn't even touched sobbing in pain. For all they knew, my function might be squeezing people's internal organs.

As though on cue, they stepped away from the cage. The cage door sprung open, and the dog lunged for one of the men, clamping its teeth around his thigh. He went down screaming. The other man swung his club wildly at me. I ducked under it, grabbed his arm, and twisted it until it snapped. I kicked him in the groin, and he crumpled to the ground. Picking up the club he had dropped, I faced the dog. It snarled at me.

"You really want to do this?" I asked.

The dog barked and leapt. I raised my hands to protect my face, but the dog sailed over me. It flew up into the sky, its scraggly tail beating the air. I watched it fly off, then turned my attention back to the men lying at my feet.

"Miss Thomas, if you wouldn't mind going for help."

❖ ❖ ❖

Clearly the Hero Brigade and I differed on our understanding of the term "help." They sent none other than Mr Indestructible, complete with his crowd of slobbering fans. As he arrested the men to the sound of cheers, I gleaned that Miss Thomas and I had accidentally stumbled across some members of a gang of animal traffickers specialising in functionables. The Brigade had no problem with people rounding up animals so long as they were put to use. Vivisection, animal engines, and transport were all considered suitable employment. But being forced to fight other animals while people gambled on the outcome, that was encouraging immoral behaviour.

With Mr Indestructible there, we would get no credit for the catch. That was fine with me. People would be more willing to take the side of the gambling ring than accept that I had done a good deed. Any offence Miss Thomas may have taken was snuffed out by the proximity of Mr Indestructible. She drank up his frosty disregard like it was refreshing to be so thoroughly ignored.

"We might as well get on with our patrol," I told her. Normally, I would have seized the opportunity to avoid patrolling by hanging around to see the arrest through to its conclusion, but Mr Indestructible was enough to boost my industrious zeal.

Miss Thomas looked at me like I was mad. "But…"

"Mr Indestructible has this under control."

She searched around for a reason to stay that did not make her sound like she did not prioritise citizens' safety. She found none.

"I suppose you're right," she said reluctantly, gazing adoringly at Mr Indestructible one last time before sighing herself down the street.

We circled towards St Katherine Docks. Once she had got over the disappointment of leaving her chisel-jawed idol, Miss Thomas was in high spirits. She must have realised what good material this night would give her for her interview.

"You're not as bad as I thought you would be," she said.

"Thank you," I said.

"You are a good fit for the Community Squadron."

That was an insult if ever I heard one.

"I expected you to be insufferable, but you are quite civilised. We make a good team."

The insults just kept coming. I turned onto Dock Street.

"I would like to be your partner in the future. Occasionally, obviously. I don't want to be seen as being too close to you. That would be bad for my reputation."

I stopped. The smell of manure was gone, replaced with the scent of damp earth. Miss Thomas did not notice I had dropped back. She was still talking as she tripped over the body.

"What are you doing in the middle of the road, you drunken fool!" she shouted.

I held the lantern high and approached the unmoving form. They were lying on their back, arms reaching up, as though trying to ward something off.

"What is it?" Miss Thomas asked in a whisper.

It had been a living person, but it wasn't anymore. I knelt beside them and brushed my fingers along their arm. A layer of dirt crumbled beneath my fingertips. The mud covered every inch of their body, thick enough to make it unrecognisable. They barely looked human anymore.

"Dirt Man," Miss Thomas gasped.

I nodded. The latest psychotic villain trying to make a name for himself. He was unlike my parents in every way: quiet, careful, uninterested in money or limelight. He used his function of controlling dirt to cover people with the stuff, clogging up their vital organs and suffocating them. There were new victims cropping up almost every night now. Whoever it was must have decided to make a full-time career out of it. He would have to slip up soon, but until then, his identity remained a secret. No one had ever seen the Dirt Man, only his creations.

Miss Thomas looked around nervously. "Do you think he's still here?"

Unlikely. If the Dirt Man was nearby, we would have been dead already.

"Shall I go and get help?"

There was no reason for Miss Thomas to sound so excited. Mr Indestructible wouldn't be taking credit for this one. Dirt Man had struck again, and he, like everybody else, was powerless to stop it.

"No," I said, "we'll call it in when we're back at headquarters. There's nothing we can do for them now."

I stood and wiped my hand on my trousers, leaving smudges of dirt on the shiny blue material.

Chapter
4

I woke up to something sharp pressing into my chest. I opened my eyes and screamed.

"You do that again and I'll kill you myself!" my neighbour yelled.

I sat up and scooted back so quickly I hit my head against the wall. The pigeon that had been pecking my chest cooed and flapped its wings to keep its balance. I shooed it. It hopped down onto my stomach and began pecking again.

"I don't remember requesting a wake-up call."

I looked at the window. No, it was still bolted shut. Either this bird had been nesting in the rafters and mistaken me for a loaf of bread, or it had a function. The latter may have been more probable, but it still did not explain why it was in my room. Maybe this hotel was one of those healthy lifestyle places which sent birds to scare you out of bed.

I tried to get up, but the bird did not like that. It cooed at me again and stuck its leg out. This seemed like strange behaviour until I noticed a metal tube tied just above its foot. In my defence, it had been a long time since I had received a messenger bird.

"Don't eat me," I begged and reached forward to free its leg.

Once released, it flew to the end of the bed. I tipped the tightly rolled parchment from the tube and peered at the tiny writing.

Walk? Head for the market. I'll find you.
Morgan.

I read the message again. I did not know which was stranger: that an assassin was inviting me for a stroll or that she could be that bad at writing letters. I flopped back onto my bed and the bird cooed at me.

"Why are you still here? Do you need a tip?"

It ruffled its feathers.

"If I buy you porridge, will you leave me alone?"

It cooed again.

"You'll have to be patient then."

Once I had secured myself in stockings, corset, petticoat, full skirt, bonnet, gloves, and everything else fashion dictated I waste my time with, I led the bird down the stairs to the communal area. The dining room was airy and welcoming in the daylight, which was probably why Morgan avoided it.

I ordered some eggs for myself and porridge for the bird, then settled at a table by a window. It was a lovely day, probably one of the last sunny ones before we plunged headfirst into autumn. It was not the kind of day for trying to make small talk with what was basically a shadow. Maybe I could get accidentally lost on the way to the market. The ominous "I'll find you" did not fill me with confidence. I would just have to make the most of this day by sucking up to Morgan to such an extent that she fell head over heels for my charm and begged me to let her go to the press and clear my name. Sounded doable.

I glanced at where the pigeon had been busy making a mess. The bird had vanished. So much for gratitude.

❖ ❖ ❖

The market was in sight when Morgan dropped down beside me.

"Morgan!" I said, like she had given me a wonderful surprise, not an awful, heart-leaping-out-of-my-skin surprise.

"Clara," she replied, as though jumping from a roof was perfectly normal. For her, it probably was. "You got my bird. I wasn't sure it would send. The updrafts around the school are terrible."

Who still bothered with birds? What was she, thirty-five? "I haven't had a bird for ages."

"What do you use?"

"Street urchins, like any normal person."

"Don't you worry about data leaks? Urchins have no guaranteed privacy."

"And birds do?"

"I've never had a problem with my bird being intercepted."

That was because her bird was a violent little bugger. Almost mortally wounding me and still managing to scrounge a meal. "Then your bird must be very dedicated, not to be sidetracked by the bread givers in Trafalgar Square."

"Victor."

"Pardon?"

"His name is Victor."

"You named your bird?" I imagined her making little cooing noises to him and feeding him grain.

"Is that strange?"

"Not at all." It was like naming your post box.

"He's the best homing pigeon I have ever had. His navigational system is spot on—unless I'm trying to send something to Hull—and his response time is so quick I swear he must travel faster than a train."

"That's impressive." Not if you considered how often trains had to stop for sheep on the line. "Does he have a function?"

"I think so, but I can't figure out what it is. No one knows how Victor travels, least of all Victor himself."

We had now entered the market, which was just a large number of drab, saggy tents full of brightly coloured trinkets. The people screamed their wares at us in unintelligible cockney. I could already feel a headache coming.

Seeing as Morgan did not seem willing to carry the conversation, I decided I would have to get the great, big, lumbering ball rolling.

"Why do you always wear your mask?"

"It helps with the smell," she replied.

I was hoping for something a little deeper and more confessional. Watching her hood turn, I tried to follow the direction of her gaze. I did not miss the extravagant luxury of my childhood. I still wore fine clothes, but because I had to look the part, not because I liked them. My neck felt a lot lighter now that it was not weighed down by diamonds. My parents had always been showing off their wealth. All things considered, it was a miracle they evaded the law for so long. The simpler life was strangely enjoyable. Living out of a travel bag, never getting attached to anything. Morgan seemed to be far more interested in the stalls than I would ever be, but maybe that was because she was trying to avoid talking to me. I tried to imagine her in a feather hat and almost snorted. Of course, Morgan chose this moment to knock into someone. The sight of the man's objection shrivelling up on his tongue when he saw who had run into him made the image even better. I had to pretend to suddenly admire some silks.

"You don't live in London," Morgan stated suddenly.

"No," I agreed.

I did not live anywhere. Dan was the closest thing I had to a home. He was usually where I left him and had a few squirrels loose in the attic, if you know what I mean. Anyone would have to be a bit mad to put up with me.

"I have a place in Dippenwick," I said. "The local scenery is quite stunning." It was a shame about the people.

"You fit in here."

I hated it. London was a city where you could be anyone, and most people found they were no one. "I was born here."

In a nice house behind a nice set of shiny gates. The places my parents and I stole from were not so shiny. Refuse oozing tracks through the dirt into the already impenetrable sludge of the Thames, poverty laid out as bare as the corpses strewn in the street. It was almost enough to make me feel bad for robbing them.

"My parents could have moved out of the city, but that might have reduced the chance of me developing a function."

"They wanted you to have a function?"

"They saw it as a gift."

"And what do you think?"

I thought our bodies had been pumped full of smoke, sludge, and silt and were now tearing themselves apart because of it. I thought that instead of rounding us up, they should have arrested the factory owners, the suppliers, and MPs, the people who turned the rivers black. But what did I know? I was not a scientist nor a politician. My opinion on the matter was not needed.

"I think it is a great responsibility," I said.

I suppose I should have been grateful. I had been lucky enough to have been born somewhere a functionable could live out their life with a degree of normality. I had heard the rumours about what happened to functionables born on plantations. The bar for human decency was low.

Dodging a group of merchants, I noticed the man. The street was crowded, but this person stood out. His face was soured by recognition. I reached out, testing the waters, seeing what pain was in the vicinity if I needed it. My nagging headache was unlikely to incapacitate him. I found some back pain, an injured knee, a few liver problems. It would be enough. I kept my eyes forward as he drew alongside us and braced.

"Scum," he hissed and spat in our direction.

Morgan froze, her head swivelling to watch him walk away. So much for lightning-quick assassin reflexes.

"I'm sorry about that," she said, her confusion ringing loudly. "That's never happened before. People are usually all right with assassins. Maybe one killed his mother or something."

"I don't think it was you he was spitting at."

Her head snapped to me. "Why would someone spit at you?"

Did she want a list? How about the fact that I was a criminal free to walk the streets while people who had committed far fewer wrongs were put on a boat and shipped to hell? Or perhaps because while an assassin worked for a corporation and paid their taxes, a villain stood outside society, robbing people's life savings, destroying their lives. I was a liar, a cheat, a backstabber, and a manipulator, and sometimes people could sense it.

"Does it happen a lot?" Morgan asked quietly.

"No," I lied.

I could expect an increase in confrontations now that the article had reminded everyone what I looked like. Thanks a lot, Maureen.

"Come with me," Morgan said. She started that quick, gliding walk that had me panting to keep up.

❖ ❖ ❖

We went to one of the larger parks, the kind they locked up at night to prevent the homeless from having somewhere soft to rest. It had huge expanses of green space, broken by large, straight paths lined with beech trees. Morgan looked out of place amongst the fashionable couples with their top hats and parasols. I was embarrassed to be walking with her, but it was tempered by a paranoia that had me struggling not to glance over my shoulder. The interaction with the man had reminded me just how many people out there hated me.

Morgan paused by a lake. The sun was high now, and her leather squeaked with sweat as she pulled off one of her gloves and dipped her hand into the cool water. I watched with fascination. Deep down, I had suspected she had skin but, still, seeing it was a surprise. I tugged my gaze away before she could catch me staring.

"This place is busier since they closed Mundmere Common," she said.

I stared across the lake at the manicured lawns. It seemed a risky move, pushing more people into these places. Those who enjoyed the feeling of exclusivity had money. The government's tenuous grip on power relied on their happiness.

Morgan had left my side and was now crouched on a bench. With an internal sigh, I settled beside her and carefully arranged my skirts in a manner I hoped communicated that she was incorrectly using the bench and drawing unwanted attention our way. I was, of course, completely unsuccessful. Suspecting her sympathy levels were running high after the little incident at the market, I decided to press for answers.

"Why did you admit to Forgo's death?"

She sighed with resignation, like she had expected the question.

"On our three-year placement before we graduate, we must take a minimum of twenty contracts. Forgo was my twentieth, and I finished with him just days before the deadline. It's the kind of thing that makes the administration suspicious. Someone else being tried for Forgo's death would make them investigate me, to make sure I killed who I said I killed. They would not have found a problem; I always followed the correct procedure, but an investigation would take too long. I wanted to graduate with the others."

I weighed up the truth of her words. I could imagine her, the nervous assassin desperate to prove herself, terrified they may find fault with her meticulous work. However, I did not believe that someone with such a high work ethic would be scrambling about only five minutes before the deadline.

"I'm surprised you cut the deadline so fine," I said carefully.

"I spent too long on a contract. It was worth it—someone very high up, lots of kudos involved—but I spent the last year desperately trying to make up for lost time. It was hard. Quentin's right, my qualifications aren't enough. People find me unapproachable. I'll never be as successful as him."

"He told you that?"

"He didn't have to."

I watched the people walking past. A nanny was ushering a group of children with the same impatience as an overbearing dog owner. Any curiosity in the world had to be scolded out of them.

"My first contract was this duchess," Morgan said. "She was dead, it was all going fine, but I hadn't realised her lover was hiding in the cupboard. My first day on the job, and I almost got brained by a naked man with a candlestick."

I laughed. "At least you got two kills in one day."

"The second one didn't count," she said morosely. "It was only self-defence."

The group of children had been marched out of sight. What wonderful, productive members of society they would make one day.

"I haven't told anyone else that," Morgan said.

I glanced at her hunched form, the gargoyle of the bench. "Why tell me?"

She shrugged. "You strike me as someone who can keep a secret. After all, this is our third conversation, Clara, and you are yet to tell me a single truth."

Chapter 5

No strange wake-up call followed my visit to the park with Morgan. Our farewells had been cordial, yet a week passed without a single assassin-related incident. The rejection frustrated me. Just when I thought I had squirmed my way into her good graces, she vanished. Her words concerning my aversion to the truth echoed around my head. Though I had laughed them off at the time, they rattled me. Could she really see through my bullshit so easily? I considered myself to be a frankly marvellous actress. If I had slightly less pride, I could have made a fantastic career on stage. Maybe middle age was getting to me, making me lose my touch. Or maybe Morgan's mask was throwing me off. It was hard to lie to someone's face when you could not see it.

I limped out of the bathroom, towelling my hair. A bath had been necessary after the day I had suffered. The Brigade had sent me to a hospital for a bit of charitable pain relief. Simply stepping through the doors had been enough to overload my senses. Who knew so much misery could exist in one place? It had all the hits: tumours, consumption, syphilis. The only part of me that did not ache was my wrist, meaning I was going to have an encounter with Quentin soon.

"Hi," said a voice at the window.

I jumped. Assassins were like plagues: think of them and they appeared to strike you down. I was going to stick bits of glass into the windowsill.

Plastering a smile on my face, I returned his greeting. I could feel his pain waiting to be lapped up. It was more than it should have been. I let just a tiny bit of my frustration show.

"You shouldn't be using your wrist so much. Don't assassins get sick leave?"

He swung himself into the room and smiled sheepishly. "I haven't been working. There's no point until we graduate. Unless you're Morgan that is; she's a workaholic. I really have been trying not to use it, but one of the guys I did a job for invited me round for a game of croquet, and I kind of forgot."

He was ruining his wrist for croquet? He deserved to do some actual damage. Reminding myself that more pain was more money, I reached out with my function.

"If you take some proper rest, it shouldn't be more than another week now."

"Thanks," he said, passing me the money. "I'm meeting some friends for a drink if you want to join us."

What maniac would want to socialise when they were in pain? There was absolutely nothing I would like to do less. "No, I wouldn't want to intrude."

"Nonsense, we'd be happy to have you."

"I should probably be going on a patrol," I lied instinctively.

"Morgan said you spent the day with the Brigade."

Great, that probably meant Morgan was one of the friends he was drinking with. The same Morgan who had been refusing to make contact but had, apparently, been stalking me.

"Crime never sleeps." God, I hated what came out of my mouth sometimes.

"Just one drink," he coaxed.

I laughed good naturedly as I fantasised pushing him down a flight of stairs. "If you insist."

❖ ❖ ❖

The Cup of Lead Poisoning had reached that delicate point between party and riot when we joined. Quentin led me to an assassin. She was with a group of artists who were taking turns weeping while their friends comforted them with epigrams. I thought the assassin was Morgan until Quentin hugged her and she did not stab him. It was a long hug, I noticed.

The assassin who was too friendly to be Morgan turned to me. Her maskless face was like a physical blow. She had rosy cheeks complete with goddamn dimples. She looked like the kind of person who would stop to lift struggling bumblebees off the path and carry them to nearby flowers. I instantly disliked her.

"Clara, this is Darcy Payne," Quentin said. "That's Payne with a *Y*, not an *I*. People always assume it's an *I* for some reason."

I wondered why. Were assassins recruited purely on a last name basis? What was Morgan's surname? Ice-Queen? Angry-For-No-Reason? Kill-You-With-A-Glare?

"Darcy, this is Clara Blakely."

Darcy went straight in with a hug. It would have been so easy for me to stick something in her jugular.

"He's been talking about you nonstop," she said. "I'm afraid he's gone all dewy-eyed for you."

Quentin shoved her playfully. "I'm not that bad," he said while making a lot of eye contact.

Two things became clear. One, Darcy and Quentin were completely infatuated with each other and blindly ignoring this obvious fact. Two, they were disgusting, and I wanted them dead.

"He'll be asking you to sign his wanted posters next." Darcy giggled.

"No, I won't. Not if you don't want to," he said to me, "but I do have some, and I thought maybe you would like to. I would pay you of course."

I joined in Darcy's laughter, a little less enthusiastically though. "I'm really no celebrity, but I'm happy to sign them. I'll even put in a good word to my parents if they ever break out of prison."

"Really?" He looked like I had just offered him a flying pig.

"Sure."

I would love to tell my parents about Quentin The Fanboy as I was being brutally decapitated by them. If they ever did get out of prison, I was a goner for sure. They had not been too fond of me even before I turned them into the police. Okay, so once, I accidentally pushed my father off a train. The key word here is "accidentally." Those things are really tricky to balance on. And yes, I abandoned my mother in a high-stakes shootout with a rival villain, Mrs Tax-Evasion. That one wasn't an accident. Yet, I would argue my foibles were inconveniences at best.

A group of grizzled men in sailors' uniform pushed past, and we found ourselves squished into a corner table.

"What have you got up to during your time in the big city?" Darcy shouted over the din of the sailors beating up the artists.

"Mostly patrols," I replied.

"Hero Brigade?" she asked.

"Community Squadron," I clarified.

She grimaced. "That sucks."

"I think it's noble," Quentin said, his inner Labrador shining through.

Darcy rolled her eyes. "I think I would have been better on the Hero Brigade than in the Finishing School. I prefer doing things, leaping into action. All this sitting around quietly bores me to death. But alas, I have no function."

Quentin shook his head. "I can't believe the Brigade still only takes functionables."

"It balances out all the places that don't take them," Darcy countered.

"Still, it's divisionary," he said.

Darcy's unwarranted support probably had something to do with the functionable sitting right next to her.

"Maybe it's because non-functionables would get their arses kicked," Quentin said with a wink to me.

"Yes, because your function is so useful in a fight," she replied.

His enthusiasm did not waver. "I mean, it may not be useful in the fight itself, but I could put people on trial after death. My slogan could be: Justice beyond the grave."

Just when I had managed to forget his terrifying ability.

"Are there any dead people here?" I asked, managing to make it sound casual and not like I thought he was a freak.

"Just the old man in the corner, but he's been here for as long as I can remember. Must have been the stubbornest man alive." He waved at the corner.

I glanced behind me. There was no one there. No one except an artist bringing a chair down on a sailor's head.

"It must make mortality rates really hit home," I said.

He shrugged. "I think they might actually be getting better. I'm more concerned about the other dead things I see. When you see the ghosts of a clear-cut forest, it makes you wonder whether our attitude to nature is sustainable. It seems like this city has a personal vendetta against green spaces."

Darcy nudged him. "You're such a softie. Maybe that's what your function represents."

I really hoped she was not one of the crazies who searched for hidden meaning in people's functions like they were not random mutations.

"Or maybe it means you can't let anything go," she joked.

He shoved her. "Okay, detective, what about Clara's function?"

She tutted like it was obvious. "Clearly it shows what a nice person she is. She wants to help people, to take their pain."

It took all my willpower not to laugh outright.

"Morgan!" Quentin hollered. "We were just debating whether functions are a reflection of some deeper personality trait. Care to pitch in?"

I looked over my shoulder and, even though I knew what I would see, jumped. Morgan was standing behind me, holding four pints. Or at least I assumed it was Morgan. With a shrug in reply to Quentin's question, she pulled a chair from a nearby table and crouched on it. It was definitely Morgan.

"Come on," Quentin persisted. "Personally, I think your function is a response to your inability to understand people."

I turned to her disbelievingly. "You have a function?"

"You didn't tell her?" Quentin was clearly disappointed. "Morgan, we've talked about this. It's not fair and a complete invasion of privacy."

"What is your function?" I asked with growing fear.

Morgan hesitated. I tried to rein in my unease. Whatever her function was, there was no need to work myself into a state. Everything would be fine.

"I read minds," she said.

I was so totally screwed.

She squirmed ever so slightly. "To be exact, I enter people's minds and witness their thoughts."

"You've been reading my mind?" A mind that was currently whirling in freefall as I remembered every mean thought I had indulged in over the past week-and-a-half.

"Yes, I've been reading your mind, and yes, you're mean," she said. "The headaches are normal by the way. It's the pressure of me squeezing into your head. I've never had someone throw the headache back at me before."

The only question now was whether she was going to send me to prison or the afterlife.

"In what way is she mean?" Quentin asked.

"Well, for starters, she finds you both annoying," Morgan said.

Their hurt was palpable. Why were assassins so sensitive?

"Don't listen to her, of course I don't," I said quickly. This was turning into a nightmare.

"She's lying," Morgan said.

"Morgan," I snapped.

She shrugged, unaffected by the fact that she was dismantling my life one lie at a time.

"Fine," I said, turning once again to the teary-eyed duo. "If it's any consolation, I find most people annoying. Are you happy now, Morgan? No one's going to employ me."

"She's a crabby one, isn't she?" Darcy mused. "And here I was thinking we could invite her into our club of optimists."

"You're including Morgan in this group?" I asked drily.

"Morgan is the most hopeful of us all," Quentin said. "You'll see soon enough."

Right now, the only thing I wanted to see was Morgan being strangled by my hands.

I would like to see you try.

I practically leapt out of my chair. It was Morgan's voice, but it had most definitely sounded in my head.

I told you I enter people's minds. So yes, I can speak to you. It's actually very difficult to avoid detection. You can hear me breathe if you're quiet, and I have to be careful not to trip over anything.

It was strange hearing her talk of my mind as a physical space. It was strange enough hearing her talk at all, but I could not help but wonder what my mind looked like. I wanted to go with ornate palace, but it was probably decaying crypt.

Morgan's voice resounded in my head again. *I don't see anything, just blackness. All minds are dark rooms, but there are still obstacles. Thoughts not quite surfaced, that kind of thing.*

I focused on forming an apology for all the horrible things I had been thinking. I had been under a lot of pressure from work recently. Of course, if she had not been such a nosey spy, then she would be none the wiser.

You're not very good at this apology thing.

"Just get out," I said aloud.

Darcy and Quentin paused in their aside flirting.

"Oh dear, Morgan's found someone new to drive to the brink of insanity," Quentin said. "Clara, if you are concerned by Morgan reading your thoughts, just drink so much she gets dizzy attempting it."

I snatched one of the cups from the table. I had best get going; I had the alcohol tolerance of a playwright.

Morgan took another one of the drinks. She pushed back her hood and pulled off her mask, laying it gently on the table like a peace offering. I turned to gaze into the face that was out to ruin my life. It was actually quite disappointing. Her features were all complementary. As in, they worked together to make her look terrifying. She had the strictest centre parting I had seen in my life. It was as though the hairs on each side of her head were locked in an idle battle, her parting forming the no-man's-land no hair bothered to cross. Her cheekbones were high, her lips pursed in displeasure, and her large watchful eyes directed solely at me.

"No facial scars," I noted.

She was almost as difficult to read with her mask off, but the slight furrow of her brows was enough reaction for me. I took a long drink, satisfied for the first time that evening.

"You should come to our graduation tomorrow," Quentin said suddenly. "You could help pad out the crowd. There are not a lot of parents; they are usually the first people killed."

"Do people actually kill their parents?" I asked.

"She says in surprise," Morgan mocked, "as though she's not thinking that she would definitely kill her parents if she thought she could take them in a fight."

That was true. I did think that.

"All right," I conceded. "But what about people without well-established mummy/daddy issues?"

"No one is off limits in our profession," Darcy said.

"What about other assassins?" I asked.

Quentin grinned. "Morgan has already told us she wouldn't hesitate to kill us if she was asked to."

"Okay, firstly, I was drunk," Morgan said. "Secondly, I wouldn't have to because, generally speaking, yes, assassins are off limits. And thirdly, yes, I would kill you both in the small likelihood I was asked, because I am a professional."

"So, graduation," I said quickly, not wanting to find myself in the middle of a knife fight. "Do I have to wear black?"

"You don't want to come. It will be boring," Morgan said with suspicious determination.

"No, it will be hilarious," Quentin countered. "Morgan has to make a speech."

The look on Morgan's face was enough to have me instantly clearing my schedule.

"She got the highest grades in the year. It's tradition," Quentin said with obvious glee.

"It's a stupid tradition," she grumbled.

"Poor Morgan has a little fear of public speaking," Quentin explained.

"I don't fear anything," she retorted.

Quentin snorted. "We both know that's not true."

"You were telling us about Sir Barnaby Cholmondeley's croquet match," Morgan said.

"A poor attempt to change the topic," he scoffed. "But the game was fantastic." He launched into a detailed description of how regular croquet, unlike the form they played at the Finishing School with grenades, was marvellous in its simplicity.

Are you mad at me for reading your thoughts?

I jumped, again. Was I mad? If I wasn't—and I most certainly was—I soon would be with these constant invasions. I tried very hard to think the word "no."

After that tirade, you think I would believe you?

The headache was back. Whether it was due to the pressure of her in my mind or her endless chatter, I did not know.

I'm sorry. And not just about the headache. I'm sorry for reading your mind without telling you.

I somehow doubted she truly was.

Okay, you got me. It's a useful asset.

It was a breach of privacy.

And sitting on someone's windowsill isn't? A disregard for privacy is part of the job.

I wondered if I asked really nicely, even fluttered my eyelashes a little, she would stop rummaging around my head like a bag of liquorice.

I would certainly be more subtle about it.

The absolute nerve.

"So, this speech you have to give," I said out loud, "what are the rules on heckling?"

Chapter 6

It was graduation day, and it was raining. Wind whipped the drizzle into a vengeful swarm that stung my face. My umbrella was more hazard than help, but I gripped it tight for no other reason than it was bright red, and I was preparing to singlehandedly add colour to the congregation.

At the gates to the Finishing School stood the small woman, her woollen cloak drenched. She saw me and gave a lengthy sigh that emanated from deep in her bones.

"I'm here for the graduation," I said, trying not to sound too smug as I presented my invitation.

She squinted at it carefully. As if I would bother faking one to clap for a bunch of people I did not know.

"Not a quitter, are you?" she said.

"Not even on my worst days."

She pointed me around the back of the building. It was easy to follow the trickle of guests heading in that direction. I soon arrived at a courtyard, with walls on all sides so high they would have blocked out the sun, had there been any. At one end was a large stage with black curtains. The rest of the space was lined with chairs. Unless there were a lot of latecomers, there were going to be some spares.

I recognised Lord Townsend amongst the few shivering bodies that littered the courtyard. He was wearing a false moustache. Considering he already had a moustache, it was not a great disguise. I had treated him after a riding accident a year previously. His eyes widened with recognition, but he steadfastly ignored me. I guessed it had less to do with him crying like a baby the last time we met and more to do with not officially being there. Being friends with an assassin must have been a nuisance. Though certainly not illegal, ordering an assassination was something people tended to keep to themselves. It was still considered impolite amongst the upper classes to murder your friends. It must have been easier in the days when assassins were just nameless shapes, a quiet footstep, the glint of a dagger in the dark. Back then, people like Townsend would never have felt obliged to attend a ceremony like this.

I found a seat and put down my umbrella. It was time to stop pretending that I was not already soaked. A woman sat down beside me, her joints clicking loudly.

"Sorry about that," she said. "Bad ankles."

"Jumping out of windows will do that," I replied.

She laughed. "How could you tell I was an alumna?"

Sun-deprived skin, dark circles under her eyes that suggested nocturnal habits, a black outfit that missed celebration by a mile. She was too old to be a student facing a deadline, and vampires did not exist, so I was going with the next logical conclusion. "Lucky guess."

"It's great weather," she stated.

"Very atmospheric."

"Who are you here for?"

"Quentin Shadow," I said, deciding he probably had the best reputation. "I've been working for him."

"In what capacity?"

"I'm a functionable, a pain reliever to be exact."

"These new assassins have no stamina," she sniffed. "Back in my day we would just carry on."

"Why not use what is available? I could take a look at your joints if you wanted."

"Or you could mind your own business."

Or I could stab her with my umbrella and see if she changed her mind.

"Sorry," I said meekly. "I did not mean to cause offence."

A hush descended as a man took to the stage. Even his billowing robes could not disguise his lamppost figure: big head, thin body, and a terrible stoop.

He cleared his throat. "As head of the Finishing School, I would like to welcome you all to this year's graduation. Seven years have passed too quickly."

He probably slept through them.

"Such a talented and dedicated cohort will be sorely missed, but it is time for them to move on to their next big adventure. Times are changing: the industry is expanding and opportunities are growing slim. With these challenges, however, come the potential for greatness. An assassin from the Finishing School is three times as likely to be employed as any other assassin in Britain."

Was this a speech or an advert?

"Congratulations to all who made it, and my condolences to the families of those who did not. Good luck with your future careers, wherever they may take you. If you live by the assassins' code of conduct, you will always have a place here. If you don't, we will divest you of your badge and your honour. So carry the ethos of the Finishing School with you in the strength of your convictions and the thrust of your dagger. *Mors Tua Vita Mea*."

Everyone clapped politely as he unfurled a large scroll. The assassins filed onto the stage to receive their seal as he read out their names monotonously. I clapped for all of them and listened for names I recognised.

"Morgan Murdur," he droned.

Was that my Morgan? Was her last name really Murdur? I hung my head in despair. These kids never stood a chance. I was thankful I had not inherited some stupidly fitting surname. I could have been Clara Mabel Evangeline Morally-Grey. I was so self-absorbed, I missed Quentin and Darcy. Before I knew it, the head was refurling his scroll.

"And now we shall hear from this year's valedictorian, Morgan Murdur." He left the stage slowly, almost reluctantly. He must have known this was going to be a train wreck. I was very pleased.

Morgan returned to the stage. Even with her face hidden, I could tell she was giving the audience a death stare. I doubted she would be reading anyone's mind at that moment, but it could not hurt to criticise her as thoroughly as possible. She clutched her speech like she could squeeze the words from the page into her mouth.

"We're taught to make deaths quick," she snapped, "so I'll try and do the same for this speech."

There were a few chuckles from the audience. I did not think Morgan had intended that as a joke.

"First of all, I want to thank you all for coming." She did not sound thankful, she sounded like she wanted to spontaneously combust. "We have an unusually good turnout this year. By this point in the proceedings, the crowd has normally thinned a bit; lots of young assassins ready to prove themselves."

There was more laughter. My neighbour joined in.

"Someone recently asked me why I wanted to be an assassin. I told her I wanted to make a difference. Assassins are known for slipping in silently and vanishing without a trace. Yet even though we might disappear in the morning light, our actions do not. We are essential, like foxhunting or hitting commoners with sticks. But just because we are part of this country's tradition does not mean we are outdated. The Finishing School is always striving forward. So, I ask the guests here today to give us a chance to show our skills by going out and making enemies. And to the graduates, I say forge your own path, and let it be strewn with bodies. Thank you." She ripped up the paper and dropped from the stage, vanishing from sight.

There were a few half-hearted claps. The rain was a more effective applauder. I was disappointed Morgan had not fainted, but I could not have it all.

"Well, that went better than last year," the woman beside me said.

"What happened last year?"

"The valedictorian tried to get the crowd to do improv." She stood. "I'm going to say hello to my professors. It was nice to meet you…"

"Clara, Clara Blakely."

Her eyes glinted with recognition, but she did not say anything.

"I didn't get your name."

"No, you didn't." She whipped around with a flourish that had me wiping rainwater from my eyes. What a pillock.

I got up and found an assassin standing behind me.

"Hello. I'm Clara."

"I know who you are," Morgan said.

Couldn't the school invest in nametags?

Couldn't you learn to pay attention?

There she was, in my head again. She must have used up all her words for the day.

"I don't see anyone else recognising you," I said.

"Morgan," a woman greeted as she sidled up to us. "You look lovely today."

She looked the exact same as she always did.

"It was a wonderful speech," the woman continued, undeterred by Morgan's silence.

"Thank you," Morgan said stiffly.

I was starting to understand that when Morgan did something that made her uncomfortable, she sounded like she wanted to bite your head off.

"We're going," she said to me as she turned and stormed off.

"Where?" I followed the wake she left as she pushed through the crowd.

Away from that conversation.

Now that I knew she had just used me to escape making small talk, I slowed. An assassin swung their arm over me. I yelped.

"Oh hush, it's just me," Quentin said. "You've sat through the boring bit, now comes the fun part. We've got the common room for the night."

❖ ❖ ❖

Quentin led me inside the school and up a set of wide marble stairs, him walking silently while I sounded like a heavily burdened horse. The halls were marked sporadically with candles, leaving plenty of shadows for people to loiter in. The common room was far more welcoming. A huge chandelier lit the many identical portraits that hung from the walls. Once you had painted one assassin, you had painted them all.

"Is this your sister, Morgan?" someone asked.

I looked around in confusion and found an assassin had materialised by my side.

"No."

I was almost insulted by how horrified Morgan sounded.

"I'm Clara," I offered.

"Her parents were the notorious villains Marie and Wyatt Blakely," Quentin said with glee.

That was something I preferred people worked out for themselves. I snatched a glass from the refreshments table. Was it the blood of their victims? No, it was wine, and a nice vintage at that. I was trying to subtly reach for another glass when an assassin came barrelling towards us. They leapt into Quentin's arms, and he spun them around.

"We are graduates!" Darcy yelled.

He let her down, and she pulled off her mask. Her face was flushed with excitement.

"You ready to go out and change the world?" Quentin asked.

"You bet!"

Ah, young hope. I could not wait to see their naïve optimism wither and die like a flower in the frost.

Wine slopped over Morgan's glass. Was her clumsiness the result of eavesdropping on me?

Darcy must have come to the same conclusion. "Is Clara thinking something mean?"

"No, I'm composing a poem to your beauty," I said before Morgan could reply.

Darcy turned to Morgan, so I concentrated on forming a rhyme. Roses are red, violets are blue. Stay out of my head, or I will bludgeon you.

Morgan snorted. I heard the sound reverberate around my head.

"She's not lying," she said seriously. "She is composing poetry."

Darcy suddenly grabbed Quentin's arm. "Oh my god, it's Claud Vedbijonsky!"

"Who?" Morgan asked.

"He's only the number one conductor in the world! And he's kind of hot," Darcy responded.

"He's twice your age!" Quentin cried.

"Maybe I like a man with a hunch. Come on." She pulled him through the crowd to where the orchestra was setting up.

I put on my socialising smile and turned away from Morgan. I could not effectively network with her snapping at everyone. My elbow bumped into an assassin, and I let the apologies turn into introductions. Before I knew it, I had suffered through three dances and got four potential clients out of it. It was exhausting work; their quadrille had more headbanging than I was used to. I kept half an eye out for any brooding figures that might be Morgan and stayed away from them. The last thing I needed was a headache.

❖ ❖ ❖

When the night was starting to wind down, I slipped past where Darcy and Quentin were sitting—very close and very carefully not making out—

and into the hall. I was probably not supposed to wander, but curiosity got the better of me. I found a window and looked down at an obstacle course. It was dark, but I could make out a group of assassins pushing each other off a climbing wall. I threw open the nearest door and found myself in an empty dormitory.

"My bed was third on the left."

I jumped. Morgan was pulling the window closed behind her. She must have scaled along the outside of the building. There was a surprising number of doors for people who never used them.

"Seems like a tough place to live," I said, gesturing to the sparse decoration.

"It's good preparation. Clients don't usually offer us a grand four-poster for the duration of our stay. Unless you're Quentin, that is. I don't know how he does it."

She had her hood off. I followed her eyes as they scanned the room.

"You don't miss your mansion?" I asked.

"I miss having my own room."

"For someone who loves solitude, you seem to spend a lot of time with me. You weren't enjoying the party?"

"It's not... I don't..." She sighed in frustration. "People."

"People," I agreed.

"You are good with people, but you don't like them."

"And you are terrible with people, and yet don't mind them."

A fleeting smile lit her eyes. "Are you reading my mind now?"

"I figured that's why you won't leave me alone, because I have what you want."

"Something like that." The floor had suddenly become the object of her interest. "What is it you want?"

There was no point lying to her. "An early retirement. As soon as my community service is done ideally. My job sucks."

She nodded.

"I'll probably buy a cottage in the woods; grow potatoes, make my own jam."

The smile was back, this time brighter, crinkling the skin around her eyes. "You? Making jam?"

"Fine, poisons then."

"I'm good at making poisons."

"You can come too, then."

I'm leaving.

"Use your words, Morgan."

"Sorry."

"You're leaving?" It was not surprising. At the rate she had been accepting jobs, London must have been drying up. I was surprised there was anyone left alive. I tried to keep the relief that would accompany her absence buried deep inside. "I suppose I might see you around. It looks like I'm going to be on call for the school for a while. Maybe you'll get grievously injured."

"We can only hope," she said quietly.

I wondered how to broach the subject of her function. I did not want her to realise how much power she had over my career, but I needed assurance she would not go around telling everyone I was a horrible person.

"Your secrets are safe with me," Morgan said.

Well, that made it easier.

"Thank you," I replied, knowing she could tell how false it was. She did not deserve real gratitude. "Where are you off to first?"

"I've heard there's work in Glasgow. I'm having a competition with Darcy and Quentin to see who can get the most contracts in the first year."

"Good luck, though I'm sure you don't need it. Just try not to act like you're about to kill your clients, and you'll be fine."

"Easier said than done."

"If you're ever in Dippenwick, I hear there's a nice sum for Maureen Butterswatch."

"I'll make a note of it." She leapt effortlessly onto the windowsill. "Will you be all right finding your way out of here? I want to get a head start on Darcy. Quentin will have to hang around until his wrist heals."

"I think I'll manage." All I had to do was follow the sounds of sickening sweetness and I was bound to find the hall in which I had left Quentin and Darcy.

Morgan paused on the ledge. *Forgo's death was paid for by Craig Little*, I heard. Then she was gone.

Chapter 7

Trust Morgan to give me the name of a ghost. Once I had dealt with the aftermath of Quentin's drunken headstands, I went straight to Eton to nose through their records for Craig Little. I was surprised to come up empty-handed. Ninety-nine percent of everyone who ordered assassinations went to Eton. I tried hunting through Ascot's membership club, but to no avail. Craig Little was an enigma.

Forgo was my best and only lead, so after I had finished with my most recent contracts and told Quentin to stop being a baby, I boarded the train and headed for Dorset. I would never understand the appeal of trains. They were terrible at making detours. I really needed to buy another horse, but the last one I had owned had ended up in a hit-and-run: I had hit the floor, and the horse had run away. At least on trains you could sleep. I planned to use the ride to catch up on some rest, but unfortunately, the other occupants had different ideas.

"Henry," the man with the drooping moustache who was sitting behind me said sternly. "Stop fidgeting."

"My name's not Henry," the child replied.

"Is it not?"

"No, it's Cuthbert."

The man frowned. "I'm going to call you Henry."

"All right, Father." The child drummed his feet against the back of my chair. "Where are we going?"

"We are going to visit your mother. She is staying by the coast to recuperate from a serious illness."

"She's sick?"

"Worryingly so. It began with the sighing. It was near constant, especially when I talked. Then she developed a problem with her eyes that made them roll of their own accord."

I rolled my eyes. It must be contagious.

"But I am sure the sea air will cure her, and if not, she can fake her death, and I'll marry my receptionist. Go to sleep now, Henry."

"But it's not bedtime, and I'm hungry."

"I'll get you a whiskey from the trolley if you go to sleep now."

If he could get the child to stop kicking the back of my seat, I would buy him the bottle. This was why I could not blame my parents for their questionable attitude towards health and safety. What sensible person would not push a slobbering, wailing child into the line of fire? I tried to shut down my thoughts on child endangerment, but then realised I could once again think whatever I wanted, safe in the knowledge that the dysfunctional family behind me could not read my mind. At least I assumed they couldn't. I had never worried about this before. Stupid Morgan and her interfering; I was paranoid enough as it was.

Thoughts of Morgan would only lead to a stiff jaw, so I pulled out the pile of post Dan had forwarded to me. The sheer quantity did not bode well. My suspicions were confirmed when I opened one.

Dear Miss Blakely,

You are the worst kind of murdering scum. You should be in prison with your lawless parents.

All the best,
Your adversary

You could probably track unemployment levels through the quantity of hate mail I got. Surely no one with a job had the time or energy to sit around doing this. I went through them all, correcting grammar mistakes before resealing them in their envelopes and writing "return to sender" on the front. Outside, the browns and greys of towns gave way to sweeping green hills and gold-trimmed trees. The whole wide world shown to me through a window frame, like an oil painting hung in a hall.

❖ ❖ ❖

I jammed all the letters into a post box as I left the station. There was no one to meet me, obviously. I had not wanted to give the locals time to sharpen their pitchforks. It was at least five miles to the Forgo estate, not including the twisting drive designed by someone with a poor sense of direction. I set off at a brisk pace. My skirts were heavy, but that would just add to my momentum downhill. At least I did not have to worry about sunstroke. The sky had put on its usual grey garb. Why did I put up with this godforsaken country anyway? Everything about the countryside I walked through was toned down; flat sea, monotonous fields, people burnt out from the constant threat of debt. Even the cliffs had the orderly look of a striped windbreaker.

The sound of wheels and the heavy, moist breathing of horses was all the warning I had before a cart pulled up beside me.

"All right, ma'am?" said a man with a west-country accent he probably exaggerated for the tourists. "Would you like a lift? It's dangerous for a woman to be walking alone."

Ah yes, Dorset was known for its crime statistics.

"A lift would be much appreciated," I said.

I stepped closer to the cart, and he squinted at my face. His eyes widened comically; he snapped the reins and urged the horse on at a gallop. They disappeared in a spray of mud.

Even if I had murdered Forgo and managed to bribe my way out of prison, that would only have been one death since my start down the road of goodness. Did they think I was about to go on a rampage?

❖ ❖ ❖

I made it to the late Forgo's estate as evening set in. The clouds had lessened to allow a few golden rays to light up the castle and highlight just how hideous it was. It was one of these modern things that tried to be Wordsworth's wet dream with a few turrets and a ruin constructed in the grounds.

I rang the bell and then settled back to wait. Everyone made appointments to see lords because their homes were impractical for unexpected guests. A knock was likely to go unnoticed, and even if it was heard, it would take someone hours to travel the length of the castle to answer the door.

Eventually, it was opened by Forgo's butler. He had a cold composure that I was sure could not be learnt. I imagined him as a baby in the crib looking up at me with the same disinterest. He was much too professional to tell me to get lost, but he did leave a long enough pause that said, "You killed my employer, and I am quite put out by that."

"Could I speak to the owner of the estate?" I asked.

"Lord Begrudd is not accepting unexpected guests today."

"Stevens!" came a distant shout, echoing down the halls.

"It is very important," I persisted. "And would probably distract his lordship from his current predicament, whatever that may be."

The briefest glimpse of relief passed over his features. "Follow me."

Due to Stevens's brisk pace, it took barely twenty minutes for us to reach the study. Inside was a very frazzled man. His sleeves were rolled up, his waistcoat unbuttoned, and his hair trying to compensate for his impropriety by drawing the eye high above his head.

"Stevens, do we have a stable?" he asked desperately.

"Yes, sir," Stevens replied.

The man threw down the paper he was holding. It floated to the floor to join the mess there.

"Damn it. I'll have to start the accounts all over again." He turned his attention to me. "Who are you?"

"Miss Clara Blakely," Stevens announced.

Begrudd's face darkened. "I am furious with you for putting me in this situation. Are you here to kill me?"

"No," I replied.

"That's disappointing. I would rather die than go through this again," Begrudd huffed.

"Sir, might I reiterate my suggestion to employ someone to do the accounts for you?" Stevens asked.

"No, you may not," Begrudd answered haughtily. "This is the running of the estate we are talking about. It cannot be trusted to some layman. In these matters, ancestry is more important than an economics degree. Fetch some brandy, would you, Stevens?"

"I will have to go to the cellar as you have drunk everything we had in the kitchen," Stevens said.

"Do it quickly," Begrudd commanded. "I'm too young to be sober."

Stevens gave a small bow and backed out of the room, probably hoping I skewered the new lord where he sat.

"What can I do for you, Miss Blakely?" Begrudd asked with a weariness suited to someone who had been working in the fields since dawn.

"I am searching for Craig Little. I remember Sir Forgo mentioning him and wondered if you might have his contact details."

"Craig Little. The name rings a bell." He drummed his fingers on the desk. "Oh yes, he's the historian. He's agreed to take Forgo's maps and other clutter."

A historian had hired an assassin to get at Forgo's map collection? People killed for a lot less; but still, maps?

"How much is he buying them for?" I asked.

"Buying? I'm paying him. It's easier than burning them. He will be here tomorrow to pick them up if you want to stay."

"I would not want to intrude."

He waved a hand. "I insist."

"The neighbours might talk. I am rumoured to have killed Forgo, you inherited his estate. If we appear friendly, they may create a plot."

Begrudd pushed himself up. "Let their imaginations run wild. They'll see how reluctant I am to be here at the next public consultation."

"You hold public consultations?"

"It was suggested to me. You can use them to stir up animosity, so everyone is too busy hating each other to get mad at the landowners. Stevens!" he shouted as he led me from the study.

"Yes, sir," Stevens replied, appearing from the depths of the house.

"Prepare the table for a guest. And sharpen the knives." He laughed at his own joke.

Honestly, you get accused of one murder, and it becomes the defining quality of your personality. Did I want to stab him with a carving knife? Yes, but that did not mean I was going to.

"I hope Little is bringing a cargo ship," Begrudd said, nodding to a room we were passing. I did not have to guess what its purpose was. Boxes overflowing with maps were piled to the ceiling.

Begrudd gave me no chance to snoop. Dinner awaited; the spoils of the estate garnished with the pleasures of empire. He settled into his seat at the head of the table with a weary sigh. I was placed on his right. I would have preferred a different spot, perhaps one in the next room. Even then, I probably would have heard him. His voice was a solid thing, used to battering its way through debates. I let him get on with it. His story was one I had heard a million times. The loving yet distant parents, their high expectations and sudden deaths. The subsequent years in which Begrudd never so much fell off the wagon as found himself dragged along behind it. Travelling from country to country, finding amazing places and leaving them with even more amazing sexually transmitted diseases. Getting summoned from his corner of paradise to rainy Britain and having responsibility thrust upon him like a large, unfashionable hat.

I swore Stevens was drawing out each course to make me suffer. I kept myself awake by taking note of Begrudd's mannerisms. He was generous with gestures, frugal on eye contact, and an unnaturally slow blinker. His eyes would stay large and round, begging for moisture until they almost leapt from his head into his wine glass. I counted his blinks. Every time I reached fifty, I made a little hum that could be interpreted as approval or disapproval. Occasionally, I added a nod.

"So, if you didn't kill Forgo, who did?"

It took me a moment too long to recognise that the question was not rhetorical, Begrudd actually wanted my opinion.

"An assassin," I replied.

"An assassin in Dorset? Now I have heard everything."

Hovering by the decanter, I noticed Stevens was paying attention.

"The assassin took responsibility for the murder, I'm surprised it hasn't circulated," I continued.

"There's been rumours, but taking responsibility is not something assassins tend to do."

"I believe it was down to a technical issue."

Begrudd ignored this uninteresting fact. "And who would pay to kill old Bart?"

"I have no idea, but I intend to find out."

I could feel Stevens's eyes on me.

Begrudd yawned. "It will forever remain a mystery. I think it's time to retire. Stevens will show you to your room. Mine's in the west wing if you feel like slitting my throat."

I laughed politely. He really shouldn't tempt me.

❖   ❖   ❖

I was shown to the same room I stayed in when employed by Forgo. It still had that smell of damp and dust that no number of roses could cover up. It was the smell of a large house with barely anyone in it.

I took some fluffy, dead thing off the bed and carried it over to the draughty window seat. When you really listened in a house like this, you could hear everything. It did not matter that Begrudd was miles away; the creaking of his floorboards ran like murmurs through the walls. All I needed was patience.

In the misty moonlight, the lawn was a dark pool, the square hedges unnatural shapes lurking in the shallows. I could see the drive winding its haphazard way to the road, like a spaniel on a scent.

It had been raining the night Morgan came here. I imagined her slipping across the lawn, using the flower beds as cover, avoiding the crunch of the gravel drive. She probably scaled the wall and climbed through his window. Had she done an inventory of the house? Did she know I was there? I wondered whether she was working at that moment, if somewhere in Glasgow, something was creeping over the roofs.

I was bored stiff, and the house had been silent for a long time now. Discarding the blanket, I slipped off my shoes. I was no assassin, and I had poorly laid floorboards working against me.

It was a good thing I had been there before, or I would never have found my way back to the map room. Closing the door behind me, I fumbled around until I located a candle. There was something in that room worth murdering for. My guess was I was looking for something old, something worth more than it would cost to hire an assassin. I should have paid attention to Forgo's cartographical rants, but that probably would have melted my brain. I started opening boxes at random and shifting through the documents. It wasn't just maps; there were copies of wills and transactions, everything that would help Forgo know who owned every piece of land in Britain.

"I see you like maps."

I spun around so fast my candle went out. There was another light though, held by the figure standing in the open doorway. The flickers threw gaunt shadows over Stevens's face.

"Is there anything in particular you are looking for?" he asked.

Going off the evidence that he had not yet thrown me out of the house, I decided to risk the truth.

"Anything Craig Little would be interested in," I replied, holding his stare.

Stevens regarded me coolly. "Mr Little seemed particularly concerned with my late master's journal." He nodded to a stack.

Carefully, I pulled a leather-bound book from the confines of the teetering pile. It was bulging at the edges, a physical reminder that Forgo had never learnt to be concise.

"I trust you can find your way back to your room," Stevens said.

I looked up from the journal to thank him, but he had already withdrawn. His light faded away with his footsteps, leaving me alone in the darkness. What a bastard.

Chapter 8

"Good morning, Stevens," I said as I entered the breakfast room.

"Miss Blakely," he replied. "I hope you slept well."

"Quite satisfactorily, thank you."

I had flicked through Forgo's journal, which had sent me straight into a deep, dreamless sleep. He was, if possible, even more boring in writing. Now the journal was safely stashed in my bag, buried under layers of frightening undergarments.

"Where is Lord Begrudd?" I asked Stevens, noting the undisturbed mountains of food.

"His lordship will not be joining you for several hours yet," Stevens said disdainfully. "I would recommend you get started."

It would probably take me several hours to catalogue all the food laid out before me. Forgo had been a fan of a long breakfast, with plenty of monologuing to fill the gaps between mouthfuls. His ghost was clearly haunting the kitchens.

I loaded up my plate with eggs, bacon, sausages, smoked haddock, crumpets with spiced pear butter, and plenty of fruit. Waste not, want not, and all that. I took it outside, away from the judgemental gazes of the household. It was a bright morning, if not particularly warm, so I found a little table in a pool of sunlight where I could listen to the fountain splash and the bees buzz. I was almost content, which of course meant Begrudd had to find me.

"Morning," he mumbled as he flopped into a chair.

I decided not to point out that it was nearly midday. With his head cradled in his arms, he nursed a coffee. I thought about offering to take his hangover in return for his hospitality but decided he might actually take me up on it. I tuned out his groans.

Stevens cleared his throat behind us. "Sir, Mr Little is here to see you."

Begrudd groaned louder. "Fine. Send him out. I never get a second to myself," he added for my benefit.

I focused on sipping my tea so I would not have to fake sympathy. Begrudd managed to get his waistcoat buttoned. It was buttoned up wrong, but at least he tried. The sound of footsteps approaching made him stand, his complaining appropriate for someone twice his age.

"Mr Little, a pleasure to see you again," I heard Begrudd say. "In a happy coincidence, I have a guest who would like to meet you."

I took my time standing and turning to greet him.

"Mr Little, meet Miss Blakely," Begrudd said.

Craig Little was frozen in place. I recovered faster than him, but only just. He was not at all what I had expected. When I thought of historians, I imagined crusty old men with beards more substantial than their bones. Little was just a kid.

"A pleasure to meet you, Mr Little. I believe Lord Forgo was a mutual friend of ours," I said with a courteous smile.

Little just stared at me.

I forged on regardless. "I heard you were relieving Lord Begrudd of his map collection. How very charitable of you. I must say I am impressed you are able take on such a large collection."

"I have space," Little managed to squeak out. He looked distinctly uncomfortable. "And I know some archives that are interested."

He was lying.

"It is a remarkable collection," I said. "I am sure there are many who would do almost anything to get their hands on it."

He narrowed his eyes at me. I smiled benignly.

"Stevens, bring Mr Little a drink," Begrudd said. He settled back into his chair, apparently satisfied that we could talk to each other without involving him.

"I must admit you are younger than I was expecting," I said. "Lord Forgo spoke of you with such esteem I imagined you would be his contemporary."

"I'm eighteen," Little said. It was clearly a lie. The kid was not a day over fifteen.

I made sure my expression was surprised rather than disbelieving. "How lucky you are to have such a youthful countenance."

"You like maps?" he asked suspiciously.

"I find them to be a useful source of information. In the right hands, they can be very valuable indeed. Of course, getting them can be a hassle. But you don't mind putting in the effort, do you?" I gave him a very meaningful look.

He scowled. "And neither do you."

"No, I consider myself to be very dedicated when the situation demands it," I said.

Begrudd was looking between us in confusion, probably wondering how a conversation about maps could sound quite so aggressive.

"Guns," he said suddenly.

"Excuse me?" I asked.

"We should go shooting," Begrudd said. "It will give us something to do while Stevens packs up the maps. Do you shoot, Miss Blakely?"

"Not for a while, but I'm sure my skills are merely dormant," I replied.

Begrudd clapped his hands. "Excellent. What about you, Mr Little?"

Little shook his head.

"Well, it's a good thing to learn," Begrudd continued, undeterred. "Stevens!"

Stevens came out with a drink for Little. Begrudd took it and downed it in one.

"Tell Gregory to fetch the guns," he said, wiping his mouth with the back of his hand.

"I shall alert him," Stevens replied, looking like he was the one in need of a stiff drink.

Begrudd ushered us around the fountain and through the rose garden to a large expanse of lawn that ran down to a lake. Beyond was a forest, where many pheasants were probably preparing to run into roads and throw themselves under carts in a final act of self-determination before they were hunted down for sport.

A man dressed in tweed came running after us with three shotguns, a trap, and a bag. Begrudd pulled a glass ball from the bag.

"I expect you have never shot with one of these before," he said to me.

The ball appeared to be full of feathers.

"No, I haven't." My targets had always been more human shaped.

"They're all the rage at the moment," Begrudd said grandly. "It's just like shooting the real thing, but you don't have any of those pesky animal-rights people marching onto your lawn to yell at you."

I was not sure the inventor had been thinking about animal safety when they created a target that would litter every aristocratic lawn with shards of glass.

Begrudd caressed his gun. "I remember when I was hunting in Africa. Nothing quite like a bull elephant charging towards you. You should go, Mr Little. It would make a man out of you."

Little scuffed the grass sullenly with his foot. I bet he would take the bull elephant over Begrudd's conversation.

"Pull!" Begrudd shouted.

Gregory fired the trap. It flung the ball up into the air for Begrudd to explode into a shower of feathers.

"Still got it," Begrudd said in satisfaction. "Miss Blakely?"

I picked up one of the guns. I was more used to pistols, but I had fired a few of these in my youth. I hitched it up to eye level. The trap let the ball fly. I followed it with my eye and pulled the trigger. The shot went wide. Dammit.

"Do not feel disheartened," Begrudd said in a show of sympathy that was ruined by his huge grin. "You gave it a shot, that's what matters. It would be unusual for someone as delicate as you to excel at a man's sport."

I gritted my teeth and resisted the urge to turn the gun on him.

"Pull!" I shouted.

This time, I was dead on. Light caught on the shards of glass as the feathers floated down to Earth. I turned back to Begrudd with a carefully constructed mask of surprised satisfaction. He scowled unreservedly.

"Mr Little, take a turn." Begrudd picked up the last gun and threw it to Little. Little let it fall. Reluctantly, he bent down to get it.

"This will put hairs on your chest," Begrudd said.

Little raised the gun half-heartedly. His grip was completely wrong, but Begrudd did not correct him.

"Pull, I guess," Little said languidly.

The ball flew up and arced through the sky. It had hit the ground by the time Little had fired in the completely wrong direction. Little let the gun drop limply to his side.

"Oh dear. I think the competition is between you and me, Miss Blakely," Begrudd said with a laugh. He lifted his gun again.

I addressed the kid. "The reason I was so desperate to meet you, Mr Little, is I am trying to track down Forgo's killer."

Little let his gun off into the ground. The bang startled Begrudd and his shot went high.

"That one doesn't count," Begrudd said.

"Of course, there is nothing wrong with hiring an assassin," I continued. "I do not wish to reprimand them, only to clear my name of any wrongdoing."

Little did not reply.

I aimed my gun at the sky. "You two were close," I told Little as I let the bullet fly. Another bullseye for me.

"No, we weren't," Little retorted. "It was strictly professional."

I bet it was. Nothing more professional than a contract killer.

"Do you have any idea who would hire an assassin to kill him?" I asked innocently.

"No," he replied quickly.

I smiled at him. "Well, if anything springs to mind, do feel free to write to me."

"Give me two, Gregory," Begrudd said.

Gregory shot two balls from the trap, one after the other. Begrudd hit them both.

"Ha! Beat that, Miss Blakely."

I put aside my competitiveness and raised the gun. I shot the first one Gregory fired and let the other fall unharmed. There was nothing worse than a bad loser in charge of a firearm.

"Better luck next time, Miss Blakely," Begrudd said smugly. "You put on a fine show. Lunchtime, I think."

❖ ❖ ❖

Lunch was served in the dark confines of the dining room. I sat opposite Little.

Begrudd sank into his seat with a contented sigh. "What good sport. It's healthy to get away from the accounts." His eyes took on a faraway look as the dread of more filing overcame him. "Stevens! Whiskey."

Stevens topped up his glass, his will to live floating away like a leaf in an autumnal gale.

"Tell me, Little, have you been on any digs?" Begrudd asked.

"No." Little could not have seemed less interested in Begrudd if he had fallen asleep at the table.

"I had the good fortune of being in Egypt when a friend was excavating. Found some wonderful busts. Helped him smuggle them out of the country," Begrudd boasted.

I gave a hum that Begrudd would probably translate to, "What a dashing and daring rogue I see before me." I was preoccupied by Little pushing a bit of veal around his plate. He didn't like shooting, so I could assume he didn't like violence. He wasn't a social climber, or he would be trying to act interested in Begrudd. What would bring a person like him to kill? Money was the obvious answer, or perhaps fear.

"Can I go yet?" Little asked, rudely cutting off Begrudd's monologue.

"Of course, of course," Begrudd replied, taking the interruption in good cheer, probably because he was a third of the way through the bottle of whiskey. "I believe I owe you some money."

He pulled out his chequebook and began scrawling on it. Was he really paying Little fifty pounds to take Forgo's collection? He handed it over to the kid, who stared at it for so long, I wondered if he could read at all.

"This is too much," he said finally.

"Nonsense," Begrudd said.

Little inclined his head. "Then I thank you for your generosity. Sixty pounds is most generous."

"Sixty?" Begrudd asked.

Little held the cheque out to him. There, where I could have sworn it had said fifty, sixty was printed in Begrudd's script.

"Sixty. Of course. That is what I decided. It's proper. Sixty..." he trailed off.

Little stood and pocketed the cheque. Begrudd stood as well, still looking confused.

"I'll see how the packing is going," he said, recovering somewhat.

This was my moment to escape.

"Thank you again for your hospitality," I told Begrudd, "but I really must be going."

"Very well." Begrudd shook my hand. "Anytime you feel like murdering me, my door is always open."

I drew a laugh from the last of my etiquette reserves and turned to Little. "Good luck with your endeavours, Mr Little. I am sure we shall be seeing much more of one another in the future."

I thought about the journal tucked safely in my suitcase. I would read it on the train. Craig Little would rue the day he got in the way of my retirement plan.

Chapter 9

"Next stop, Dippenwick."

Damn. I had fallen asleep. How was Forgo continually able to bore me into unconsciousness? I had barely made it through ten pages of the infernal journal. At this rate, Little would be able to grow facial hair by the time I had finished.

I rushed off the platform and walked as fast as I could through the village without looking like I was hurrying. Stares and whispers followed me as I went. People shut their doors and drew their curtains as I passed their homes. If I saw Maureen, I was going to push her into a ditch, witnesses be damned.

Dippenwick may have been the central meeting point of all the surrounding hamlets, but it was still small. Thirty houses, a church, Brigade clubhouse, and a jail. That was it. The ratio of sheep to people tipped heavily in favour of sheep. Dan owned the only boarding house. It was full of people whose stay in Dippenwick was supposed to be temporary, but they were kidding themselves. It was a charming place, but not one you admitted to moving to voluntarily. If you failed, you went abroad, or you went to Dippenwick.

I threw open Dan's door. "Dan! Stop whatever inconsequential thing you are doing."

Dan was standing on a chair, feather duster in hand. "Inconsequential? That's rich coming from someone who has never done a day of housework in their life."

"I need your help."

He clambered off the chair. "Does this mean I am being upgraded to sidekick?"

"If I were getting a sidekick, you wouldn't even make it to the interview stage." I slammed the journal on the table. "An important clue to Forgo's death lies within this journal, but it is too dull to read."

"Why are you always so dramatic? It cannot be that bad."

I settled myself in a chair and watched him pick up the journal. He flicked it open and began to read. His eyes gained a foggy film as they glazed over. He rubbed them and looked up at me in horror.

"How is this even possible? I've written tax returns with more soul. This is the guy who was assassinated?"

I nodded.

"I think the question you should be asking is who wouldn't want to kill him."

"Be serious."

"Fine. If I'm going to tackle this, I'm going to need drugs. Coffee?"

"Coffee," I agreed.

I held the door for him while he grabbed two mugs and his hat, and then we went outside onto the dirt track. The industrial revolution had yet to reach Dippenwick, which was why I liked it. Life was simpler when you could be late for work because you lost both of your shoes in the mud.

"Tell me more about this assassin friend of yours," Dan said, taking my arm.

"She's not my friend."

"No, because Clara Blakely would never stoop low enough to have a friend."

I pushed him away. "That's not what I meant. She's dangerous."

"Yeah, she's an assassin."

"Yes, but that's not the real problem. She has a function. She can read minds."

Dan stopped walking. "You're kidding."

I shook my head.

He laughed as he jogged to catch up with me again. "Of all the people in the world, with all the different functions they could have, this has got to be the worst, most catastrophic turn of events for you. She can see through all your lies?"

"Yes."

"That is priceless."

"I'm glad you find my predicament so amusing."

He took my arm again. "What does she think of you?"

"It's hard to tell. She gave me the name of the person who contracted Forgo, which has got to be good, right?"

"Maybe she's trying to stir up trouble, get you involved in whatever plot Forgo was mixed up in."

"I don't know. She's bemusing."

We reached the stall set up in the street where someone was serving coffee out of a large pot to all the farm labourers heading back from the fields.

"Hi, Carrie," Dan said.

"Hi, Dan," Carrie replied, smiling at him and avoiding eye contact with me.

Dan handed her the mugs. She ladled a thick brown liquid into them that smelt nothing like coffee.

"Tell me more about this illegal gang of animal traffickers you stopped," Dan said to me.

I smiled. Dan had a tradition of trying to talk me up in public, as though he could change public opinion one fool at a time.

"I can't take all the credit," I said modestly. "If Miss Thomas had not been there, I don't know who would have gone for help while I held the mob of cruel criminals back. Mr Indestructible was very impressed by our work. He said he has been trying to track them down for some time."

"The Brigade is lucky to have you. Thanks, Carrie," Dan said, handing her a couple of coins. "You should drop in and see Arthur Todd while you're here. He's been asking after you again."

We were far enough from the cart now that I could talk freely. "I would rather boil myself in Carrie's pot. Maybe that's how she makes it."

I took a swig from my mug. It was better not to let it touch your tastebuds. Behind us, I could hear the small crowd convening around Carrie as she repeated everything she had overheard.

"I see everyone still loves you," I told Dan.

"That's what happens if you are a polite, respectful person who genuinely cares about the community."

"Sounds like an awful lot of effort."

"It's even more effort when people keep asking me whether you've murdered everyone in the house yet."

"I'm surprised you can still stand to be seen with me."

"It's my good deed of the day, tainting my reputation through you."

"The vicar must be very proud."

"Actually, he told me I should leave you in a ditch somewhere. Everyone tells me you're no good. I got an hour-long lecture from Maureen the other day."

"Did you tell her to take her parish news and shove it up her—"

"No. You know I hate confrontations. I told her that you were lovely and I did not believe that you had a single bad thought in your head. She was adamant that you are a raving, homicidal maniac. So I said we would just have to agree to disagree, and could she please stop yelling at me when I am trying to buy a cauliflower."

I pushed open the little gate to Dan's house.

"Look at my petunias," he tutted, stepping off the garden path to examine some ragged flowers. "I've got another acid-spitting slug. It must have come from London."

"Put salt down," I suggested.

"It spits acid, Clara. I don't think a bit of salt will stop it."

I opened the door, catching sight of someone running up the stairs.

"Hi, Mrs Winow," Dan called.

"Hello, Dan," Mrs Winow said, failing to cover up the sound of the cat stuffed beneath her jumper meowing loudly.

I put my empty mug on the table and leant over the journal. Dan joined me.

"We should start at the end, just before he died," he said, flipping to the back.

I read one page while Dan read another. I was starting to understand how gold miners felt. A cloud of helplessness overcame me as I stared at the wall of words, knowing I might read them all and never find a nugget.

"It looks like some mayor has been land grabbing," I said unenthusiastically. "They pushed their fence back."

"Yeah, like three feet. It's immoral, but it isn't something you kill someone over."

"I would."

"Yes, but you're you. A lord blocked a footpath, but again, I doubt anyone would kill Forgo just because he was demanding they reinstate public access."

"Clearly, you know nothing of the landed gentry."

He flicked back another page.

"Wait." I grabbed his arm. "I saw a name I recognised."

Dan turned the page and there it was, **Craig Little**.

Dan began to read. "As previously noted, I contacted Sir John Blythwood III to inquire about my findings. Today, he sent a representative. He was some young historian called Craig Little, and I did not like him one bit. Not only was he rude and scruffy, but he was also not at all interested in my maps. He handled them with a negligence unbecoming to a supposedly professional historian. He was dismissive of my accusation of forgery. He merely suggested my copies were faulty, advising me to view the originals in person. As previously noted, I have viewed the originals in person and have seen how different they are from my copies. However, I do not doubt the validity of my sources. I intend to get to the bottom of this, starting with how such an incompetent boy ever became personal historian to Sir John Blythwood III. I suspect perhaps he is being duped. First, however, I must cure my gout. It is making me quite irritable."

Dan broke off and looked up at me. "Craig Little is forging documents."

"For John Blythwood," I completed.

Dan looked back through the pages. "Blythwood bought Mundmere Common, but he shouldn't have been able to. Forgo claims it was registered as common land, until suddenly it wasn't. Boundaries moved, records changed, legal documents altered overnight."

"Documents don't lie." My thoughts wandered back to our meeting. "At least, we assume they don't. But what if you were able to change documents? What if you had a function that allowed you to rearrange the ink on paper? You could, for example, turn a fifty-pound cheque into sixty pounds in the blink of an eye."

"That would certainly be convenient."

That sneak. If Little went away and changed the cheque, he would be accused of forgery, but if he did it in front of our eyes, we accepted it.

"Why put so much effort into buying a piece of land?" I asked.

"They wanted to conserve it."

"Sure they did," I scoffed.

Dan turned the journal to a page with a map. "Look. Right next to Mundmere Common is a factory owned by Blythwood. Maybe he wants to expand."

I shook my head. "He's had the land for a year, and we've seen no expansion. Isn't that weird?"

"I don't know."

"I think it's time I paid Mundmere Common a visit." I picked up the journal and stuffed it back into my bag. At least I hadn't unpacked.

"Surely this can wait till tomorrow," Dan said.

"I need to figure this out before they realise the journal is gone."

"The journal itself is worthless. If you don't have the maps he refers to, you can't prove anything. In fact, even with the maps, people will just say Forgo's are wrong."

"Then I will just have to do more snooping, won't I?"

I picked up my bags. Dan grabbed my arm.

"Clara, stop."

"Why?"

"Why?" he asked incredulously. "Forgo is dead! And if you carry on with your usual single-mindedness, you could be next!"

"Unlike some stuffy lord, I'm used to looking after myself."

"Even if it comes to blows with Blythwood? He's way above your usual circle, Clara. He is rich, powerful, and used to getting his way."

"Then he'll be grateful when I offer him a simple solution to tie up all his loose ends."

"Clara, I know you think of me as that boring voice of caution in your head you choose to ignore, but please, I am begging you, go carefully on this one. John Blythwood invented a whole theory of evolution to save himself from bankruptcy; if his grandson has any of his political shrewdness, you may have met your match."

I slung my bag over my shoulder. "Your lack of faith in me is inspiring, but I have a trespass to commit. Don't wait up."

Chapter 10

Mundmere Common was in the middle of the East End, bordered by Mundmere Factory, where BW Incorporated had churned out my Squadron uniform and so many other one-size-fits-all replicas. I had opted to wear it for this little excursion. It was, unfortunately, the most practical outfit I owned, and I was less likely to be thought suspicious if caught roaming the streets in the dead of night.

The common's twenty acres of forest and scrubland had once been the perfect place for workers to take their lunchbreak and perhaps engage in a harmless bit of deviance. Now, even the illiterate could not fool themselves into thinking they were welcome. The ten-foot-tall fence topped with barbed wire was unnecessary, the No Trespassing signs already formed an impenetrable wall of unfriendliness.

The main gate was far too conspicuous, so I followed the fence, sticking to the road and trying not to look too obvious as I scanned it for the best point of entrance. It was not long before I saw what I was looking for. There was a small hole under the fence, dug by one of the many animals who lived in the common and did not appreciate this rude obstacle suddenly blocking their way. I scanned up and down the street. There was no one around.

Kneeling beside the fence, I began scooping great handfuls of dirt away, widening the hole until it was a far more practical size. I went headfirst, pushing and wriggling myself through like a worm. It had to be up in the top five most embarrassing things to be caught doing.

With a final squirm, my head broke from the damp, musky earth on the other side. I managed to get my arms through and drag myself the rest of the way. I was covered in mud, and my dignity was a little bruised, but I was in. What was Dan so worried about? It was only a harmless bit of trespassing. It was worth it if it would allow me to put my days of colluding with assassins behind me. I wanted to work with people who wore colour and let me sit in comfortable chairs while they bored me to death.

I stood and looked around, squinting into the darkness. It was not what I was expecting. The trees, the dense undergrowth, it was the same as it had been before, if not thicker. Blythwood had trumpeted conservation, but that was usually just an excuse. You would expect someone like him to seize the opportunity to cut and slash and cause a bit of wanton destruction in the name of profit.

Having absolutely no idea which way to go, I began to put distance between myself and the fence, fighting my way through bracken, brambles, and clumps of stinging nettles. Eventually, I found what had probably been a man-made footpath once. Now, it had shrunk to a narrow animal track. I followed its meandering line, wondering if I was going to get lost in this forest forever, and if I did, how long I would last. That was the problem with all this city living. I didn't know where I would be without easy access to metallic-tasting water and slightly mouldy meat.

I was cursing myself for not bringing a lantern when I stumbled onto a path. Unlike the track I had been following, this one had been used by humans recently. The mud was churned by footprints, hoofprints, and deep ruts caused by carts. To my left stood the main gate, which I must have circled back to accidentally. I set off in the opposite direction. Mud squelched underfoot, leaking into my supposedly waterproof boots. The night was dark and overcast, but even though I stuck as close to the trees as possible, I felt exposed. I resisted the temptation to reach out with my function to see what was around. The last thing I needed was to sense five-hundred squirrels with sore paws.

A glimmer of light up ahead made me freeze. I ducked behind a tree and peeked around its trunk. The light was still there, but it was not coming any closer. I crept on as quietly as I could. The light steadily grew brighter until it began to separate into individual pinpricks. They were lanterns, raised on poles and illuminating a clearing. After the dark of the wood, they seemed blinding.

"Did you hear something?"

I crouched low. The man the voice belonged to came into view, silhouetted against the light.

"It was nothing, come on."

A second figure joined him. The first man scanned the wood where I was hidden, holding his own lantern above his head. Finally, he lowered his arm and both men set off together, walking away from me. They were approaching two more people standing farther down the bank next to a cluster of barrels and tools.

"About time you two showed up," one of them called.

"Forgive me for trying to postpone a gruesome death," the first man replied.

I stood up and, keeping myself within the treeline, crept forward so I could follow their conversation.

"Grow a spine, would you. It's been eight days since it attacked one of us, may Susan rest in peace."

"You know why they recruit us from workhouses? Because we're desperate enough to put up with this."

They shared a laugh, but it sounded nervous. I squinted at the water, sure the lamplight had to be playing tricks on my eyes. It was as though an invisible water wheel was churning it into a dark froth.

The two latecomers picked up shovels and began spading a white powder from the barrel into the lake.

"That's enough," one of the others said.

The men put down their shovels and stepped back. The other two took their place. One of them collected a sample from the lake, while the other made notes in a thick ledger.

"We have movement," one of the shovel men said.

There was something about the absolute dread in his voice that raised the hairs on the back of my neck. A gurgling, sucking sound reached my ears. The lake seemed to be rising in the centre, as though something was pushing its way out. My mind went unbidden to the stuffed animals I had seen in cabinets in large houses: the scaly bodies of reptilian creatures pulled from swamps in far-flung places. Yet as it rose higher, I realised this was no animal. Its body oozed and shifted, unable to commit to a single shape. It was not so much rising from the lake as building itself from it. Out of the corner of my eye, I saw the shovel men stepping back. They were afraid, but they were not running. Surely, if it was dangerous, they would run. The thing was still rising. At seven feet tall, it seemed to stand on top of the lake. It was as far from human as you could get, and yet my mind picked out a head, legs, and arms that were reaching towards me. It looked like a man made of dirt, and that was what made me think of Dirt Man. Did this mean one of the men by the barrels was the psychopathic serial killer Dirt Man himself? None of them seemed surprised to see the clay giant. Horrified, yes, but not surprised.

Whoever was controlling it was steering it in my direction. It was gliding across the lake like a dense, damp dust cloud. I had an unjustified and completely ridiculous feeling that it could see me. There was something purposeful about its movement.

"We get to live another night. It looks like it's on its way out," one of the men said.

"Wait. Is someone there?"

One of the lights swung towards me, spurring me into action. I turned and dived back into the woods. As famous as Dirt Man was, I decided to pass on an introduction. Brambles snatched at my clothes as I ran, and branches reached out to form barriers every way I turned. I glanced back. There was no sign of the men, but that swirling mass of dirt was coming up behind me, visible in the diminishing light from the lanterns. It was flying just above the ground, passing through every obstacle that ensnared me. I snatched a glance forward just in time to avoid a tree. I could hear the thing smacking into the trees behind me with a wet *thwack*, but that didn't slow it down.

It was instinct, reaching out with my function. I had been forced to run for my life on numerous occasions, and incapacitating my pursuer was my go-to method of escape. My function landed on a pain so great it hit my senses like a physical blow. I tripped over a root and went sprawling in the dead leaves. I flipped onto my back, scooting away as the monster loomed over me.

The pain I felt was not coming from a person, it was coming from this thing, this lump of mud. It was not possible. It could not be possible. Dirt couldn't feel.

The thing lunged, and I did the only thing I could think of.

I took its pain.

I had never taken someone's pain when they were on fire, but I imagined it would feel something like what I experienced then. It was too much for me to even to cry out. My body locked up. My eyes were trapped open as I watched the Dirt Man dissolving in front of me. It piled into a mound, looking no more threatening than a large mole hill. I could not comprehend what I was seeing. The only thought passing through the white-hot agony consuming my mind was that I had to get away.

I rolled onto my stomach and crawled forward. I could barely get my limbs to do what I told them to. The pain was in my head, I told myself. It wasn't real. My hands came to rest on the base of a tree, and I used it to claw upwards, pulling myself onto my feet. There was nothing behind me: no more monsters, just the lights from the lake.

I staggered away from them, lurching from tree to tree. It wasn't real. The pain I felt was an illusion. It was hard to convince myself any of this when it felt like my body was tearing itself apart.

❖ ❖ ❖

I had never been more pleased to see a fence before. I dropped to my knees, somehow convinced I had magically returned to the hole I had dug. It wasn't there. I had no idea which part of the fence I had stumbled upon. Digging a new hole seemed impossible, and even though I did not care one jot about the barbed wire anymore, climbing the fence seemed even further out of my reach. If I was to get out of there, I had to get rid of the pain. I reached out with my function. There was no one, not even an unsuspecting rabbit.

Using the fence to prop me up, I edged forward, prodding the area with my function. There had to be someone out there. I could not be the last person in the city, in the world. Perhaps there were hordes of people on the street, but I was so overwhelmed that I could not feel them.

For a second, I thought I had imagined it. But no, there it was. There was a crowd somewhere on the other side of the fence. It could have been a pub or a fight or the grand opening of a new garden centre for all I cared. The important thing was there were people. This was not going to be a pleasant experience for them, but if there was anything that was going to stunt my moral growth, it was the searing torment I was currently experiencing. Sharing the pain amongst a group meant it would not be nearly so bad for them. Sending the organiser of whatever event I was about to ruin a silent apology, I began shunting my pain into the crowd.

With every push the fire burnt a little less bright. It was like waking up and realising the horrors were all dreams, like discovering the cup of poison you drank was just apple juice. The agony faded away like it had never existed. As the last of the pain was extinguished, I sank to my knees, sobbing. I was filthy, scratched, and faintly embarrassed at my reaction. I probably looked like I had just gone through hell and certainly felt like I had. But I was alive, and that felt amazing.

Never had I thought I would feel quite so grateful kneeling in the mud, listening to the far-off screams of people in pain.

❖   ❖   ❖

The trip back to my hotel felt like no time at all, probably because after I had dug myself out of Mundmere, I ran like my life depended on it. I told myself it was because I had to put the last of my adrenaline to good use, not because my senses were returning to me, and with them, my fear was rising like a crescendo.

I shut myself in my hotel room, bolted the door, and slid down so my back was pressed against it. I needed to eat, but I was too exhausted to move. I needed to sleep, but I was shaking so hard, I was sure I would shake myself out of bed. I felt like I wanted to cry again, but my tear glands were lazy things, and I had already used up my crying quota for the year.

Instead, I focused on the important question: what had just happened?

Chapter
11

I woke abruptly and flinched at the sudden move from the position I had moulded into. I had fallen asleep sitting against the door. I deserved every inch of my discomfort. A perfectly good bed was less than three feet away.

I got up carefully and made my way to the window, massaging my neck. The traffic was building as the morning rush hour got underway. Horses were stamping their hooves while their impatient riders shouted and threw things at each other. Could I have dreamt last night? No, my dreams were not that interesting. Besides, I hadn't tried to make a snow angel in the middle of the street, and I could not think of any other explanation as to why I was so mucky. I picked a person shovelling manure and gave them my pain. They dropped their shovel as their hand went to their back. I was breaking my rules, but my mental state was a little fragile, and I did not want any excuse to lose my wits.

I trudged downstairs to ask for hot water and got a few odd stares and a bowl of tepid, brown water out of it. I supposed I looked quite the sight. What story would they make up? That I was digging a tunnel into a bank vault?

Back in my room, I began to scrub the dirt from my hands. On the bright side, I might have been the only person to have ever survived a Dirt Man attack. It did not feel like a victory.

What was the Dirt Man? Not a man, that was for sure. The thing I had encountered had come from the lake, it was not a functionable. But if it wasn't an animal, how could it have been in pain? And how was John Blythwood mixed up in this? He had bought Mundmere because of it. Of that, I was sure. But why? And why all the secrecy?

I threw down my cloth and submerged my face in the bowl. Bubbles surged past my skin as I breathed out. Whatever was happening at Mundmere, John Blythwood had a good reason for not wanting people snooping around. I may not have had the faintest clue what was going on, but I knew enough to cause him a lot of hassle if I wanted. I pulled my face out of the bowl. Water streamed down my face, soaking the collar of my suit. It was time to blackmail a powerful person.

❖ ❖ ❖

I walked into the London Historical Society looking like a respectable woman, not someone who had spent the last night crawling through dirt. My Squadron suit had been washed in water dirtier than it and hung up to drip on the floorboards. I would be long gone from that dump by the time the mould grew.

An old man was hunched over a tall mahogany desk. The whiteness of his skin, scraggy beard, and bushy eyebrows made him look like he was coated in a layer of dust.

"How may I help you, Miss…"

I decided not to give him my name. "I'm looking for the contact details of Mr Craig Little. I understand he is a historian and was hoping he might be a member here."

"Mr Little is a member," he sneered. "But if you want, I can point you in the direction of a real historian."

"Is he not a respectable historian?" I asked with fake surprise.

"There are some people who respect him."

Blythwood being number one.

"But he is young and inexperienced. There are others here who have far more training. Perhaps you would like to take a look at the latest edition of our journal to see what the more distinguished members of our society specialise in."

He pushed me a hardback denser than the tree it had once been.

"How interesting." I read the list of contents. Potsherds, mapping post holes, clay pot analysis. Incredible, a list of everything I didn't want to read.

"Or I would be happy to introduce you to those who are here," the overly helpful man offered.

I looked to the door leading into the society common room, where many old men were doubtlessly engaged in alcoholism and a gossip.

"That is very kind of you," I said sweetly, "and I will bear it in mind should I ever have need of a historian, but the matter I wish to discuss with Mr Little is a personal one. His mother is very sick, and I must ask Mr Little to hasten to her side immediately. Mrs Little gave me his address, but alas, I have mislaid it. I fear if I do not find him soon, it may be too late."

"I am terribly sorry. Here." He scribbled down an address and passed it to me. "Do tell Mr Little how sorry we are for his loss."

They were only sorry Little wasn't the one with the incurable disease.

"I'm sure he shall appreciate it. Good day."

Now all I had to do was find Little before he heard his mother was gravely ill. Forget Morgan and her speedy bird, rumours travelled the fastest of the lot.

❖ ❖ ❖

I knocked on a door. The sign outside said it was a boarding house. Craig must have been making a pretty penny if he was able to board at a place as well-placed and well-kept as this.

The door was opened by a neat woman with a pinched face.

"Can I help you?" she asked.

"I am looking for Mr Little."

Her face lit up. "He's out at the moment, but he should be back soon if you would like to wait."

Bemused by her enthusiasm, I allowed her to escort me through a narrow hall with a nice, understated wallpaper that I could barely see due to the number of boxes packed against it. In the sitting room, she moved a box from a chair and indicated that I should sit.

"I tasked Craig with fetching some milk. It's the least he could do after filling my house with old books. What's he trying to do, start a library?"

I picked up a stray map that had stuck itself to the back of my chair. I had to agree with Forgo on this: for a historian, Little did not seem to hold much respect for the past.

"It's so nice to finally meet one of Craig's friends," she said as she threaded through Forgo's collection with a tea tray.

That explained the warm welcome.

"I must admit we have only known each other for a short time." A day, in fact.

"I'm sure your friendship will be a lasting one. He's a good lad, just a little moody sometimes."

Puberty could do that to you.

"How long has he lived here?" I asked.

"Almost a year now."

She handed me a cup of tea with too much milk.

"Where are his parents?" I asked.

"They live up in the North." The North for Londoners being anything above Luton. "I don't think they have a very good relationship. He doesn't write to them often."

Maybe because he knew his landlady was snooping through his mail.

"But then, that's Craig, isn't it? Always mooching around in his room. I wish he would go out a bit more, comb his hair, and stop listening to all that loud music. I've heard of concerts where cellists smash their instruments and the conductors jump into the crowd. I don't want him getting mixed up in any of that."

"It's probably just a phase."

The front door opened and slammed.

"I've got your sodding milk, Mrs Morris!"

"There's someone here to see you, Craig!" she shouted back.

"Who is it?"

She turned back to me. "I'm sorry, I never asked your name."

"Clara Blakely," I said.

Her hand jerked, spilling tea onto a pile of Forgo's tithes. Craig came through the door.

"What are you doing here?" he demanded.

"Hello to you too. I thought I would pop in and see how the map sorting is going. I guess you've been hard at work going through it. Did you get what you were looking for?"

He folded his arms. "I don't know what you're talking about."

"I think you do. Mrs Morris, would you mind leaving us alone for a moment?"

Mrs Morris nodded so vigorously her bun came loose. She fled, leaping over the boxes with the gymnastic dexterity of a cat.

I stirred my tea. "You've got a nice place here. Better than I would expect an amateur historian could afford."

"I'm not an amateur," he snapped.

"Where did you study?"

"Cambridge."

I smiled. "Really? Can you prove it?"

"Yes," he said defiantly. "What do you want?"

"Clearly, you never had a real formal education, so I'll spell it out for you. Stop me if I'm going too fast." I put down my teacup. "I know that your function allows you to change documents and that you have used it to help John Blythwood buy Mundmere Common."

Little went very pale.

"I have proof that you did this, courtesy of Forgo's journal." A journal that was tucked safely under the mattress in my hotel room. It was unlikely anyone would notice one more lump. "I also know Blythwood doesn't want anyone looking too closely at what he's doing at Mundmere. If people were to investigate his actions, the consequences would be…awkward. The scandal would ruin both you and Blythwood. There would be prison time involved, I suspect."

He was now sweating.

"Of course, you already knew the risks when you got involved, I'm just reminding you of them to convey to you the seriousness of the situation and how appalled I am that someone of John Blythwood's calibre would get involved in such heinous crimes. However, I am a charitable person, and I'm happy to make this all go away. All I ask in return is that someone goes to the press and admits responsibility for Forgo's death, thereby clearing my name. I don't care who this person is or what they claim the reason to be. You could say you did it because Forgo made fun of your acne for all I care. And to sweeten the deal and apologise for wasting my time, I want one-hundred pounds. I'm giving you three days. By the end of those three days, I want to read an article in *The Times* proving my innocence and see a nice fat cheque waiting for me at my bank."

I picked up my tea and sipped it, watching over the rim as Craig relearnt how to swallow.

"How?" he gasped.

I raised my eyebrows. "How what?"

"How did you know?"

"That you and Blythwood are both scheming little cheats?" I asked.

He nodded.

"I suppose it takes one to know one." I flashed him a smile. "Now, do you accept my terms?"

He nodded slowly. He seemed dazed. The reality would hit him soon enough, give him the motivational boost he needed to see this through.

"Good." I stood. "I'll be going then. And please don't disappoint me. You have a bright and shining career ahead of you, and I would hate to destroy it."

He seemed frozen in place. I had to manoeuvre round him to reach the door.

"Thank you for tea, Mrs Morris," I called.

"That's quite all right," came a muffled response from behind a closed door that was probably barricaded with a table. I expected Mrs Morris would change her mind about trying to get Craig to leave the house more. It was a dangerous world out there, full of evil souls like Clara Blakely.

Chapter
12

Being teamed up with a retiree named Sally for patrol gave me a new perspective on life that had me wondering if I had been too hard on the kid. She wanted to give back to her community by using her earthquake-inducing voice to scream at any youths enjoying themselves. I did not want to be a cantankerous old woman who forgot what it was like to be young and full of schemes. Then again, I thought—as I passed my ringing ears to a poor bystander who was already suffering too much to notice—I would threaten a kitten if it meant I could walk away from this endless suffering.

By the time I had convinced Sally she had done enough world-saving for one day, it was long past lunch, and I was starving. I was trying to decide how I could get food without any social interaction when someone dropped down into the street next to me.

"Clara."

Heavens to Betsy! Were heart attacks Morgan's speciality? I took a moment to catch my breath and glare in the general direction of her hood.

"Morgan. What are you doing here?"

"I was contacted by a previous client."

Craig Little echoed in my head.

Ah. I could probably take a stab at who that commission was.

Clara, came Morgan's severe voice. *Do not tell me I am about to be contracted to kill you.*

It was probably a complete coincidence he sent for her after I threatened him.

You threatened him? That isn't why I gave you his name!

What a fool I had been. Craig was probably kicking around his house, writing to assassins and laughing over me for being a gullible idiot who thought she could take him down with a stern talking to.

If only I could kill him before he killed me. Unfortunately, I did not have the savings to hire an assassin, and even if I did, would I be entirely comfortable killing a fifteen-year-old who had not yet done me any bodily harm? He was not a very nice fifteen-year-old, but could I really blame him for trying to kill me? I had been around his age when I plotted my parents' downfall. If I was honest with myself, I couldn't condemn him for trying to make the best of a bad lot.

Besides, I had a feeling Morgan would be disappointed if I asked her, and though it was pathetic, I didn't want to give her another reason to think I was the worst kind of scum. I would just have to hope Craig had other unfinished business that did not involve me, or failing that, that Morgan "Would Kill Her Friends If Asked To" Murdur, would listen to reason.

"Do you want to go out?" Morgan asked.

I realised we had been standing in the middle of the street in apparent silence for some time now.

"Don't you have to see Craig?" I replied.

"It's still light."

"Oh, of course, The Rules."

"Do you want to go out?" she repeated.

I could be living on borrowed time. Did she really think I would want to waste it with her?

What else would you do? Go volunteer for the Squadron?

That was a fair point. "Where to?"

She shrugged. "You probably know better than me. Most of the places I frequent are where the aristocracy go to seek us out. They like to pick rough areas; it's part of the experience of hiring an assassin."

How sweet; she thought the places these well-groomed people chose for a bit of local colour were dodgy. I had belonged to the criminal underworld. The places I knew would break through that stoic exterior.

Want to bet?

I grinned. "All right. But you asked for it."

❖ ❖ ❖

I took her to The King's Head on a Spike. It had no direct links to the monarchy as far as I was aware, but many a head had rolled in this fine establishment. It was sandwiched between a butcher and a morgue, a convenience for when they were carting off the bodies. If one was full, you could just go to the other.

We stepped over an unconscious person in the doorway. Candles burned down to stubs gave just enough light to feel our way to the bar.

"Hi, Clara," the man behind the bar said.

He looked familiar in an old, grizzled man sort of way, but I couldn't remember his name.

"Hello. Great to see you again," I lied.

His name is Frank, Morgan supplied. *He thinks you've forgotten it.*

Had Morgan just been useful? Perhaps I was dreaming.

"How's business been, Frank?" I asked.

He gave a gap-toothed smile. "We redecorated."

"I thought so." The bloodstain in the corner looked new.

"How goes the road to redemption?" he asked.

I quirked a smile. "Rocky."

"How about a drink to send you on your merry way?" he offered.

I nodded. "Two please, the best in the house."

He reached for two brown glasses and a dusty bottle with a label too mildewed to read. I doubted it was rosé, though, as black, viscous liquid splattered into the glasses. I thanked him and took them to a corner table far away from the group playing cards. It looked like they were gambling on their spleens. My Community Squadron costume was getting a few looks, but having Morgan as my shadow seemed to stop even the intensely inebriated from making a move.

Morgan threw back her hood and put her mask in a pocket. I raised my glass, and she clinked hers against it like a challenge. The liquor burnt all the way down and up again before I managed to stop my gag reflex from painting Morgan a new shade of black.

"Did you know he's fifteen?" I asked after I had finished coughing.

Morgan wiped the tears from her eyes and looked around. "Who?"

"Craig, he's fifteen."

"You're kidding. What fifteen-year-old is called Craig?"

"This one."

Morgan seemed genuinely upset by this knowledge. "In my defence, we met in a dark alley."

"Do you not take commissions from minors?"

"I try not to implicate anyone under the age of eighteen. It feels wrong."

"If they're old enough to work in a factory, they're old enough to hire an assassin."

"But five-year-olds work in factories."

"My point exactly."

She shook her head at me. "Did you get to the bottom of Forgo's death?"

"Yes, I know who killed him. It was an assassin."

"Very funny," she deadpanned.

"Little is working for John Blythwood III."

"Blythwood?"

"You know, grandson of John Blythwood, defender of functionables, merchant, and philosopher."

"That Blythwood? What does Little have to do with him?"

"He's got a function that allows him to change documents. I don't know exactly how it works, but it's best with functions not to think about it too much."

"So, he's changing documents for him?"

I nodded. "Helped him buy Mundmere Common less than legally. Forgo was a map collector."

"I know. I could barely find him under his collection."

"He found the proof to show what a devious little weevil Little was being."

"Drama amongst academics isn't the usual thing I get involved in. Why was Blythwood so interested in Mundmere?"

I shrugged, blocking out all thoughts of what I had seen there. "I don't know, and I don't care."

Something banged in my head, and Morgan flinched.

"Did you hear that? What was it?" I asked, panicked.

"I tripped over a thought you are trying to hide. Don't worry, I'll leave it alone."

That was strangely decorous of her.

"This is awful, by the way." She gestured to the glasses.

"I know. No idea what they put in it, but the last time I had it, I went blind for three days. There's a one-in-eight chance of fatality."

Her face changed slightly. There was a glint to her eyes and a pull on her lips. She was smirking, I realised and catalogued it for future reference.

"I can beat those odds," she said.

❖ ❖ ❖

Morgan's pub was situated down a maze of side streets. I did not try to figure out where we were. Frank's mystery drink was making me all warm inside. I had lost the feeling in my toes, but it was a small price to pay. I looked up at the Seven Arms sign hanging wonkily from a chain.

"Where are the arms?" I asked.

"Mary keeps them in the back."

It looked like they had simply built the pub on top of whatever was there before. There were layers to everything. Morgan pulled open the door, and half of it stayed closed.

A woman behind the sloping bar looked me up and down.

"We don't want any trouble," she said.

"Then don't cause any," I suggested.

Morgan sorted the drinks with her tactic of glaring at the barmaid silently till she passed us two tankards. The drink was an innocent brown but seemed to be crackling.

"How are Quentin and Darcy?" I asked as we took our seats. Mine creaked ominously. Maybe Morgan's preference for crouching on chairs was so she could land on her feet if it collapsed.

"I don't know," Morgan replied, and I remembered that I did not actually care how Quentin and Darcy were. "I expect I'll hear from them soon. I think Victor has gone off to find them. He does that with people he likes."

"Victor, your bird? That's not how carrier pigeons work."

"It's how Victor works."

"You really have no idea what his function is?"

She shook her head.

"It's rare to find a bird with a function, isn't it? They don't usually live long enough to develop one."

"With the way pollution is going, I think we'll see functions developing a lot earlier. There will soon be many more pigeons like Victor."

"What a terrifying thought."

"What's your deal with birds anyway?"

"They have such tiny brains. There must only be room for one emotion in there, and what if that emotion is hatred?"

"You're paranoid."

"I have enough people watching me, I don't need any birds." I took a sip of my drink. It felt like swallowing an electric eel. "Maybe I would feel less paranoid if they let me carry a gun."

"They don't?"

"No, we must rely on our functions and our wits. Of course, Miss Fortitude carries whatever the hell she likes, but it's always one rule for them, another for the rest of us."

"What about when you're not on duty?"

"That would be completely unladylike."

"What's the point in all those voluminous skirts if not to conceal weapons?"

"What weapons do you carry?"

A spark lit up her eyes. She pulled a dagger from a sheath on her hip and one from her boot. She held out the thinner blade. "This is a dirk, good for thrusting. And this thick blade is a cinquedea, good for slashing." She slipped a tiny dagger from her sleeve and closed her fist around its T-shaped handle. The blade stuck out between her knuckles. "This is a push dagger. It's like a knuckleduster, but more pointy."

"You like knives then."

"They're quiet and efficient. Plus, the school really pushes the dagger module in third year. It's traditional, after all. But I also carry this." She reached for her other hip and laid on the table a miniature crossbow. "It's collapsible."

It was precious how excited she was.

"I have three different types of bolts. There are the regular, of course, and then I have ones dipped in opium and ones dipped in a special poison I make myself. It contains toxins found in frogs. It's shipped all the way from the Spanish Main. I add some—"

She broke off suddenly and turned from me. A man was approaching our table with a purpose and a leer. He walked with the confidence of someone who had once been attractive. Perhaps he had not owned a mirror for several years.

"What is a pretty thing like you doing in a place like this?" he asked.

Was he talking to me or a piece of the furniture? He was looking at me, but then again, I was not a "thing." I did not want to stand in his way if he was trying to pick up a chair.

A small movement to my side caught my attention. Morgan was shaking. For one fearful moment, I thought she was crying, but then I realised she was laughing. Morgan was publicly, visibly laughing. She was displaying an emotion. Incredible.

Morgan started laughing harder. The man looked very offended.

"It's not you," I explained, "it's my thoughts, they get to her sometimes. Why don't you take your sexual frustration and go screw a chair?"

His face contorted with anger, and I realised I had said all that out loud. He leant across the table, pointing one of his huge, scarred fingers at me. I heard a squeak of leather, and suddenly, the man was howling and clutching at a finger that was about half an inch shorter than it had been before.

Morgan was on her feet. "Go near her again, and I'll cut the tip off something else."

There was blood all over the table. The man was still screaming, and his friends were yelling too. Whether they were yelling in support of him or us, I couldn't tell. But the proprietor was coming towards us holding a bat, so I guessed we had overstayed our welcome.

I took the ugly man's pain and passed it onto her. The unexpected agony in her hand made her drop the bat. Morgan was right behind me as I tore from the building. I kept running until I had to stop because I was laughing too much. Morgan was barely out of breath.

"Come on," I panted. "I know a super dodgy place we can get some food."

❖ ❖ ❖

Bricked Street looked like a dead-end, but there was a small gap in the wall that, when squeezed through, led you into an open space lined with stalls that were always changing, usually because their owners were arrested.

I followed the aroma of pastry to a stall stacking pies like architectural follies.

"What can I get you?" the owner asked.

"If I said I had an allergy to horse meat, would that affect what I could buy?"

She frowned. "If that were the case, I would say the meat pies you'll be fine with, but you might want to avoid the apple tarts."

I bought two pies and handed one to Morgan.

"Roll up, roll up! This is the fight of the night! An invisible fox against a levitating cat! Place your bets people!"

Morgan weaved over to the loud man. There was a large cage. In it was a cat with half a tail and a chewed ear. It was hovering a couple of feet above the ground, hissing at the audience.

"Release the fox!" the seller cried.

He opened a side of the cage that backed onto an adjoining one. The small crowd cheered. Nothing happened.

"Is it there?" someone asked.

The seller thumped the cage. The cat curled up in the air and began grooming its paws.

"I guess the fox doesn't want to fight," Morgan said.

"Or they got the wrong cage," I responded.

There was a crash down the end of the street.

"Hero Brigade!" someone shouted. "Scram! Scram!"

Through the panicked mass of people, I could see the glittery uniforms of the heroes heading towards us. Mr Indestructible was there, drawn to the scene like a moth to the limelight. Miss Fortitude stood beside him, in a uniform that was just as patriotic as his but lower cut. I was betting it had been designed by a man. Behind them were Mrs Grace, who could manipulate temperature, and Mr Righteous. I could not remember what his function was, but he always looked very smug.

It would be slightly awkward if the heroes caught me in a dive like this. Most of their intelligence had been beaten out of them at some point, but even their addled minds might find the sight of me holding a pie, watching a flying cat, and talking to an assassin slightly suspicious.

Morgan grabbed my hand and tugged me after her. I was sorry to drop my pie, but needs must. Behind us, we heard the man with the flying cat being beaten up and his stall being destroyed.

Faster, Morgan said.

I glanced behind. Mr Righteous was chasing us. I doubted it was his function, but he sure could keep up a steady sprint.

We were nearing the dead end. Morgan leapt forward and scrambled up a wall like a lizard. She stopped at the top and reached down to haul me up. We dropped down onto the cobbles. A thump on the other side of the wall suggested Mr Righteous's function wasn't climbing.

We ducked down a side street. I pressed my back up against the wall and peeped around the corner. No one was following us. I sighed in relief and let my head fall back against the wall. What a day. Who would have thought Morgan could be so entertaining. She was leaning against the wall beside me. She still had her mask off, and I could see her smile glinting in the dark.

In the dark.

I tried to stamp on the thought as soon as it surfaced, but Morgan must have caught it because the smile vanished, and the professional mask slipped back into place. She covered it with her actual mask.

"I should go meet Craig," she said. "It's impolite to leave a client waiting."

I nodded. "Give him my regards." And, if he happened to be plotting my demise, perhaps a kick in the teeth too.

Morgan turned and began pulling herself effortlessly up the side of the building closest.

"See you around," I called after her.

I wondered if that was true. Maybe I would only see her knife.

❖ ❖ ❖

The walk back to my dingy little hotel gave me time to sober up and mull over my impending death. On the bright side, to be killed by an assassin would make me seem far more exciting. Though, come to think of it, I could be killed in a run-of-the-mill horse trampling and people would still make up wild stories about it.

What I needed was a nap, but changing into my nightdress felt like asking for a stabbing. I decided to stay in my Squadron uniform. Maybe Morgan would feel bad for me and let me live. No one wanted to be an unattractive corpse.

Settling at the rickety desk, I began to compose a letter.

Dear Dan,

If you are reading this, then I am dead and have exceeded your expectations for my theatrics. Mrs Winow's cat is going to have kittens. Good luck.

I folded the letter and put it in an envelope.

Don't scream.

I screamed.

"Is that you again?" came a shout from next door. "Do you get murdered every day of the week?"

I righted the pot of ink I had spilled and glared at the assassin on my windowsill.

"Saying 'don't scream' in my head is not going to stop me from screaming."

"Sorry," Morgan said, slithering in through the window.

I grabbed the pillowcase and threw it on the desk to soak up the ink. It had probably been used for worse things in the past. By the time I had finished, Morgan was standing completely still in the centre of the room. Somehow, it was more annoying than pacing.

"So, will I live to see another dawn?" I asked unnecessarily. She had resorted to shadow mode, a sure sign of bad news.

"You are the contract," she said quietly.

I sighed. "I really thought I had this one in the bag." I threw the pillowcase into a corner. "How is it going to happen?"

"He wants it to look like an accident."

"I trip down the stairs and break my neck? I drink too much and choke on my vomit?"

"Actually, I was thinking you get crushed by a falling piano. It will make a better eulogy."

"Right." I turned back to my desk. I could not believe I was going to spend my last moments filing. "I need to send these papers to Dan." I paused as the realisation hit me. "My will gives him everything. Is it too late to add a stipulation that he has to change the wallpaper?"

"You know the piano was a joke, right? I made a joke."

I was glad I had my back to her so she could not see me smile. She was so adorably pathetic. "Don't worry, I figured a piano would be a lot of faff. I'm assuming you'll just clobber me when I don't expect it. But if you could wait until I've sorted this out, I would be much obliged."

"I turned down the contract."

I looked back at her, bank statement forgotten. "What?"

She ripped off her mask and scrubbed a hand down her face. "He's fifteen. It would be irresponsible to further facilitate his choice of lifestyle. Plus, it's you."

"You said you would kill Quentin and Darcy if asked because 'you're a professional.'"

"But you're not Quentin or Darcy."

"Then what am I?"

Her gaze dropped to her feet. She was scowling the way she did when she was nervous.

Oh my god, she had a crush on me. The realisation was like getting hit by a cow. How had I not seen this coming?

She was reading my mind. I knew because a faint blush was creeping up her cheeks. As soon as I noticed, the blush accelerated.

"Why?" I managed to croak out.

She shrugged. "It's not like no one's ever fancied you before."

"But you can see into my mind."

"I like your mind."

And wasn't that like a punch to the gut, to have all your flaws laid bare before you and have someone say they liked you because of them.

She adjusted her stance, just slightly. Getting ready to run, I realised.

"You are in my head a lot more than I am in yours," she said steadily, like she was reading out this year's corn prices. "In Glasgow, I saw someone that reminded me of you, but when I read their mind, they were nothing like you. Compared to you, everyone is boring."

I opened my mouth, then closed it again. What the hell was I supposed to say to that?

"It's all right that you don't feel the same," she said. "In fact, I like the way you think of me. It brings my ego down a notch."

She gave me a small smile, and I knew she meant it. Perhaps I was more charming than I had realised.

"Or perhaps, it's your ego that needs to be taken down a notch."

I searched around until I stumbled on some words. "My respect for you has gone down significantly now that I know about your crush."

She huffed out a laugh. "See, this is the content I'm here for."

Her stance relaxed. The tension was gone, and that made me inexplicably angry. I stormed over to her, crowding her personal space.

"I mean it. That you of all people would fall for someone as callous, self-centred, and utterly despicable as me is frankly disappointing. You might be the worst assassin ever, turning down a contract because of something as boring as feelings."

She stood her ground. "You're like a dog: all bark and no bite."

"And you are like a stewed fig."

"Because I didn't do market research?"

I poked her in the chest. "You're sweet and mushy."

My hand was still on her chest. Rather than remove it, I flattened it. Beneath the layers of leather, I could hear the whisper of a heartbeat. How had she trained even her heart to be quiet?

"Are you sure?" she asked softly, and I didn't think she was talking about the fig thing.

"Read my mind," I whispered.

A knock from the door had us leaping apart. I smoothed down my uniform, not looking at Morgan. You would think I had just kicked a cat by how guilty I was acting. Hoping I was not flushed, I opened the door. There was a dirt-streaked urchin on the other side, no older than ten.

"Message for you, miss," he said.

I gave the stupid, interrupting kid a warm smile as I took the letter from his grubby paws. "Thank you."

"Miss?" He tugged on my trousers, leaving a brown smear.

I bent down.

"There's an assassin in your room," he said in hushed tones.

I glanced behind. Morgan was crouching on the dresser. I wondered if this was her version of acting natural.

"Don't worry, she does that." I flicked him a coin, kicked the door closed, and ripped open the letter. It had better be a knighthood.

"It's an urgent summons from the Brigade. The commander probably stubbed his toe."

"You need to go," Morgan inferred.

"Can we finish this when I get back?"

She blushed again. "I'll go to the school. If Little finds someone else to assassinate you, there's nothing I can do about it. But if I spread a rumour that he doesn't like paying up, it might slow him down."

"You know that this was my plan all along, right? I was nice to you so you would offer me protection."

"That was you being nice?"

I grinned. "I'll be back soon. Try not to miss me too much."

Chapter 13

I stepped out of the hotel onto the street. A man gave me a strange look. I realised I was smiling. I had to force myself to stop; people were going to think I had committed a crime. It was all Morgan's fault, making me happy. Damn her. I took a deep breath and quickly regretted it as the stench of smog made me gag.

I set off at a brisk pace towards the Brigade. It was late. If I had been in Dippenwick, I would have been able to see the stars. I didn't know any of the constellations. It had never seemed important before. Maybe Morgan knew them. I could ask her.

God, listen to me, talking about stars like some lovestruck teenager. What was the matter with me? I didn't even like Morgan. She had no social skills and no respect for boundaries. I didn't like Morgan. At most, I liked that she liked me.

I craved admiration, that was all. I wanted someone to see me, to truly see me and not be disappointed. Morgan could do that. She could see me for all that I was, with her dark eyes and her stupid cheekbones and silky hair. Was her hair silky? I had never thought about it.

All right, so she was pretty, but lots of people were. She was also intelligent, which was something the world regularly lacked, but she wasn't the only intelligent person out there. She made me laugh, but a lot of people made me laugh. Usually, I was laughing at them rather than with them, but still. There was nothing special about Morgan. She was unlike anyone I had ever met before. That was it.

I stopped. I had been so absorbed I had walked right past Brigade

Headquarters. This was getting ridiculous. I could not afford a distraction. I had a plan, a plan involving early retirement and long isolation. What would have happened if someone had seen me with Morgan? I could imagine the headlines: Miss Take Beds Assassin, and a Woman at That. They would eat me alive.

I needed to rush through this job and then go threaten the living daylights out of Craig before he sent any more assassins my way. This stupid crush stopped now.

I retraced my steps to the Brigade.

"Hey, shouldn't someone put that criminal in handcuffs?" a hero lurking by the entrance joked to his friends.

I smiled good naturedly at them to show that I didn't mind being the butt of their unintelligent, unthoughtful, immature jokes. I felt my confused emotions settle into irritation and bitterness. I breathed a sigh of relief. This was the me I knew.

❖ ❖ ❖

The Brigade was fairly empty, just the usual people gearing up for patrol. I loitered by the entrance, hoping that no one would notice me and I could just go home.

"Miss Blakely."

One of the commander's lackies was walking briskly towards me with the air that I was already holding him up.

"Come with me." He turned abruptly on his heels and led me down a hall towards the back exit. Standing at the door was a man wearing a Union Jack.

"This is Mr Indestructible," the lacky said unnecessarily. "He has something he would like to discuss with you."

Mr Indestructible bowed low in greeting. The lacky withdrew, leaving us alone.

This was not necessarily as bad as it looked. Yes, Mr Indestructible had decided to meet me at night in an empty part of the building a couple of hours after we had crossed paths in an unsavoury part of town, but there was every chance he just needed my help and was too proud to talk to me in public. I reached out with my function, but he was not in pain. It was unnerving. People were usually always in some sort of discomfort, but Mr Indestructible was a blank space.

"Miss Blakely, would you do the honour of accompanying me on a short drive?"

Okay, this was leaning towards bad.

"Would it be possible for you to tell me what this is about first?" I replied in my young, sweet, innocent-girl voice.

"I will explain on the way."

"Naturally, I do not believe you mean me any harm, but you must understand that, as an unmarried woman, I would feel more comfortable with a chaperone."

"It is not my intention to make you uncomfortable."

Yet, he was succeeding.

"It is a rather sensitive matter. Please," he opened the door, "indulge me."

Lacking any other option, I nodded and slipped past him into the alley behind the Brigade. There was a carriage waiting for us. It was not the one with his name printed on the side and an excess of bunting trailing behind it that Mr Indestructible normally used. This was just a typical cab. Mr Indestructible did not want people knowing where he was or where he was taking me. He held the door of the carriage open for me. I smiled as I took his offered hand and climbed up the step into the velvet-clad interior. He may have been travelling incognito, but he was still travelling in style. He took the seat opposite me, his huge form consuming three quarters of the space.

With a lurch, the carriage lumbered forward. The curtains were closed over the windows.

I folded my hands in my lap and gave him a smile. "I hear you are making good headway on the animal traffickers. Congratulations."

"You have always been a thorn in my side," Mr Indestructible said.

He wasn't so polite behind closed doors. I arranged my features into a picture of confused hurt. "I'm sorry to hear that. I have always had the highest respect for you. If I have offended you in some way, I will try to make amends."

"Unbelievable," he said to himself with the closest thing I had ever seen to a smile. "You never stop, do you?"

"I don't know what you mean."

He leant towards me. I could see his eyes looking out through his mask. I had once heard them described as "bluer than a summer sky," but in this light, they looked as grey as steel.

"This evening, Mr Craig Little turned up on Lord Blythwood's doorstep in near hysterics."

I closed my eyes. Of course. Stupid, stupid me.

"He was most perturbed. It transpired that you had threatened him and his employer quite severely. Now Little, being the great upstart that he is, thought he could deal with this problem by himself. Yet when he attempted to hire an assassin, he was refused. It was quite a shock for him."

"You're working for Blythwood," I said. I had dug myself a nice little hole to die in. "Why?"

"I wouldn't expect you to understand."

"Then help me understand," I said earnestly. "I'm sure there is a reasonable explanation for your actions, so please reveal it to me so I can continue to consider you a true hero."

"You don't think I'm a hero. You think I'm a fool. You are a liar and a villain, just like your parents. You think you are above the rules, that you can laugh in the face of your betters and use good and honest people to raise yourself higher on your pedestal of blood and greed. If you honestly want to make amends for the trouble you have caused, then I'll tell you how you can: you can die."

There was just no reasoning with some people. I opened the door of the carriage and threw myself out. We were travelling faster than I had realised, and I hit the cobbles hard. Mr Indestructible jumped out after me. He landed with a similar lack of elegance but bounded right to his feet. His stupid function had me at a disadvantage. My fall had given me plenty of pain to work with, but I held back. Running from Mr Indestructible was one thing, but attacking him would seal my fate.

"Get back in the carriage," he said, stalking towards me.

I struggled to my feet. "No. If you want me, you'll have to arrest me." I gestured to the people who had paused in their suspicious, late-night deeds to watch us. "Go on, I dare you. The law has rules." Ones it frequently ignored, but there was some comfort in knowing they existed. "I will enjoy my day in court. I have some things to say about your employer."

Mr Indestructible clenched his fists at his side. It was like facing down an avalanche.

Suddenly, two hands grabbed me from behind, latching onto my forearms. I struggled against the hold, but the world blinked out. It reappeared a second later.

I was no longer on the street. The sky had been replaced by a high ceiling which was spinning nauseatingly. I fell to my knees.

"I told you my way was easier," a voice said.

The world spun faster. Darkness crept in at the corners of my vision.

"I had it under control," Mr Indestructible said peevishly.

"Sure you did," the other person replied.

I tried to turn my head to see them. It was a mistake. The black fog consumed my sight as I was dragged down into unconsciousness.

Chapter
14

Waking up in pain was not a novelty. Finding myself tied to a chair was. These were the kinds of situations I tried to avoid. The weak light filtering through grimy skylights showed I was in a large warehouse. There were unlit furnaces, huge tanks of water, and machines with more wheels and conveyor belts than they could possibly need. A disgusting smell of chemicals hung in the air.

I noticed a piece of material pulled taut on a rack near me. There was no mistaking that shade of blue. If they made BW Incorporated synthetic here, then I had to be in Mundmere Factory. The next closest place that made the stuff was in Manchester. I looked at the machines again. Now, I could see the various places functionables would stand to help with the process.

I flexed my wrists. Whoever had tied them must have been a sailor. I blew a stray bit of hair out of my face and settled back to try and enjoy my unexpected day off.

The door to the warehouse flew open. Only one person had a shadow that looming. Mr Indestructible walked in, cape billowing behind him.

"Good afternoon," I said.

"It's morning."

I plastered a charming smile on my face. "Your radiance makes the day seem brighter."

He did not look impressed. I decided to skip the foreplay. "This is all very unnecessary. I made it perfectly clear to Little that my silence can be bought."

"You're a woman. We can't trust you to keep your mouth shut."

"Now that's just blatant stereotyping."

He was right in front of me, muscles glistening like he had bathed them in oil.

"If you wanted to kill me, why not just kill me?" I asked. "Renting a warehouse, finding an uncomfortable chair, buying rope, it all seems a waste of valuable resources."

"Because you still have one use." He grabbed my face in a meaty hand. "Put that big mouth of yours to work, and tell me what you know and who else knows it."

"But I'm a woman, you said so yourself. Head full of cotton wool, not a thought there."

He squeezed my face slightly. It was not enough to hurt, just enough to remind me how much time he spent lifting boulders.

"Funny how my impending death isn't putting me in a chatty mood," I said.

"There's plenty of time to make you more cooperative. Pain seems to do that."

I couldn't help myself, I snorted. "You know who I am, right?"

His hand released me only to shoot back in a fist. The shock as my head snapped sideways was enough to stun me, but only for a moment. I threw the pain right back. His hand flew to his face as it contorted with surprised rage.

I smiled at him through my split lip. "I'm a pain reliever, you moron. Were you so busy hating me that you forgot how our fights used to end?"

His face took on an unfortunate look of determination, and he raised his fist again. His stupidity in the face of pain was almost admirable. This hit got me just behind the ear, a cheap shot if you asked me. It must have been painful, according to his reaction.

"I must say," I said, "I'm surprised that Blythwood managed to buy your services. I thought your moral convictions had the quality of a brick wall. The pay must have been pretty tempting for you to deign to work for such a lazy, greedy, vacuous thug."

He threw a punch at my nose. The thick, wet feeling of blood was as unpleasant as the knowledge that he had just ruined one of my best features. Mr Indestructible clutched his perfectly unharmed nose and moaned. The thing about being indestructible was you weren't used to getting your arse handed to you. This had to be an annoyingly unusual experience for him.

"John Blythwood is a man of honour," he managed to say between his groans.

"Yes, I've heard there's honour amongst thieves." The dripping blood was making my face itch. "I'm just repeating what everyone else says about him. Although, they do say it's his sister, Edith, who's the real sociopath."

His backhand had me seeing stars.

"Why do you care so much about the Blythwoods' reputations?" I asked. "I thought you were too self-centred for that."

He raised his fist again. Miss Fortitude appeared beside him and caught his hand in hers.

"I told you the usual methods wouldn't work," she said.

Mr Indestructible glared at her, then slowly lowered his fist. If I could have applauded him for finally admitting defeat, I would have.

Miss Fortitude looked down at me with cold disgust. If I looked as bad as Mr Indestructible felt, it could not have been a pretty sight. I gave her a bloody smile.

"Why do you refuse to talk to my good friend here?" she asked.

"Because he's not great at communication, and I'm only interested in talking if it's a conversation," I said. "I'll tell you what I know, but first, tell me something I don't."

Miss Fortitude surveyed me with her dead-eyed gaze. She had blue eyes too. It must have been a hero thing.

"You are a peculiar one, Miss Blakely. I thought you were smart, weaseling your way out of trouble whenever it found you, but then you went and threatened the Blythwoods. That wasn't very smart at all."

"I know you feel all high and mighty because I'm tied to a chair and you're not, but it sounds like you want something from me, so I would hold back on the condescension if I were you," I said.

Her lips pursed. "All right. Let me tell you a story." She rotated on the spot, looking up at the rafters like they were the most beautiful thing she had ever seen. "This factory was built forty years ago under the instruction of John Blythwood II. He recognised a need for uniforms for the Hero Brigade and beyond to cope with the strains of their work and the functions they had. Creating this material was a difficult process, and there was, naturally, a moderate amount of waste. Factories along the Thames dump their excesses into the river. They don't have that luxury here, but right next door is Mundmere Common, a large tract of unpopulated land."

I could guess where this was going.

"The waste accumulated in the lake," she said. "The fish quickly died, and most people avoided the area all together because of the smell. It was perfectly safe."

It sure didn't sound perfectly safe.

Miss Fortitude examined her perfect nails. "However, there was an unexpected complication. It would appear the concentrated wastage has resulted in the development of an unforeseen function."

My brain finally caught up. Perhaps I had always known but had not wanted to accept it. "The dirt in Mundmere has a function."

"That would be absurd," Miss Fortitude scoffed. "Only living things can get functions. No, we believe it is something in the soil—a creature too small for the eye to see—that has developed the function."

"You are trying to tell me that one tiny creature is responsible for all the dirt monsters?" I asked.

She shook her head. "No, that is one of the many fascinating things about this case. We are looking at millions of microscopic organisms, all with the same function and operating as a collective to form these dirt 'monsters,' as they are known colloquially."

"And they're attacking people," I added.

"*Lutum gigantos*, as we call it, does not 'attack' anyone," she replied coldly. "It does not have a brain nor a motivation. However, when a collective manifestation encounters a person, it does tend to end in loss of life."

She could say it how she wanted; it was still murder. "Why those victims?"

"Again, they are not victims," she said with a tight smile. "*Lutum gigantos* does not choose who dies. We suspect there is a scientific reason for how far it travels before latching onto a person, but we are yet to understand it. It tends to be those on the street, so we do try and conduct our experiments at times when most of the population are in their houses."

"And at times when most hero patrols take place. What about all your mates on the Brigade?" I asked.

"They are willing to walk the streets while thinking there is a human trying to kill them with dirt, what is the difference if it is *Lutum gigantos*?"

she replied.

I had a feeling the difference had something to do with lies and corruption, but I decided to move on to a more pressing question.

"Why aren't you stopping it?" I asked.

"Why would we want to?" she replied. "There is huge potential here. It is a microscopic weapon, one that can be spread covertly and activated when needed. Imagine being able to weaponize the dirt of an entire country. There would be no more long-drawn-out wars full of senseless violence. We could bring about world peace."

Ah yes, world peace, the greatest money-making opportunity there was. "If, for some completely unknown reason, Blythwood decided he wanted to stop the Dirt Man, could he?"

"The manifestations are naturally occurring, Miss Blakely," she said condescendingly.

There was nothing natural about them.

"Our addition of certain substances may accelerate the rate at which they appear, but they would happen either way," she continued.

"Could it be killed?" I pressed.

"Well, we can't know for sure without trying." She seemed to consider it. "But in my opinion, no, it would be like trying to kill a disease."

Or trying to kill human greed. "So, Blythwood is trying to mould it into something sellable, but he needs to be able to control it first. And you haven't managed that yet, have you?"

"Not yet," she relented. "But that actually brings me nicely to the topic I would like to discuss with you. Two nights ago, our watchmen reported seeing someone in a Community Squadron uniform fleeing the lake at Mundmere, being followed by a *Lutum gigantos* manifestation. To their surprise, they were unable to find a body, only a pile of dirt. Mere hours after this extraordinary event, you spring up from nowhere. Did you visit Mundmere Common two nights ago, Miss Blakely? And if you did, how are you still alive?"

So that was what it all came down to. They wanted to know if I had somehow found a way to control their precious dirt. It was tempting to remain silent, but I had a feeling the truth would annoy them even more.

"I took its pain," I said simply.

I watched Miss Fortitude's eyes harden with disbelief. "That's impossible."

"One of the other fascinating things you have failed to notice is that your little monster is in agony," I told her. "Pain the like of which I have never experienced, and I have experienced a lot. All your efforts to control it are just pissing it off. No wonder it's out for revenge."

"You speak as though it thinks. This is not a complex organism. It cannot have a motive," she said with confidence.

"I don't know," I replied casually. "The Dirt Man has already broadened my ideas of what is possible, who's to say it can't know enough to recognise that humans are responsible for its pain. Maybe it just wants it to stop."

"She's lying," Mr Indestructible told Miss Fortitude.

"No, she's not," I countered.

"We'll soon find out whether she's telling the truth or not," Miss Fortitude said.

"How?" Mr Indestructible asked.

"By causing her fear, not pain. She can't project that," she replied.

"What is she afraid of?" he asked.

Why bother kidnapping me if they were going to talk like I was not even there? "Being released," I offered.

"Bring her," Miss Fortitude commanded.

Mr Indestructible cut me from the chair, tied my hands behind my back, and dragged me out of the warehouse. We were surrounded by more buildings, every one of them silent in the early morning light.

Miss Fortitude led the way up some rickety stairs adjoining the warehouse in which I had been a guest. Once we were two flights up, she stopped. I was pushed into the space where the handrail was missing. Beneath me was a large vat full of something old and congealed. I had a bad feeling it was some kind of nasty, skin-shredding acid. Mr Indestructible reached out, and I instinctively stepped back. My heels floundered on nothing, and Mr Indestructible fisted one hand in the front of my jumpsuit to stop me from falling. This was not looking good for me.

"How did you survive?" Miss Fortitude asked.

Typical. The one time I told the truth, and no one believed me.

Mr Indestructible shook me. "What do you know?"

"I know that your sideburns don't suit you," I said.

His hand loosened. My back arched as I tried to rewrite physics.

"I'm telling the truth," I said quickly.

Miss Fortitude curled her lip. "Forgive me for struggling to believe a criminal that is so used to being deceitful."

"Be careful who you call a criminal," I replied. "Those in glass houses and all that."

Mr Indestructible's grasp loosened.

"Okay, okay, let's not overreact," I said hastily. "Listen, you don't want to kill me. My function can help you control the Dirt Man."

"Perhaps," Miss Fortitude conceded. "But a world in which you can control *Lutum gigantos* is not one I want to be a part of. We'll keep looking for a way to control it. I have faith that we will succeed without the need for your pathetic little function." She patted Mr Indestructible's arm. "She's all yours."

She was gone in the blink of an eye, leaving me in the hands of someone who was definitely dramatic enough to think of me as their archenemy.

"I don't know about you, but I feel that this could be a turning point in our relationship," I told Mr Indestructible. "I always thought you and I had this real enemies-to-lovers thing going on. Don't you agree?"

He let go.

❖ ❖ ❖

Whatever breath I managed to retain throughout the fall was punched out of me the moment I hit the surface. The substance in the vat was thicker than water, but not solid enough to break my spine. It sucked me under and dragged me down with a vengeance. A stinging on my hands, neck, and face gradually built to burning. It would have been nice to push my pain onto Mr Indestructible as a final petty revenge, but I was too disorientated to find him. I could no longer tell which way was up, or if there was a bottom to this pit of despair.

It hit me with sudden clarity that I was going to die. Imminently. What a waste of a life. I should have run when Dan told me to, should have found peace and happiness and all that stuff.

Clara.

Lack of air was starting to mess with my head. It was unfair that I could hear heavy breathing when I could not breathe.

I'm here, Clara.

That was Morgan's voice.

Hold on.

And then she was gone, and I had never felt more alone. Perhaps I had imagined it to give myself hope, to find the strength to fight for a few seconds longer. There were flashes of light as my brain sent out a final, desperate signal to my body. No one was coming to save me.

I opened my mouth. The rotten gunk seared my tongue as it forced its way into my lungs.

Where are you?

The shout pounded on my brain, demanding an answer, but my thoughts were bubbles bursting all over the place.

❖ ❖ ❖

There was something on me and I couldn't breathe. I rolled onto my side and retched, gasped, and puked, all seemingly at the same time. I was shaking and hurting all over, and in a moment of panic, I pushed the pain out to whoever I could. I heard a clatter and a thump, and then hands were grabbing me and pulling me up. My back was slammed into a wall. I opened my eyes, but everything was hazy. There was a face in front of me. The mask looked familiar.

"You think some lousy assassin can kill me?"

An assassin? What assassin? I looked past him. There was a lump of black on the ground. It was trying to get up but was failing. I was pulled back from the wall to be slammed against it again.

Clara.

That was Morgan's voice.

The pain.

Oh god. I had put my pain on her. I tried to draw it back, but I was so tired. It was impossible, like trying to pick something up with both arms nailed to the ground. I didn't want to hurt anymore. Mr Indestructible slammed me against the wall again, and stars flew in front of my eyes. Man, I hated him. Gritting my teeth, I latched onto Morgan's pain and pulled with all my might. It was awful. I threw it onto Mr Indestructible. He let me go, and I crumpled to the floor.

Morgan leapt, knife out. The knife broke against Mr Indestructible's back.

He roared, turning on her. "Will you cut it out! I'm indestructible, you can't kill me!"

"I'm pretty persistent," Morgan replied.

Morgan pulled out another knife. He made a grab for her. She slipped through his legs, coming up behind him. Jumping onto his back, she wrapped her legs around his waist and put an arm around his neck. Her knife glinted in the sunlight as she raised it high before bringing it down into his eye. He screamed. Morgan withdrew the knife, and blood spurted from his eye socket. He dropped to his knees, and Morgan clambered off him.

"I guess it's only your skin that is indestructible," she said.

She pushed his body away from her. He tumbled over and lay on the ground screaming. Morgan ran over and cut my hands free. They dropped like lead weights at my side. She hefted me up. I leant heavily on her as we stumbled away from Mr Indestructible.

"How did you know that would work?" I asked.

"I didn't."

I focused on trying to move my feet, but despite my utmost concentration, Morgan was still practically dragging me. "What happened?"

"You fell in a vat of toxic waste."

"I did not fall, I was pushed."

The buildings around us started swaying, and the ground rippled beneath my feet.

"Stay with me, Clara." Morgan's voice was thick, like she was shouting at me underwater. I had just been underwater, hadn't I? Maybe I was still there, floating in an endless pool. It didn't sound so bad.

Chapter 15

My throat was a canyon of dust and rocks. I opened my eyes and let the white spots dancing in my vision grow tired enough to let me see a rather unexciting ceiling. Every hair on my body recoiled from the touch of the sheet covering me. It felt like a shroud. The intense odour was not helping me feel any more alive. Stale sweat and vomit were the nicest scents I could discern. Whatever had happened must have been the worst.

"That's the first coherent thought you've had in days."

I rolled my head to the side, my stiff neck complaining. Morgan was crouching on a chair by my bed. You could have hidden a body in the shadows under her eyes.

"How long was I out?" My voice came out like a croak. No, that was insulting to toads.

"Three days. You had a fever. It was bad."

I nodded, but that made my vision swim. Morgan helped me sit up enough to give me a few sips of water. The relief to my throat was temporary.

"Inventory report?"

Her voice came out clipped, professional. "Severe bruising to face, rope burns on your wrists and ankles, and I had to reset your nose. The vat you fell into was a skin irritant, but there doesn't seem to be any permanent damage. I'm less sure about the damage to your lungs from your near-drowning."

Could have been worse. "Where are we?" I asked.

"A safe house. I normally use it as somewhere to hide when Darcy invites me to parties."

"Did you carry me here?"

"You walked most of the way, but you were babbling. It took me a while to realise this wasn't your usual verbal nonsense."

"Careful. One more insult to my fragile heart and I'll go back to hammering on death's door."

She scowled at me. It was probably one of her concerned scowls, but I was too tired to analyse it.

"The Hero Brigade has put out a warrant for you. You were seen arguing with Mr Indestructible shortly before he disappeared."

I raised an eyebrow. "Disappeared?"

"Last I saw him, he was right as rain, sans an eyeball."

That I could remember. It was a vivid memory, and not one I was likely to forget. Just thinking of it put me in a better mood.

"How did you find me?"

"Victor."

I levelled her with my most unamused stare. "Your bird did not find me."

"He did. I was coming back from the school when I heard about your confrontation with Mr Indestructible in the middle of the street, so I went to the Brigade and threatened the commander."

My stare grew incredulous.

"Only a little. But he didn't know where they had taken you. I was searching for you, and then suddenly, Victor turns up. I read his mind, and he was thinking about you. I followed him straight to Mundmere Factory."

"Wait. You can read animals' minds?"

"Of course. Humans aren't special. He associates you with porridge by the way."

I looked around, almost expecting to find Victor hanging from the ceiling like some stalkerish, porridge-eating demon.

"That bird is seriously weird. I vote we cook him in a stew."

Morgan frowned. "That's not funny."

I swung my legs off the bed. The world tipped sideways briefly before I managed to regain my bearings.

"You need rest."

"I need a bath. And new clothes."

Morgan went to a small cupboard in the corner. She threw me something black. I knew it was going to be leather even before it hit me in the face.

"Do you have anything that's not leather?"

"No."

"What do you sleep in?"

She gestured to herself. "This."

"I am introducing you to the marvels of cotton."

I used the bed to stand. I was shaking like I could shake myself to pieces. From beneath the sleeves of my ruined Squadron uniform peeked the raw skin of my rope-burned wrists. My face must have looked like a ripe, puffy, oozing plum. I hobbled over to the door I suspected led to the washroom and pushed it open.

"Don't!" Morgan yelled.

There was a chair in the middle of the room. Tied to it was Craig Little.

"What the hell is this?"

Morgan joined me in the doorway. She shifted uncomfortably. "I asked him to come with me willingly, but he refused."

"So you kidnapped him?"

"What else was I supposed to do?"

"Not kidnap him!"

"We need him, and he needs us."

"In what way does he need us?"

"He needs a role model."

I snorted. "And you think you are the right person for that?"

"Not just me, you as well."

I blanched. "Me?"

"I can't take care of him by myself."

"Apparently, I can't take care of myself by *myself*. What makes you think I'm ready for adoption?"

"We can't just leave him with them."

"Sure we can."

She looked horrified.

"The kid just handed me over for a nice torture session," I explained.

"I'm sure all parents say the teenage years feel like torture."

I groaned. "I want to go back in the vat of toxic waste."

Craig mumbled something beneath his gag. I raised my hand to shut him up.

"There's no use complaining. If you had agreed to my terms, you wouldn't be in this mess."

My legs were starting to cramp. I ignored them and ventured farther into Craig's holding cell.

"I'm going to take this off," I told him, reaching for the gag. "Don't scream."

I untied the gag, and he let out a scream that would make a banshee cover their ears in horror. I clamped a hand over his mouth.

"What did I just say?" I asked.

Something moist pushed up against my hand, and I pulled it back in disgust. "Did you just lick me?" I asked with a grimace.

"You're both insane," he spat. "When Blythwood finds you've taken me—"

"He'll kill you as well as us," I interrupted. "If we let you go, how long do you think it will be before a hero drags you off for questioning? Not everyone wears the post-interrogation look as well as me."

He pouted.

"Like it or not, you are on our side now, so you might as well make yourself useful. What were you doing for Blythwood?" I asked.

"You already know," he grumbled. "I was changing documents. My function allows me to make things read whatever I want them to."

I nodded. "I was just guessing that was your function, I didn't really know."

"What?" he spluttered.

"What kind of documents were you changing?" I asked.

He glared at me. I waved the gag at him.

"Some maps, records, legal documents. Anything that would help them persuade the courts that Mundmere Common wasn't common land," he said sullenly.

That confirmed what I already suspected. "Did you know what he was doing on the common?"

"No. She hired me to do a job, and I did it," he replied.

"She?" I repeated.

Craig squirmed. He had not meant to let that slip.

"You weren't hired by John Blythwood?" I asked.

He chewed on his lip a moment before replying. "Edith Blythwood was my point of contact."

The sister was in on it too. It made sense. From what I had heard, Edith was basically John's manager. I should have realised it sooner. Damn patriarchal brainwashing strikes again.

"And when you're dealing with Edith Blythwood," Craig continued, "you don't ask questions, you do what you're told. She brought me back to deal with Forgo, and I dealt with him."

"Like how you intended to deal with me," I said wryly.

He really doesn't know what they are doing on the common, Morgan said in my head.

I tried to stop all my thoughts on Mundmere rising to the surface.

You know what they are doing there, don't you?

I pulled a hand through my lank, greasy hair. I really needed a bath. If only I could scrub my brain at the same time. I sighed. There was no use avoiding it, Morgan would spy it out of me eventually.

"What I am about to tell you may get you killed. Do you accept the risk?" I asked solemnly.

"Yes," Morgan said at the same time Craig said, "No."

I dismissed him. "You don't get a say, Craig."

"Why not?" he demanded.

"Because you ratted me out to your psychotic overlord." I sat on the floor. This could be a long conversation, and I did not want to faint in the middle of it. "The Blythwoods created the Dirt Man."

"No way," came from somewhere outside the washroom.

"Who's there?" I shouted.

Quentin stuck his head around the door and waved.

"What are you doing here?" I asked.

"I sent for him when your fever wouldn't break," Morgan said quietly. "If you didn't make it, I wanted you to know that I was…" she shrugged, "sorry, I guess, that I didn't get there sooner."

"And I was all too happy to watch the woman who hates me die," Quentin said cheerfully.

I may not have learnt sign language, but Quentin seemed to have no trouble deciphering the meaning behind my hand gesture.

"I brought food." He shuffled into the room and passed Morgan a bundle. I reached for one of the others, but he slapped my hand away.

"That food is for people who haven't just woken up from a three-day fever. People who fall into vats of toxic waste get dry bread," he said, tossing me a piece of bread.

I glared at him. "I will choke on this, and all your safety precautions will have been for naught. Who is the rest of the food for?"

"Hi guys," Darcy said, slipping in behind Quentin. "What are the odds? I was just passing through and accidentally ran into Quentin."

Oh yes, London was a small city after all.

Darcy hit me with her most sympathetic gaze. "Quentin told me about your kidnapping. I'm really sorry, Clara." She made it sound like the worst thing about it was the embarrassment of being kidnapped. I hated to admit she had a point.

"How am I supposed to eat that?" Craig asked as Quentin held a bundle out to him.

Morgan flicked a knife from her sleeve and sliced through the ropes around one of his wrists. Craig yelped.

"Go on, Clara, tell us the story," Quentin said, settling down cross-legged and taking a large bite out of a currant bun.

This room was clearly not big enough for all of us, but I could not be bothered to argue. Maybe by telling them this information, they would go out and get killed, giving me some much-needed peace and quiet.

"The Blythwoods' factory has been dumping its waste in Mundmere Common for the last forty years," I said. "The dirt, or something in the dirt, has gained a function and started flying around London, attacking people."

A heavy silence descended on the room. I ripped off a bit of bread and chewed it. It wasn't just dry, it was stale.

"The dirt has been flying around London?" Quentin asked sceptically.

I inhaled loudly. "Miss Fortitude may have used a couple more scientific terms, but that's pretty much the gist."

"The dirt has been flying around London?" he repeated.

He was getting on my last nerve. "Tell them I'm telling the truth, Morgan."

Morgan squirmed. "She thinks she's telling the truth."

I turned my indignation on her. "What are you trying to say, Morgan?"

"You had a fever, Clara. It made you see things that aren't real," she said.

The betrayal. How could the one person who knew I was telling the truth not believe me? What was the point of her function if she was going to doubt me?

"You think I dreamt the whole thing up?" I asked.

"I think you might be confused," she replied.

They were looking at me with such awkward pity.

"I met a Dirt Man monster on Mundmere Common long before I was kidnapped," I practically shouted. "It was in pain. The dirt itself was in pain. I was trying not to think about it when we were in the pub, Morgan. Don't you remember?"

"You two went to the pub?" Quentin asked.

I ignored him.

"I knew you were hiding something, but I never saw what," Morgan said. "I told you I wouldn't pry, and I didn't."

She thought my dip in toxic waste had knocked my brain loose. They all did. I pushed myself to my feet.

"You want proof? Fine. Let's go to Mundmere Common. You can come too, Craig," I added.

"No, he can't," Morgan said.

"Why not?" I asked.

"It's called child endangerment," she replied.

"I'm eighteen," Craig whined.

"No, you're not," I said.

"We'll go," Morgan said, nodding to Quentin and Darcy. Turning to me, she said, "you stay here and watch Craig."

I folded my arms. "If you leave me on babysitting duty, he'll end up going out the window, chair and all."

"Stay here, Clara. You'll only slow us down," Morgan said.

I could not believe those words had just come out of her mouth. Forget Dirt Man. That was the first truly unbelievable thing I had heard. I would slow them down? I supposed that was Morgan speak for, "I care about you and don't want you getting hurt when you may not be operating at your absolute best."

I pushed past Morgan and stepped over Quentin and Darcy. I may have crushed some fingers, but they would assume I was just clumsy. Morgan followed me into the bedroom, which, I realised, was the only other room. It was not a safe house, it was a safe cupboard.

"You should stay here to rest."

"I can rest when I'm dead," I snapped.

"Then give me your pain."

"No, thank you."

"Clara, you don't have to prove yourself to me. I know you're tough."

She clearly had no idea what I was capable of. "I wouldn't want to slow down our group any more than I doubtlessly will through my mere presence. Besides, I don't know you, Morgan. I don't know how tough you are. I'm not sure you could handle it. But I can. I'm used to it."

"Fine," she said shortly, and I knew she was hurt. Who needed a function? Passing on pain was easy.

❖ ❖ ❖

It was dark, because, of course, assassins can't do anything at a time when they can actually see where they are going. And for that night, I was one of them. It turned out being an assassin was harder than it looked. I couldn't breathe because of the leather jacket, the hood gave me tunnel vision, and the mask kept slipping down. The smell of leather was so strong I was beginning to think my bath had been a mistake. I would rather smell like a vat of chemical waste. The trousers were too short, and I was worried the display of ankle would make me too sexy for Morgan to resist. She seemed to be coping just fine, probably because I wouldn't stop complaining.

You're drawing attention to us, Morgan reprimanded. *Act like me.*

I tried to channel my inner Morgan. Look like a stone, be the stone. Morgan did have every reason to be nervous. I had never seen so many heroes on the street before.

"Is all this for me?" I whispered.

Quentin nodded. "Mr Indestructible is a national treasure, and you are a national disgrace. It's the manhunt of the century."

He seemed far too happy about it.

"Maybe I should pick an assassin name. How about 'Clara De'ath?'" I offered.

I was proud I could tell by the slight downward tilt of Morgan's head that she was smiling somewhere deep inside her hood.

"I knew a Kevin De'ath once," Darcy replied.

We lingered in the shadow of a house until a group of heroes had marched past, then we darted forward to the fence that surrounded Mundmere Common. The assassins crouched low. I leant against it. There was no one there to see us anyway.

How are you feeling? Morgan asked me.

My spite was still fuelling me.

"Okay, let's do this. Be fast, and don't get seen," Darcy said.

"If we do, can't we just say we're here to kill someone?" I asked.

She shook her head. "Mundmere Common is technically listed as a conservation site."

"So?" I asked.

"We're not allowed to assassinate people in sites of conservation. There is a risk to the wildlife," Darcy replied.

She said it like it was perfectly rational. I tried to make out her expression, but that was impossible. "So, houses, castles, even prisons, they're all fair game, but not conservation sites?"

She nodded.

What the hell was going on at that school? Did they spend their evenings volunteering at the local animal centre and their weekends sowing wildflower meadows?

"We have no reason to be on this land," Darcy said. "If we are caught, we will have our seals revoked. It will be like we never went to the school."

Quentin piped up. "It's worse than that. If the school ostracises us, we'll never work as assassins again. They've got the power to make our lives miserable."

"Are you sure you want to do this?" I directed the question at all of them, but I was thinking of the obsessively professional Morgan.

"We won't get caught," Morgan said.

"I'll give you a foot up, Clara," Darcy offered. The sympathy radiating from her made me feel worse than any torture could.

With Darcy underneath me and Quentin cutting the wire as he went over, I could not help but suspect I was being led on an assassin-themed school trip. At any other time, I might have enjoyed the preferential treatment, but my pride was feeling a little ragged. I pretended not to notice Quentin's open arms and dropped onto the ground without so much as a rolled ankle.

I did not wait for them but set off trudging through the undergrowth, wondering how I came to be doing this again. It did not even feel like I had company this time. The assassins crept silently over the dry wood and dead leaves. I couldn't even see them most of the time, but that was probably because of the damn hood. Compared to them, I might as well have been skipping along in a jester's uniform, bells and all. I had a feeling they were not mentioning it to be nice. It made me want to hit something.

The lights of the lake blinked into view.

"There it is," I whispered, turning round to try and find an assassin. There was no one there.

Someone dropped down from a tree beside me, and I almost screamed.

"That's what we're heading for?" Quentin asked.

I resisted the urge to bang his head against a tree and walked on. I stopped at the edge of the clearing. There was no one around. I ran to the lake and crouched behind a barrel. One by one, Morgan, Quentin, and Darcy dived into a roll to join me by the lake. I sighed.

"Okay, I'll agree, that's pretty weird," Quentin said.

The lake was swirling. Now that I knew what it was, I could convince myself it looked angry.

"You were telling the truth," Morgan whispered.

She had the audacity to sound surprised.

"Are you sure?" I asked in mock concern. "Don't you think I should give you more proof? I mean, I wouldn't want you to have to take my word for anything."

"I can feel it," Morgan said.

I momentarily forgot I was mad. "You can read its mind?"

She shook her head. "No, it's different. It's not thoughts. Not visual, or any sense I recognise, but there's something. It's strange. I don't know how to explain it."

"Can you talk to it?" I asked.

She shook her head again. "No. I can't understand, and neither can it. It can't recognise me. But I believe that it can feel."

I reached out with my function. There was pain all right, an ocean of it, but I couldn't get a grip on it. It did not feel like the wall of pain I had encountered the other night. This was more spread out, like each speck of dirt was screaming, and I had no idea where to begin.

We have company, said Morgan in my head.

She was right. Two figures were approaching the lake. I watched them over the top of the barrel. They were heading straight for us.

"It's this one tonight," one of them said, stopping beside a large sack not far from our hiding place.

"Right," the other replied. "So how does this work?"

"Just tip it in, and I'll take the measurements."

It ended up needing both of them to empty the sack into the lake. I waited, dreading what would happen. It took less than a minute for that slurping, sucking noise to set my heart jackhammering. Something was rising from the sludge. The assassins beside me tensed. Morgan had a blade in her hand, as though it would do any good. The thing floated above the lake for a moment, seemingly directionless. I held my breath. I knew what I would have to do if it came our way, but I didn't want to. I reached out with my function and flinched. That was the pain I knew.

Suddenly, it shot up into the air and flew away over the trees.

"Do we track it?" one of the people at the lake asked.

"No, just note down the direction it went," the other replied.

That dirt could go anywhere. I could have stopped it, but I didn't. I was a coward. Some poor, luckless soul was going to end up as another dirt-covered husk, and they wouldn't even know who was responsible. They would die thinking it was some jumped-up villain, not a corporation so set on profits it didn't care that it was killing people. The Blythwoods had a history of making things worse in the pretence of making them better. Perhaps it ran in the family.

"Well, well, well."

I jumped at the sound of the voice right behind us. It was Mrs Grace, backed up by two guards.

"Did you somehow miss the Private Property signs?" she asked.

The assassins rose slowly to their feet. I did the same. The two people who had been mixing chemicals abandoned their measurements to shuffle behind Mrs Grace. We were outnumbered.

"I know one of you is Clara Blakely," Mrs Grace said. "Drop the masks."

Morgan pushed me roughly, making me fall backwards over the barrel. I barely stopped myself from rolling into the lake. Cursing her, I clambered up. The assassins had already launched themselves into the fight. Forget Craig, I was the one being babysat. I leant against the barrel and folded my arms.

"Don't mind me, I'll just stay right here."

It must have been Bring Your Own Weapon to Work Day. There was a bizarre show of clubs and knives. It looked like somebody had a mace. No guns, I noticed. Screams could be explained away as foxes mating, but gunfire would raise suspicions if it originated in a conservation site.

Darcy and Quentin would have been a lot more efficient with the guards if they didn't keep getting in each other's way.

"Sorry!" Darcy cried as her roundhouse kick caught Quentin's shoulder.

"That's all right! I was in the way!"

Clearly, the Finishing School did not focus on teamwork. Morgan was staying well away from them, taking on Mrs Grace in a battle of blades. Morgan was just that little bit faster than the other assassins. Every move was slightly more fluid, with a touch more strength. I could see how easily she would deal with her usual targets. But Mrs Grace was not some inbred lord who had cheated on his wife; she had been doing this hero thing for years.

The temperature was steadily dropping. Morgan was slowing down, while Mrs Grace, impervious to the effects of her function, was becoming more aggressive. Their knives screeched as they came together. Morgan was on the defensive now. Her breath rose in clouds as her moves became jerkier and weaker. She made a desperate lunge at Mrs Grace but slipped on a patch of ice. Mrs Grace was on her before she had hit the ground.

I pushed myself away from the barrel with a sigh and put all my pain on Mrs Grace. With an unexpected gasp, she collapsed by the side of the lake. I supposed feeling the effects of a torture session, near-drowning, and life-threatening fever all at once must have been really something. I walked leisurely over to her, past the last few guards that were battling Quentin and Darcy. I picked up a shovel, spun it in my hands, and whacked Mrs Grace over the head. The temperature returned to its normal, mildly chilly state. I kicked Mrs Grace's body over. Her empty eyes stared up at the sky.

I turned my attention to Morgan.

"Oh, I'm sorry, was I slowing you down?" I asked.

Morgan stood. She picked up her knife from where it had fallen and threw it at one of the guards. I picked up his pain and passed it onto another.

I'm sorry.

I cupped a hand to my ear. "What was that? I didn't quite catch it."

Morgan looked down at her feet. "I'm sorry. What I said was wrong. Thank you for saving me."

"You are the one person I can't deceive, Morgan. You are at a distinct advantage, so don't waste it by doing what everyone else does and underestimating me."

"Oh my god. They're in love."

My head whipped round to Quentin. A body lay at his feet, but he was staring at us with wide eyes.

"What was that?" Darcy asked, skipping over.

"Nothing," I said quickly. "You did not say anything, did you Quentin?" If it came out sounding like a threat, that was because it was.

Quentin shook his head vigorously.

"We should get out of here," Morgan said.

"Should we get rid of the bodies?" I asked.

"There's no point," Morgan replied. "They might guess it was assassins, but they won't be able to prove it was us. Staying will just increase the chance of us getting caught."

No running, no hiding, no burning bodies or stuffing gold into our bags. It felt like a rather sudden way to leave a fight, but I wasn't going to complain.

"How's Mrs Grace?" I asked Quentin as we walked away from the lake.

He looked over my shoulder. "Not very happy."

Pulling his piece of paper from his pocket, he ran his finger through a spray of blood on his jacket and modified it so it read, **She's sorry she killed you**, followed by a sad face.

"Did it help?" I asked.

Quentin shook his head. "No. If anything, she looks angrier, which is weird."

"I'll tell you what's really weird," Darcy said. "Not getting paid. I think being an assassin may have ruined killing for pleasure for me."

I decided to ignore this rather worrying statement.

Chapter
16

I stumbled into Morgan's safe house knowing that if I didn't lie down soon, the ground would rise to meet me. The excitement of the fight had burnt away, leaving me with a hollow tiredness. The worst pain was temporarily gone thanks to Mrs Grace, but those leathers gave me terrible chaffing.

The others were already inside, pulling the window closed.

"If someone doesn't untie me soon, I'm going to piss myself," Craig called.

"I'm on it," Darcy said.

I leant against the doorframe as Darcy cut Craig's restraints. "Don't you want to know what they saw in Mundmere Common?" I asked him.

He looked up at Darcy questioningly.

"Clara was right," Darcy told him.

He gaped at her, then searched the faces around him, as though someone would suddenly say no, we had actually found a kitten sanctuary.

He stumbled over his words. "They can't... I wouldn't..."

"You wouldn't have...what?" I asked. "Helped them cover up mass murder?"

"The question now is what are we going to do about it?" Morgan said.

Ignore it, run from it, use our knowledge to make a small fortune. These were all valid options, yet for some reason, I found myself saying, "We need to stop the Blythwoods from pumping more chemicals into the lake, and we need to expose them and their gang of heroes."

"Are you sure we should expose them?" Darcy asked.

I raised my eyebrows. "You better not be taking the Blythwoods' side."

"Just hear me out," she said. "If people know dirt can get a function, it may reinvigorate the anti-functionable movement. Functionables will be hated. I'm speaking as someone whose three best friends are functionables."

I hoped she wasn't including me in that group.

"It's going to come out sooner or later anyway," Quentin said. "We do this, and we may be able to stop it before it kills all of us."

Quentin and Darcy embarked on a bout of long eye contact. I let them get on with it. There were other things to think about. I had been able to stop the Dirt Man by using my function. It was like taking away its pain took away its motivation to kill me. But stopping one manifestation was not enough, as another would just rise to take its place. If the Dirt Man was a person on fire, then all I had done was take the pain from their little toe.

I think it has a centre, Morgan said.

I looked over at her. She was chewing her thumbnail. It was the greatest expression of worry I had seen on her.

Maybe thinking of the manifestation as a little toe isn't so far from the truth. When one formed at the lake back there, its thoughts—if I can call them that—seemed weaker.

But its pain had been stronger.

I think the thoughts came from somewhere. Somewhere in the lake. If I could somehow find the centre, it might give you something to focus on.

Allowing me to take the pain of the entire thing. Would it work? And if it did, how long would it last? I wouldn't be curing anything, just appeasing it.

And could you do it? Morgan asked. *If the little toe hurt that much, would taking all its pain kill you?*

The honest answer was I did not know, and I was not all that keen to find out. I never wanted to feel pain like that again. I was not some self-sacrificing hero, willing to put my life on the line to solve one of the world's many problems. Especially if it helped the Blythwoods cover up their mistake. I was not going to lift a finger against the Dirt Man until there was a photograph of it on the front of every newspaper, next to a shot of John and Edith Blythwood in those rather fetching prison overalls.

Darcy finally nodded and tore her gaze away from Quentin's.

I pinched the bridge of my nose. "Okay, let's sum up. We have a huge conspiracy, people trying to kill us, a dead hero, and no plan whatsoever. Does that cover everything?"

"I still need to pee," Craig offered.

"I'm going to bed," I said. If I had to interact with one more person, I was going to scream.

"We should all get some rest," Quentin said. "I'll take the floor."

He seemed far too willing.

"Clara, you and Morgan can take the bed," he finished.

He had the nerve to wink at me.

"Can I go home yet?" Craig asked.

"They will kill you, Craig," I told him.

"You can join me on the floor," Quentin said.

"Death doesn't seem so bad," Craig mumbled.

I fell onto the bed. I would never complain about the ridiculous clothes of polite society again. It turned out that there were some luxuries I could not live without. Being able to breathe was one of them.

Morgan lay carefully on the other side of the bed, as far away from me as possible without the use of levitation.

"Mind if I join you?" Darcy asked.

"Come sleep next to me," Quentin said quickly. "We can gossip."

Darcy scoffed. "And miss out on a bed? Budge over Morgan."

Reluctantly, Morgan edged over until we were pressed together. The tension was so thick, it was probably changing barometers across the country. It filled me with an inappropriate urge to laugh. Beside me, Morgan was lying as stiff as a corpse.

"Relax," I murmured. "I don't bite." Unless she asked nicely.

Morgan shifted onto her side to face me. "Stop it," she whispered seriously.

"Stop what?" I asked innocently. "I'm just trying to make you more comfortable."

"What are you guys talking about?" Darcy asked, raising herself up on her elbow. I could hear Quentin screaming into his pillow.

"Just talking about corn prices," I said.

Darcy flopped back. "How boring. Hey Quentin, did you hear the rumours about the Clicking Assassin?"

I closed my eyes to the sound of their dull ramblings. It wasn't quite as relaxing as rain, but it was just as constant. The waves of exhaustion washed in, growing steadily closer and rising, gaining ground like water, or something else. Something darker and thicker that I couldn't escape.

A hand found mine. Morgan laced our fingers together and squeezed.

I'm right here.

I could hear her breathing in my mind, and it was comforting. I really was losing it.

"Stay out of my dreams, Morgan," I told her.

"I'm not promising anything," she whispered back.

❖   ❖   ❖

I had no idea where I was. There was a bright light in my eyes, and my legs were bound. No, they weren't. It was these damn leather trousers. I looked around blurrily. I was alone in the bed, and Craig was still asleep on the floor. The assassins were poring over a paper in a corner.

"What's going on?" I asked.

Darcy hushed me. "The kid's sleeping."

"What's going on?" I asked louder.

Craig sat up with a jerk.

"Nice work," Darcy scolded.

I untucked myself from the bed and tried to stretch some feeling back into my legs.

"*The Times* is saying one of your accomplices has been arrested," Quentin read.

"It's Dan," Morgan said.

"Dan? My Dan?" I grabbed the newspaper.

There was a sketch of a very confused Dan being taken into custody. It said he had been arrested on suspicion of aiding and abetting me. The Blythwoods were trying to draw me out of the woodwork.

Poor Dan. His only fault was knowing me. Well, that was not strictly true. He had plenty of faults. His desire to be a knight in shining armour led to him giving me a room in the first place; his hatred of confrontation resulted in Mrs Winow's cat; his eagerness to please allowed me to walk all over him. And then there was his abysmal cooking and terrible taste in wallpaper. Any of these deserved life imprisonment in my book, but still, it was Dan. He had warned me not to get involved. I had not listened, as always.

Someone had probably searched my hotel room and found the letter I penned to him. They must have deduced he was far more valuable to me than he really was. Sure, he was important, but in the same way that a leg is important. If I had to, I could live without him. The one consolation was he did not know anything important. He didn't know Morgan's name, even if he knew her function, and that wouldn't be enough to lead them to me. He had knowledge of Forgo's journal, but he had no idea of Mundmere's significance. The Blythwoods were probably in possession of the journal now. Hiding it under the mattress had been stupid. A toddler could have found it.

Dan's ignorance was for the best; he would definitely crack under pressure. Would they torture him just for the hell of it? Would they invent a crime and execute him?

Yes, I had lied to him and flirted with him to win his favour like I did with everyone. But at some point, I stopped pretending with him. He was the closest thing to family I had left. Now, there was a chance I would have to read about his hanging. I would not even be able to attend to heckle him.

"So, now we know the Hero Brigade, the police, and the newspapers are all against us," Quentin said.

I flicked through the rest of the paper. There was an unflattering cartoon of me. I knew there was such a thing as artistic license, but my head was nowhere near that big. It served its purpose though; I was the evil mastermind once again. When would these people get it into their thick skulls that I was just as lost and stupid as they were?

"It's not a bad tactic," I mused.

"What isn't?" Quentin asked.

"Using the papers," I replied. "People like to read them in the morning before they're awake enough to employ critical thinking. They believe what they read, or at least think about it. If only we had someone who could get an article printed in a credible newspaper."

They followed my gaze to Craig.

"We're not exploiting the kid," Morgan said.

"Not exploiting, employing," I replied.

"It's too dangerous," she pronounced firmly.

"What's too dangerous?" Darcy asked.

I smiled. "Craig has a very useful function, don't you Craig?"

Craig puffed out his chest. "I can change ink on paper, make it say whatever I want it to say."

"That's so cool," Quentin exclaimed.

"Let's not inflate the kid's ego," I said.

"Why don't we just kill the Blythwoods?" Morgan asked. "That way no one gets hurt. Except for the Blythwoods, of course."

"We could," I agreed. "But personally, I would rather destroy them. I want them to lose everything: their money, their reputation, their little empire of influence. I want them to experience the same level of suffering they have caused. I want John and Edith to become the least popular names of the next generation."

"That's good with me," Quentin said.

"I vote we send Craig to the printers and get him to add an article telling everyone the truth. Or an edited version of it, anyway," I said.

"They will be looking for him," Morgan observed.

"We can go at night," Darcy offered.

"That's not how newspapers work," Morgan snapped. "We would have to go during the day, and we can't just disguise him as an assassin. We won't blend in there."

"I think it's time to test whether your skills as assassins go beyond leathers," I said.

Darcy and Quentin practically squealed in excitement.

"We get to wear disguises!" Darcy said, clapping her hands.

Quentin grinned at her. "What fun!"

I decided not to mention that they would, for once, be wearing regular clothes.

"You can't go," Morgan told me.

"I am aware," I replied. My face was probably more known than the Queen's.

"We should get Dan," Morgan said.

"Get him?" I asked in confusion.

"Break him out," she clarified.

I shook my head. "We can't."

"They may torture him, even kill him," she said.

"Then he'll regret ever meeting me," I replied with a shrug. "It was bound to happen eventually. I'm surprised it took this long."

"Surely, you're not that heartless," Darcy said.

"You know nothing about me," I shot back.

The worst possible thing I could do was make the Blythwoods think I cared about anyone. Going after Dan would seal his fate.

We can get him out and bring him here, Morgan said in my head. *The Blythwoods can't know about this place, or they would have sent someone for you already.*

And how did she expect us to break him out?

We go in as assassins. The police will think we are there to kill him, not rescue him.

It was madness. The police were probably under explicit instructions not to let anyone kill their valuable prisoner, and even if by some miracle they let us in, assassins didn't go around saving people. They might realise I was disguising myself under a skin of leather. What happened if Morgan was implicated? Was she willing to risk her career, possibly her life, for someone she had never met?

He's your friend.

He was my inconvenience.

"Fine," I said. "I'll go break my stupid friend out of prison, you guys get Craig into the printers."

"I'm coming with you," Morgan said. *And don't bother arguing. If you try and go without me, I will just follow you. You can't hide from me.*

Morgan and I were going to have a talk about her use of ominous phrases.

"What about Craig?" I asked. "I thought you were concerned about his safety." God only knew why she had decided to protect the little brat.

"I trust them," Morgan said, nodding to Quentin and Darcy.

"Morgan, you just said something nice," Quentin said, tearing up.

Darcy threw herself at Morgan and hugged her tight. Morgan stood stiffly, receiving the affection like a beating.

"All right," I relented. "I expect Quentin and Darcy are far superior to Morgan at pretending to be normal."

"We can pretend to be married and that Craig is our child," Quentin offered.

There would not be much pretence needed.

"Do I look like I have a fifteen-year-old?" Darcy asked, offended.

"I'm eighteen," Craig mumbled.

I waved him off. "Nobody is believing that."

He folded his arms. "No one has actually asked if I want to go."

"Do you want to stop the Blythwoods from murdering London one flying dirt monster at a time?" I asked.

He picked at a thread on his sleeve. "Yes."

"Then what's the problem?" I asked.

"Edith scares me," he said quietly.

I inhaled deeply. "Morgan, would you like to give Craig a pep talk?"

I did not need to be able to read minds to see Morgan would rather light herself on fire. She looked more terrified than Craig was claiming to be. I knelt beside him. This would have been easier if I had been a bit nicer to him.

"Listen, Craig. It's good that you're scared," I told him. "It shows you've got some sense. But you're going to have to put that aside for now. It's not fair that this responsibility falls on you, but you're the only one who can do this. We need you."

"Why does it have to be us?" he whined. "Why can't someone else take on the Blythwoods?"

"Because we're the only ones who know what they're doing," I said. "We've got the knowledge and the ability to do something about it, so it's got to be us."

Craig chewed his lip. I let him have his moment, even though my knees were getting sore.

"What do you want the article to say?" he asked.

"Good lad." I patted his shoulder. "If the people want me, then give them me. Make it sound like an exclusive interview. Explain how on my way to prove my innocence in Forgo's death, I came across a journal hinting at how the Blythwoods had illegally acquired Mundmere Common. I was on my way to the authorities when I was kidnapped by Mr Indestructible and told the dirt in Mundmere has acquired a function and is out there slaughtering innocent people. The Blythwoods know this and are doing nothing to stop it because they hope they can weaponize it and make another fortune. I have not seen Mr Indestructible since I escaped his cruel clutches. Keep everyone else, including yourself, out of it."

"Thanks," he mumbled.

"They'll call you crazy," Quentin said.

I shrugged. "But hopefully they'll also get curious."

"Come on." Darcy tugged Quentin's arm. "We need to go shopping. What look are you going for?"

"Don't get carried away," I warned. "I don't want to see any wigs or fake moustaches."

Darcy rolled her eyes. "Fine, Mum."

"Trying to change each individual paper will take forever, so we'll need to time it when the copy has left the editor but not been printed yet," Craig said. He still sounded nervous. "Even changing just one copy will take me a while."

"We'll need a distraction then," Darcy cried with glee. "Perhaps I could pretend to faint, or we could have a huge argument. Have you been cheating on me?"

Quentin put a hand over his heart. "I would never!"

"I saw the diamond necklace, Francis!" she shouted.

"I bought that as a gift, for you!" Quentin shouted back.

Darcy sniffed loudly. "Sure you did. You can't even remember our anniversary, but you suddenly start buying me jewellery? How could you do this to our family? What about little Robbie? He's only ten."

"I'm not ten!" Craig shouted.

"Crouch down a bit," Darcy suggested.

They were going to get arrested. I had seen pantomimes with more realism. "It's a marvellous idea. You work out the stage directions, and we'll get going to Dippenwick. How do we get there?"

"We'll take the stagecoach," Morgan said.

"Assassins can take the stagecoach?" I asked.

"Of course," Morgan replied. "How did you think we travelled? On horses as dark as night?"

"I did," Craig said.

"That's because you're stupid, Craig," I fired back.

Morgan slapped my arm. "Stop bullying him."

"What part of 'he gave me to Mr Indestructible to torture' do you not understand?" I retorted.

"Clara will need a seal," Quentin interrupted.

"And a gun," I added.

"No," Morgan said.

"Why not? I have had ample experience with them," I pointed out.

"I don't have a gun, but you can have my dagger," Darcy said, handing me her seal and a large knife.

"I'll also need a uniform for Dan so we can get him back here," I said. "Quentin, have you got a spare?"

I followed Quentin to the bed. He pulled a suitcase from under it and rummaged around in it until he had a bundle of clothes. I had no idea when he had decided he was moving in. He stuffed them into a black leather bag for me. "Here you go."

He glanced around. Darcy was talking animatedly to Morgan about dresses while Morgan stared at her blankly. Quentin looked back at me. "I'm sorry about Darcy. She can be a bit oblivious sometimes." He shot a longing glance at her, reminding me that Darcy was not the only oblivious one. "At least now you and Morgan can have some alone time."

I wrenched the bag from his hand. "Good. We'll use it to plot your murder."

Chapter
17

At the coach station, Morgan scowled at the man selling tickets.

"Two tickets to Dippenwick," she snarled.

The man gulped visibly.

"Please," I added.

Morgan snatched the offered tickets from the man's shaking hands and stalked over to the waiting carriage. I found her sitting stiffly on a seat, arms folded, glaring out of the window. I settled into the space next to her, allowing myself to slouch. This was one of those rare occasions I did not have to play the role of sophisticated lady, and I intended to make the most of it.

The silence stretched between us. I knew this was a good opportunity to thank her for everything she had done. She had saved my life twice now, which was once more than I had saved hers, and she was helping me rescue my helpless landlord. The problem was that gratitude slipped so easily from my lips. It was the simplest thing in the world to fake, and the hardest to make sincere.

"I suppose I should mock you," I said.

"What for?"

"For being a terrible assassin. Not only did you help murder a bunch of people in the one place you're not allowed, but I was the only one with a price on my head in that warehouse, yet I was the one you saved."

"If I can't kill you, no one can."

The door opened. A man put one foot in, saw us, and clearly considered getting out again.

"Move along, Hector," came a voice behind him, one I had the misfortune of knowing quite well.

Hector climbed in. Behind him, forcing her voluminous skirts through the door, came none other than Maureen Butterswatch. Two hours of Maureen and myself in an enclosed space. Someone was going to die.

With a great amount of yelling and lurching, the carriage lumbered its way out of the station. The aches from my previous occupation as hostage were building again, along with the headache I was learning came hand in hand with Morgan's company. I picked a person on the street and lobbed my pain at them as we sped away. If there was going to be any chance for Maureen's survival, I was going to need to remain as calm as possible.

"Excuse me, but are you assassins?" Maureen asked in her skin-flaying voice that somehow imposed her superiority while remaining whiny.

"What gave us away?" I asked drily.

Clara, Morgan warned.

"And what would two assassins be doing travelling to Dippenwick?" Maureen asked.

There she went, sticking her nose in where it wasn't wanted.

"My grandmother is sick," I said.

Maureen pursed her lips. "Is that so?"

I did not care that she did not believe me. Let her imagination run wild.

"We've been in London attending an event." Maureen preened.

Had I asked? "How fascinating. What kind of event?"

"For journalists," she replied smugly. "I wrote an article about Miss Take, the criminal."

Miss Take, the criminal. That was what they would write on my tombstone. *Affectionately missed by absolutely no one.*

"I heard she's completely innocent," I said.

"Unlikely," Maureen sniffed. "I know her quite well. She had a room in Dippenwick, so I thought it best to keep an eye on her. She was an unsavoury character, full of airs she inherited from her new-money parents. They were criminals too, of course."

I could get Craig to forge a contract for her, Morgan offered.

It was a very thoughtful suggestion, but it would be better to simply prove my innocence. That would be worse than death for her.

"They recently arrested her accomplice," Maureen continued, unasked.

"I knew him too. He was a very suspicious individual. No young man should be running a boarding house. He should have been a soldier overseas. That's what my sons do."

Ah yes, if you fail in England, export your failure abroad. I could just imagine the kind of damage they were doing with their inherited snobbery.

"How interesting," I said. "Now, if you would please excuse us, we should try and get some sleep."

"Are you planning on staying up late?" She had the subtlety of a bull in a tearoom.

"No, we're just nocturnal," I replied. "It's a symptom of the job."

I tilted my head back and closed my eyes. Maureen continued to talk at Hector in a voice loud enough to wake the dead, but I resolutely faked sleep. If I did not distract myself somehow, I was going to throw myself out of the carriage. To do that twice in one week would be pushing my luck. Maybe Morgan was listening in on my thoughts. I started composing a poem. Roses are red, violets are blue. Pay attention to me Morgan, I want to be amused.

How do you expect me to do that?

I would settle for anything so long as it prevented me from putting my fist through Maureen's teeth. She could philosophise on the meaning of life, regale me with anecdotes from her past, give me a dramatic retelling of a fairy tale. Once upon a time, there was a prince who wished more than anything to be a frog.

I'm not sure that's how the story goes.

He wanted to spend his days hip-hopping, not trudging through the tedious bureaucracy of state affairs.

I can't say I know that one, but have you heard the story of the Clicking Assassin?

No. It sounded like a type of praying mantis.

Do you want to hear the story or not?

I begrudgingly admitted that I wanted to hear the story.

The Clicking Assassin came to the Finishing School fifteen years ago. She had weak ankles that clicked whenever she moved. The teachers told her she would never be an assassin with ankles like that, but she paid for the first year upfront, so they were willing to let her try a few classes. They expected her to drop out or die in an exercise within the first week. She didn't. She graduated top of her class. She has become, without doubt, the most successful assassin to have ever come from the Finishing School. Reports arrive from all over the country of her work. People hear a terrifying clicking noise, and the next thing they know, they find a body. Nothing can inspire fear quite like her dodgy ankles. I heard a rumour that a mark once died of fright upon hearing them drawing closer. She turned what everyone saw as a flaw into her greatest strength.

That was a surprisingly sweet story. Morgan clearly wanted me to glean some moral lesson from it. Probably that it was fine to be different, that we can turn our weaknesses into strengths and all that.

Actually, I just think she's really neat.

How adorable, Morgan had a crush.

Fine. No more stories for you.

Assassins were so sensitive. I conjured an insincere apology in my mind and asked for another story, adding many a "pretty please."

I don't know any more.

She was sulking. Everyone had stories. What had her life been like pre-assassin?

Why do you want to know? she asked suspiciously.

Because there was nothing else going on, and it might have been one of the few occasions when someone's life story wouldn't bore me.

Not much to tell, she said.

It was like drawing blood from a stone. She had not materialised from mist or risen from a bog. I knew she had parents and a sister, so she must have done some form of mundane growing up.

I did all the normal things children do. Playing, crying, hiding in a coal mine.

I had to admit I had never experienced the latter.

My parents owned it. Me and my sister used to sneak down there. I got good at hiding. She got good at telling on me.

Did I sense some sibling rivalry?

Not really.

I could always reveal my identity to Maureen. That would certainly make the ride more entertaining.

Fine, but it's not at all interesting. I suppose there was a little bit of tension between us. My parents were very proper, not ones for communication, so they enjoyed being able to talk to me without actually talking. I became a sort of go-between for them, so naturally, my sister was a little bit jealous of me.

I had never asked if Morgan's sister had a function.

No. I was the only one.

That must have been tough. Despite all that the original John Blythwood had done for our image, a lot of old-money families still looked down on functionables. They saw us as dirty. It was rather progressive of Morgan's family to accept her.

They had the complete works of John Blythwood. They would quote bits at parties. His philosophy conveniently allowed them to continue maximising profit.

Made sense.

They wanted me to be a perfect example of a high-society functionable, but I fell woefully short of everyone's expectations.

I bet her parents wouldn't be saying that if they were still alive. She had won a scholarship to the Finishing School and graduated top of her year.

Yes, they would, and you know why. The things that are easy for people like my sister just aren't for me. That is why her jealousy has always been so unfounded. I could never smile and curtsey and talk to people. I tried, but a conventional life has never been on the table for me.

I wanted to reassure her that it was all right. People were overrated. Being able to talk to them just meant you had to do it more often.

I told you something. Now it's your turn.

I was an open book. Anything she wanted to know, she could weasel out of my unprotected mind.

How did you meet Dan?

Technically, the first time I met him was when I was robbing him. Well, he worked as a clerk at the bank I was robbing with my parents. He lost his job because of it, which he said was the best thing that ever happened to him.

Does he like his job now?

Running a boarding house? No, he hated it, but he must have hated it less than the bank.

He clearly means a lot to you. I'll try not to embarrass you in front of him.

I snorted, turning it quickly into a snore when Maureen's monologue came to an abrupt stop. The idea that Morgan could embarrass me in front of Dan implied I cared what he thought of me. The only reason I listened to Dan's advice was so I could do the opposite of it. Yes, Morgan was embarrassing, but her lack of social etiquette was growing strangely endearing to me. She did not bow to any of the pressures I hated. She was a lot braver than I was.

I realised she was listening to these thoughts and that I would now quite like to throw myself out of the carriage for reasons other than Maureen.

All right, I'm gone, Morgan said.

She might have left my head, but she had not left my thoughts. That was the problem.

❖ ❖ ❖

Dippenwick did not have a coach station, so the carriage dropped us outside the most prominent architectural feature: the Brigade clubhouse. The smell of cow manure wafting in from the fields greeted us like a welcome parade as we climbed down the step onto the street.

"Have a good evening," I told Maureen.

"Give your grandmother my regards," she replied.

I would have to get hold of the next copy of the parish news. It would doubtlessly describe hordes of assassins descending on Dippenwick, setting fire to barns, and threatening the occupants.

"It's not as miserable as you remember it," Morgan said, looking around with interest.

"That's because it's raining. You should see it on a fair day. That really is tragic."

The police station was right next door to the Brigade so they could both keep an eye on each other. Officially, having multiple agencies kept everyone accountable, but in practice, it just encouraged coercion and conspiracy. As we made our way around the Brigade, I noticed Arthur Todd standing in his window, looking even more saggy than usual. I hoped he was in trouble for providing a glowing recommendation of my character. One unexpected benefit of the whole affair I had not considered was that I was looking at a future free from Arthur's proposals. There was only so low his pride was willing to sink, and marrying the suspected killer of Mr Indestructible was well below that point.

I made sure to keep my hooded head pointing at him as we passed. He disappeared as his knees gave out from terror. It was nice to frighten someone as an assassin, not as Miss Take. I had gone from being feared because my face was well-known, to being feared because I had no face at all. The huge ego instilled in me since birth would start clawing under my skin eventually, but I could enjoy the anonymity briefly.

Morgan eyed the window of the police station. I doubted she was reading the notice stuck on it that said: Do you have a history of gambling, blackmail, and grievous bodily harm? Come inside and ask us about our administrative roles. Functionables need not apply.

I opened the door for her. "Come on, you can do it."

She glowered at me and stalked past so fast, I wondered if she actually had a phobia of doors.

Leaning across the front desk and breathing all over the constable was Mrs Winow.

"Could you just ask him where he keeps the iron?" she pleaded.

"I'm sorry, ma'am, but passing unsanctioned messages between outsiders and a prisoner would be considered a felony. Could you please stand aside while I talk to these folks?"

Mrs Winow backed away grumbling. Her cloak gave a twitch. It was almost as if there was something cat shaped hidden beneath it.

"How would you do this normally?" I murmured to Morgan under my breath as we approached the desk.

"I'd tell him I'm here to kill someone, and he would let me through."

"All right." I put on a smile the constable couldn't see and spoke up. "We're here to kill one of your prisoners, is that okay?" I didn't quite have the same menacing tone as Morgan. It was hard to shake the habit of politeness.

Morgan held out her seal to the constable. I followed suit.

"Not this again," he sighed.

"On the bright side, you'll have less filing to do," I coaxed.

"That's always a plus." He hesitated. "Which prisoner are you after? I've got a special one that I'm under strict instructions to protect till they can transfer him."

"What's your name?" Morgan asked suddenly. No one could do sinister quite like her.

"Why?" he asked nervously, voice cracking.

"I heard of a contract for someone in the police force," she said ominously.

The man quailed at the threat. His hand shook as he slid the keys across the table. "Go right ahead."

Morgan looked at the keys disdainfully and stormed past the man towards the cells. I picked up the keys, thanked the constable, and followed her.

Dippenwick was one of those places that prided itself on the comfort of its prisons. Most of the time, they were used as somewhere to sleep off a hangover if home seemed too far away. They didn't want any of that chains-hanging-from-the-ceiling, water-dripping-down-the-walls nonsense.

There were three prisoners, and I knew them all. In the first cell was the man who pretended to have an alcohol addiction so he could use the prison's superior lighting to read. He was smoking his pipe and perusing a copy of *The Odyssey*. In the cell opposite him was a kid I had once picked up for propping horses on bricks and stealing their shoes.

Morgan pulled her miniature crossbow out and fired two shots. Both cell occupants slumped over. The constable was going to get the sack. One missing prisoner, two dead. He would be clearing horse dung by the end of the week.

They're not dead. I used the sleeping draught.

She sounded aghast that I would think she had killed them. An assassin? Killing people? Preposterous.

In the cell at the end was the person we were there for. Dan was sitting on the floor, knees pulled up to his chest. He looked upset, but unharmed. I slipped the key into the lock, and he looked up.

"Oh god no, please," Dan said, scooting backwards to put as much distance between us as the tiny room would allow. "Clara, what did you do?" he whispered to himself.

How unfair. He just assumed that if an assassin was after him, it was my fault. "Why do you blame me?"

"Clara?" he stuttered. "Why are you wearing a mask?"

"Because it's good for hygiene. Why do you think? I'm a wanted fugitive. Put these on. We need to go." I threw the bag full of leathers at him.

The bag fell to the floor. Dan gawked at me for several moments longer before he shrugged, picked up the bag, and started pulling out the clothes.

"Who's your friend?" he asked as he stripped off his shirt, nodding to Morgan.

"Just that," I replied.

He finished pulling on the clothes and looked down at himself. "These leathers do no favours to my butt."

I held the door open for him. He still managed to walk into it.

"How is anyone supposed to see out of this?" he asked, trying to prevent the hood from falling over his eyes.

"Be quiet," Morgan snapped. "You both take the door. Walk quickly, and don't talk. They may notice one of you is taller than when we came in."

"Are you taking the window?" I asked.

She nodded.

"We'll meet you out front," I said.

Morgan hopped onto the ledge, jimmied the window open, and dropped out of it. A gust blew in and extinguished the lights. I sighed as I closed it. Assassins and their dramatic exits.

"Your friend is scary," Dan whispered to me.

"That's Morgan, the assassin who can read minds." I headed for the door back to the reception.

"What?"

I kept walking. Dan ran after me.

"Whatever happened to, 'She's dangerous,' 'She's not my friend?'"

I pushed open the door. Mrs Winow was talking to the constable again.

"How long should I hold the iron over the fire?" she asked.

"Until it's hot."

"How do I know when it's hot?"

"When you touch it and go 'ouch.'"

I nodded to the constable.

"My poor tenants," Dan whispered as we left. "Most of them don't know how to feed themselves."

"This is a great time for them to learn."

"Or burn down the house."

"What a shame that would be."

"For god's sake, Clara, the wallpaper isn't that bad."

I stopped. In front of us, standing on the steps leading down from the police station, was Arthur Todd. There was a small crowd gathered behind him.

"Now. I want an honest answer here, no lollygagging. What, so to speak, is your business here?" Arthur demanded, his voice barely shaking.

I prayed that Dan would keep his cool.

"I'm afraid I cannot reveal the particulars of our operation," I said calmly. "That would be a breach of client confidentiality."

The crowd began whispering fiercely. What was the point in telling them the truth? They would make it up anyway.

Arthur's brow furrowed. "Your voice sounds somehow familiar. Have we met before?"

"I think you would remember it." If I ripped off the hood, would he be sufficiently distracted by my neck to allow us to make our escape?

"Look, we're a small, tight-knit community here," he began. "We don't usually get your type. There's no one for you to assassinate, so why don't you just, well, get on your way."

"I don't know, you seem like a valuable gentleman," I suggested smoothly.

"Thank you," he said puffing out his chest. Then, he realised the implications and bristled. "Now look here."

"No, you look here." I took a step towards him. He fell back one. "I came to this place seeking employment. I thought, 'Nice landscape, easy access to London. There's probably a few moneybags around here who would like to off each other.' But clearly, this is the kind of backwater town where people come to die, making my work superfluous. There's no one here who could afford me."

Arthur spluttered wordlessly.

"Are you here for Miss Take? Do you think she's around here?" someone yelled from the crowd. I located Maureen as the source. I should have kicked her out of the carriage and left her to hitchhike.

"I am not aware that there are any contracts out for Miss Blakely," I said loudly. "I would advise you to query the police over her whereabouts, or perhaps your local Hero Brigade commander. She is one of them, after all."

Arthur continued to find nothing in his mouth but spit. I grabbed Dan's arm and pulled him down the steps.

"Has your friend got anything to say?" Arthur said, finally locating a sentence.

Dan shook his head.

"She's antisocial," I said.

The door to the police station flew open, and Mrs Winow barrelled towards us, her cat leaping behind her. She threw her arms around me. "Dan. Dan, is that you? Where is the iron kept?"

I tried to prise her from me, but her claws were latched onto my skin.

"You have to come back, Dan! It's all falling apart without you!" Mrs Winow cried.

"What is the meaning of this, Mrs Winow?" Arthur demanded.

The constable came running out, blowing his whistle. He pointed at us, and the whistle screeched. Realising his mistake, he spat out his whistle and tried again. "They took the prisoner! They took Dan!"

If I was going down, I was taking someone with me. I pulled out Darcy's knife. Mrs Winow decided it was time to let go of me. I grabbed Arthur and pressed it against his neck.

"I hear another whistle or a scream or someone even blows their nose, and I'll be painting these steps with Mr Todd's innards," I shouted.

The policeman shifted his weight from foot to foot but didn't advance. Either he wanted to preserve Arthur's life or, more realistically, he didn't want to spend the week scrubbing the steps.

I felt Arthur's Adam's apple bob against my knife. "Clara?"

I turned the blade to press the point up into the folds of his chin. "It's nothing personal, Arthur, dear."

"What happens now?" Dan whispered, dithering as he tried to decide whether he should be putting me between him and the policeman or him and the crowd.

Now, we hoped for a miracle.

A loud whinny pierced the air as a carriage tore into the street, two wheels in the air as it rounded the corner. Morgan sat on the box, snapping the reins and urging the horses faster. I threw Arthur out of the way and shoved Dan forward.

"Catch that carriage!" I shouted.

He jumped through its open door as it passed. I ran after it and grabbed the doorframe. My feet dragged through the mud as I hauled myself inside. Dan was lying on the floor. I reached out of the carriage for the open door. The crowd was yelling obscenities after us. A few of the sprightlier amongst them had given chase, but they were falling behind. I slammed the door and stuck my head through the gap that gave access to the driver's seat.

"They'll come after us," I told Morgan.

"They'll find it difficult. These were the only horses I could find. All the others were up on bricks, and they didn't look like they were coming down anytime soon."

I grinned and pulled my head back into the carriage. Dan pounced on me.

"Dan! What are you doing?"

He peppered me with weak slaps.

"What did you do, Clara? Yesterday, everything is fine, and suddenly, I'm being arrested, dressed up as an assassin, and thrown under a horse!"

I grabbed his arms.

"You better start explaining yourself!"

"I would if you would stop the physical assault!"

His arms went limp, and I let him go. He took a seat opposite me. I leant back and took off my mask. Finally, I could breathe again.

"Clara, what happened to your face?" Dan asked, horrified.

"Mr Indestructible happened."

"Did you actually kill him?"

"No, I did not. But I did kill Mrs Grace."

He gaped at me.

"Relax. Everything is under control."

"It sure doesn't look it!"

"Do you want to know what is going on or not?"

He huffed and folded his arms. "Go on then."

I hesitated. It was difficult to know where to begin. I scratched my chin. "So, you know Dirt Man? Well, it's not exactly a person."

Chapter
18

The sound of flirtatious laughter reached us before we could even get inside Morgan's rooms. I concluded that Quentin and Darcy must have made it back safely. It was good news in the overall scheme, but a few injuries might have taken their energy levels down a bit.

Dan stood on the stairs behind me, staring blankly at the wall. He was still recovering from our chat in the carriage. He had found the idea that tiny little invisible creatures in dirt could have a function a little hard to swallow, but once I had made him breathe into a paper bag for a while, he was okay.

I pushed him inside and locked the door. Morgan closed the window behind her.

"You're back!" Darcy came spinning towards us, wearing a pink dress and looking like she had taken a wrong turn out of a baroque painting. Quentin was on her heels, twirling a top hat and making his tailcoat swing with the intensity of his strut.

Darcy hugged all of us in turn. Dan took the hug, bemused. His eyes were round, like twin moons reflecting Darcy's light. Oh dear. He had always had a taste for that he could not have. If I was any sort of friend, I would warn him now. Good thing I wasn't.

"It went off like a blast," Quentin said.

"I hope you don't mean that literally," Morgan deadpanned.

"Come on, Morgan, you know I don't," he retorted.

She was unconvinced. "Your style is quite flamboyant."

"How's Craig?" I asked, not that I cared.

"I'm fine," Craig said, slouching out of the washroom. "Although I'm thinking I may have made a grammar mistake in the last line."

Quentin threw an arm over his shoulder. "He was superb. He acted the reluctant kid being dragged out by his parents very well. That reminds me." He withdrew his arm and pulled off a tacky fake wedding ring. "Suppose we don't need these anymore."

Darcy did the same. She looked at it sadly. "I liked them."

"I know. It was fun, wasn't it?" Quentin said.

"You two aren't married?" Dan asked hopefully.

They looked at each other and laughed.

"God, no," Darcy said. "Can you imagine what that would be like? I'd have to put up with his skincare routine."

"And I'd have to put up with her snoring," Quentin replied playfully.

Dan sent me a sideways glance.

"You must be Dan," Quentin said.

"Sorry, yes," I said. "Everyone, this is Dan. Dan, everyone. Dan is an old friend."

"Only friend," Dan corrected.

I rolled my eyes. "Well that much is obvious given the fact that they bothered using you as a hostage. You've already met Darcy, the hugger. This is Quentin."

Dan went to shake Quentin's offered hand.

"They're both assassins," I added.

Dan aborted his hand.

"And that's Craig, a child we kidnapped," I said.

"What?" Dan spluttered.

"I'm starving," Darcy said. "What about we get some food?"

"Why don't we go to a music hall?" Quentin suggested.

I raised an eyebrow. "I'm a wanted criminal, Dan is less wanted but still a suspect, and Craig has got to be on a watchlist somewhere. I don't think we can just go and take in a play."

"We can't stay in, it's Dan's first night in the city," Quentin said.

"It could be his last if anyone sees him," I retorted.

Quentin waved away my concern. "You can wear assassin clothes."

I looked at Morgan.

"It should be fine," she said reluctantly. I did not know whether her disinclination was because she feared for my life or for the unnecessary social interaction. "Just stay clear of any other assassins. They will know you aren't one of us."

Dan adjusted his leather trousers to get rid of a wedgie.

"How could they possibly tell?" I asked.

❖ ❖ ❖

I preferred theatres to music halls. The loud, intimate setting of halls made them harder to sleep in. We got seats on the ground floor, where the tables were, rather than the galleries upstairs, where the hordes jostled for a better view. It was one of the cheaper halls, but still gaudy. Huge chandeliers lit the brightly coloured plaster decor. The stage was bare except for a piano, on which an old man was playing some popular rubbish. People in the galleries lobbed their empty cups down onto him.

I left Quentin and Darcy in charge of ordering the food, which was probably a mistake. I wouldn't be surprised if their idea of eating was feeding sweetmeats to each other. I noticed that Dan chose a seat next to Darcy.

A woman walked onto the stage, and the assault of cups stopped as the crowd cheered instead. She was dressed in a dark-red jumpsuit and matching mask trimmed in fake gold. The ruffles around the shoulders were too excessive, and I knew this because I knew the original very well.

Quentin was bouncing up and down in his seat. He recognised it too. As, it would seem, did a large portion of the audience if the jeering was anything to go by.

"Thank you all for coming," the woman shouted above the din. "There's nothing I love more than attention. Except, perhaps, your money."

The crowd laughed. I prayed for a sinkhole to appear beneath me.

"Am I supposed to know who that is?" Morgan asked.

"Come up from under the rock, Morgan," Quentin said, eyes sparkling as he looked at me. "That outfit is iconic."

I threw my napkin at him.

The man at the piano started up a jaunty tune and the woman began to sing.

> *"My name is Miss Take, tonight I'm running the show.*
> *I've always been a criminal and now everyone knows*
> *That I'm a villain's daughter."*

Quentin and Darcy started clapping along. I sank into my chair. How humiliating.

> *"I was robbing banks before I could walk*
> *Then I ratted on my parents soon as I learnt to talk.*
> *Cos I'm a villain's daughter."*

Dan was sniggering into his hand. Craig looked scared, like he was worried I would leap into the crowd and start ripping people apart with my bare hands. It was a valid fear.

> *"I put down my sword, swore that I'd reformed,*
> *But then I had to kill a lord because he was a bore*
> *And I'm a villain's daughter."*

It wasn't even a good tune. The rhymes were forced and made absolutely no sense. I had never once used a sword. I would have cut off my own arm if I tried.

> *"So I seduced a hero and we ran away.*
> *Now we're lying on a beach in the south of Spain.*
> *He likes a villain's daughter."*

The performer did a few lewd gestures. It was not difficult to gather what she was insinuating. Dan was cackling, Quentin and Darcy were cheering. The piano changed its tune and the woman launched into a new song that went into far more detail about my apparent seduction of Mr Indestructible.

I signalled a passing waitress. "Can I get a drink please?"

Quentin slapped me on the back.

❖ ❖ ❖

By the time we had eaten the offal the hall treated as a delicacy, I had mastered the act of drinking with a mask on. It involved a straw. Darcy pulled out a pack of cards.

"I don't know how to play," Craig said.

"I'll teach you," I told him. "Gambling is something all fifteen-year-olds should learn."

Clara, Morgan warned. *This isn't what I had in mind when I said he needed new influence.*

I pushed Craig my glass. "Here, have a drink."

Clara!

"It's busy tonight," Quentin said.

Dan leant back nonchalantly and looked around. "I suppose it is."

"I was talking about the dead people," Quentin said.

Dan choked on his drink.

"Quentin, don't scare Dan," Darcy admonished.

"I wasn't doing it on purpose," Quentin said.

Dan relaxed. "I probably just misunderstood."

"It's his function," she explained.

"I see dead people," Quentin said.

Dan choked again. Darcy patted him on the back.

"Ghosts are real?" he rasped.

Quentin shrugged. "They're real to me anyway."

"You should do séances," I said. "They're weirdly popular at the moment. You would make a mint."

Dan rolled his eyes. "Trust you to see everything as a money-making opportunity."

I plastered a fake smile on my face. "Obviously, what I meant was you would make a lot of people very happy by strengthening their illusion that there is a life beyond this one and giving them a feeling of self-importance. How anyone could wish for even more life post-life is beyond me."

"I think the idea is that your post-life life is better than this life," Darcy said.

I snorted. "Yeah, if you're what classifies as a good person, but what are the chances that anyone makes the grade? Look at how our government punishes every stupid little transgression. If there is a cosmic overlord, they'll be just the same. People in power are petty little hypocrites. Always have been, always will."

Darcy laughed. "Oh Clara, you really are a little cloud of misery."

I shrugged. "None of it matters. If there's a hell, I'll be going there, but I doubt I'll notice the difference."

"When did you realise Clara was such a downer?" Darcy asked Dan.

"I don't know. At first, she was so sweet and polite, asking if I needed help making dinner when she had clearly never cooked a day in her life. Then, flash forward three years and she's verbally degrading me." Dan shook his head. "It's amazing what becomes normal."

Darcy laughed again.

"Do you have a function, Dan?" Quentin asked, trying to draw Darcy's attention back to him.

"No, do you?" Dan asked Darcy.

"No, I suppose we are the odd ones out here." She nudged him playfully. "I can already tell you and I are going to be best friends."

I could see Quentin's scowl beneath his mask.

Darcy got up. "Clara, come get some more drinks with me."

I would rather have gone up on stage and done an encore of the Clara Blakely song. Darcy grabbed my arm and manhandled me towards the bar. I tried mouthing, "Help me," to Morgan, but the mask ruined it. Darcy ordered a tray of drinks and leant against the bar.

"Your friend is very handsome."

"Is he?" I looked back at Dan, who was tossing his hair around. "I guess so." If pathetic was your sort of thing.

"I always see these guys who are really cute, but there's always something missing, you know?"

A facial scar, perhaps.

"Somehow, it doesn't matter how amazing they are, I always end up sitting on a windowsill with Quentin."

If I started banging my head against the bar, could I pass it off as drunkenness?

"Have you considered that maybe everything you are looking for is right in front of you?" I asked.

"So you think I should give it a shot with Dan?"

If I spent any more quality time with Darcy, her stupidity was going to rub off on me. I grabbed two drinks and headed back to the table. Morgan was explaining to Craig how to throw a knife.

"It's all about the wrist movement," she said solemnly. "Technique is more important than brute force."

I smiled fondly.

"Here, try with this." She handed him a playing card.

Craig tried to throw the card. It fell limply from his hand.

"No, no, like this." Morgan picked up the card and gave it a sudden flick. It whipped through the air and hit a passing waiter.

"My eye!" he cried, clutching his face.

"Perhaps now would be a good time to leave," I said.

Morgan grabbed Craig by his hood and tugged him towards the exit. I downed both drinks and followed.

❖ ❖ ❖

There was a light rain puddling on the cobbles. It floated like clouds in the soft glow of the streetlamps. A group of heroes were going door to door, demanding to search each house and be offered light refreshments.

"Come on," Darcy called, taking Dan's hand and starting to skip. Their leather squeaked in unison.

Quentin fell into step beside me.

"Do you think Darcy likes Dan?" he asked.

"They do seem to be getting along very well," I said mildly. "They look good together, don't you think?"

"I suppose," he said morosely.

"You don't sound sure."

"I'm not really sure what she sees in him."

"She said he's attractive."

"But he's so…"

"Kind, helpful, good at ironing?"

"I guess."

"Why does it bother you?"

"She's my friend," he said defensively. "I want her to be happy."

"She looks happy to me."

"Yeah, she does," he said bitterly.

Darcy had stopped skipping to twirl around a lamppost. Under the light, the rain on her jacket glowed gold. Quentin slouched off to eavesdrop on their conversation.

"That was cruel."

I was almost getting used to Morgan's sudden appearances.

"They've had years to get together. It's not my fault they are so slow." I beckoned Craig over. "Word of advice, kid, all assassins are fools."

Craig looked nervously at Morgan.

"It's okay," I reassured him. "That's her happy face."

Chapter 19

I sat up blearily. Darcy and Dan were talking quietly in a corner. Darcy had her head rested on her hand and was looking up at him through her lashes. Dan was playing with his hair again. I put the pillow over my head. It seemed like an eternity since I had last had a minute to myself. I felt the mattress move and peeked out from under my hiding place. Craig had rolled over in the bed next to me and was now drooling onto the sheet as he snored gently. I kicked him and he sat up.

"Where's Morgan?" I asked Dan and Darcy, the hormonal teenagers. I flung the pillow at Craig and stood, clicking my back.

Darcy snapped her gaze away from the window it had drifted to. "In the washroom. She's been in there for a long time."

I opened the door to the washroom without knocking. Morgan was sitting on the chair Craig had been held hostage in, sharpening her knives.

"Did you get any sleep?" I asked her.

"I'm fine."

"I have no respect for people who don't like sleep. Where's Quentin?"

"He went to get the paper. He's been gone a long time."

It looked like Morgan wasn't the only one hiding from the happy couple. Add a sulking Quentin into the mix, and I was almost inclined to hand myself over to the Hero Brigade.

I sat on the floor and took out Darcy's knife. She had not asked for it back, so I considered it mine now. Morgan passed me the sharpening stone. I worked on the blade in silence. Morgan watched me.

"Are you going to tell me I'm doing it wrong?" I asked eventually.

She shook her head. "You do it well."

"You're surprised?"

"I just thought you didn't like knives."

"They weren't my first choice, but my parents wanted me to be competent with a wide variety of weapons. They were sure my function would be speed and strength and that I would be a weapon enough by myself, but they wanted to cover all their bases."

"How old were you when you developed your function?"

"Ten. You?"

"Eight."

"My condolences." I passed her sharpening stone back. "I thought you broke that knife on Mr Indestructible's back." I nodded to the dirk lying on her lap.

"I did. I replaced it."

When had she had time to do that? There was only one answer. "You went shopping while I was lying on my deathbed?"

"After your fever had broken."

"Was a three-day vigil too boring? I thought assassins had patience."

"I thought I had ample patience, but you test my limits."

The way she said it, so straight-faced, made it impossible not to laugh.

"Quentin's back!" Darcy shouted from the next room.

"We could bolt the door?" I suggested.

Morgan smiled as she sheathed her knives. Back in the bedroom, Darcy was throwing herself all over Quentin, but his response was half-hearted. His usual delight for life was absent. I took a certain glee in being partly responsible for the personality change, but the credit had to go to his own obliviousness. Darcy was practically slobbering over him. It was disgusting.

I snatched the paper from Quentin. Craig's article was on the front page. The heading read: In Her Own Words: Miss Take Framed to Cover Up Dirt Man Conspiracy. I scanned the article.

"Good job, Craig. You should consider a career as a journalist," I said.

Craig glowed. That was why you dished out the compliments frugally. It made them seem like they meant something. I passed the newspaper to Dan.

"I still can't believe it," he said. "It's awesome and terrifying at the same time. Is anyone else afraid that the dirt on the bottom of their shoe is suddenly going to come to life?"

"That's the response we're hoping for. What's the general feeling?" I asked Quentin.

"It's mixed. Disbelief, outrage, mostly at you and *The Times* for printing it, but also at the Blythwoods. The best thing is the Hero Brigade is going round confiscating copies, which seems suspicious even to the sceptics. They are doing a really good job at making themselves look guilty."

This was excellent news.

"I'm going to watch the Blythwoods," Morgan said.

Without bothering to stay for acknowledgement, she jumped out the window. I waited until I was sure she was out of range.

"I'm going to listen to the gossip," I told them.

"Are you sure that's a good idea?" Dan called as I headed out.

I pulled up my hood. "I'm an assassin."

"A real assassin would use the window," Darcy called.

I slammed the door behind me.

❖ ❖ ❖

You could tell something was happening. People were walking fast, trying to look like they had a purpose. Any groups of loiterers were being broken up by the Brigade. There seemed to be even more heroes on the streets now.

"Empty your pockets!" a member of the Community Squadron screamed at a man he had pinned up against a wall.

Tensions were clearly running high. I slipped into a tea shop where people were gossiping behind the thick fog of tobacco smoke. I joined the queue.

"Have you read it?" the man at the front of the queue asked the man behind the till in a hushed tone.

"Yes, have you?" he replied.

The man nodded.

"I haven't," said the woman in the queue behind him.

"Here." The man beckoned her to the till. I saw him pass her a rolled-up newspaper. She ducked under a table to read it.

"What do you make of it?" the man getting tea asked.

"Clearly, Miss Take has someone inside *The Times*."

"Do you believe what she said?"

He snorted. "Course not. It's ridiculous. She's probably working with the Dirt Man. I wouldn't be surprised if they teamed up to kill Mr Indestructible."

"Have you heard the rumours about Mrs Grace?" the woman under the table put in. "They are saying she's missing too. Maybe Mr Indestructible went off with her."

The man stepped aside with his cup, and I moved forward. It was the kind of tea leached from leaves spilled on the dock. Occasionally, you got the odd mollusc in it. I took a cup to a table and pretended to drink it through my mask.

"I don't know," a woman at the table next to me said. "Don't you think it's strange the Brigade is confiscating copies? If there was no truth in it, they wouldn't care."

"You actually believe it?" her friend asked her in surprise.

"Well, we all thought it was weird when someone bought Mundmere Common. No one really knows what they're doing there."

"It's conservation."

"What are they conserving? Badgers? I'm just saying, I wouldn't put it past those Blythwoods."

"You believe there's some tiny animals in the dirt that are going around attacking people?"

"We know there are tiny animals in the dirt. They proved it with science and stuff."

"If I can't see it, it doesn't exist."

A couple queued up at the till.

"Look, I don't know if I believe everything Miss Take is saying," one of them said, "but I would like to see what's going on in Mundmere."

The woman at the table next to me leant towards her friend. "What I'm trying to say is, who would make something like this up?"

"I wouldn't put it past Miss Take."

The woman who had been under the table shuffled out and handed the paper back to the man behind the till.

"I think Miss Take has been framed," she said.

"You read the article two minutes ago and suddenly you're an expert?"

"You know anything I don't, Clive? All we've got are her words, but I believe them. If *The Times* printed it, they must have evidence, right?"

The door banged open. Curls of tobacco smoke wafted around the hero that stood on the threshold.

"All right everyone. Empty your pockets."

Chair legs scraped on floorboards as people scrambled for the back door. The hero plunged into the fray. I waited until someone had thrown a pot of boiling water at him, then slipped out of the door and headed back to the safe house.

"Stop!"

I stopped. The order had come from a hero I recognised from the tabloids, Mr Keen or something like that.

"State your business," he said.

You would think the mask would have given it away. "Killing people for money," I replied sweetly.

"A lot of assassin activity on this street," he noted. "I thought you were supposed to only operate at night."

"We're having a party," I lied. "It's my friend's birthday. I was just out ordering the cake."

He regarded me suspiciously. "All right. Carry on with your business."

I walked off, making a mental note to tell the others to limit their movements. The last thing we wanted was unnecessary attention.

❖ ❖ ❖

Darcy and Dan still had their heads together when I returned. Quentin was as far away from them as possible, throwing a knife in the air and catching it as he glared murderously at Dan.

"Any news?" Darcy asked.

"Some fascinating debates on my morality," I replied. "From what I heard, we may actually have a chance of winning public favour. We can only wait and see."

A breeze swept through the room, and Morgan leapt in through the window. She was still wearing her mask, but I could see from the tension in her shoulders that it was bad news.

"What happened? Have the Blythwoods done a runner?" I asked.

"No. Well, maybe," she replied. "They did send a telegram to Australia, but we have bigger problems than their travel plans. They are saying that you dressed as an assassin from the Finishing School and broke Dan out of jail. The Prime Minister is going to pass an emergency action to make it a legal requirement for all assassins to show their faces. He says once you are caught, he will reverse the act. There will be nothing saying he has to, but we're expected to take his word for it."

There was stunned silence.

"They can't do that!" Darcy cried.

"They say it's in the profession's interest, to 'boost confidence' in them after what they are calling a breach of trust." Morgan shook her head in disgust. "They are suggesting the school is working with Clara."

Were the Blythwoods behind this? They could be putting pressure on the Prime Minister to try and force me out of hiding. Of course, it could be the minister himself, desperate to make progress in the case against me, or it could come from a genuine fear that assassins were overstepping their place.

"Politicians getting involved with assassins. I've never heard of anything so ridiculous," Dan said.

"He's been looking for a reason to restrict us for ages, and we just handed it to him," Morgan divulged.

"We should assassinate the Blythwoods now while we have the chance," Darcy said.

Morgan shrugged. "We can, but we don't need to. If this is somehow traced back to them, they'll have the whole school after them. It's an attack on our independence."

"And it's our fault. We never should have gotten involved," Quentin muttered darkly.

"You don't mean that," Darcy said. "You hardly ever wear your mask anyway."

This made him angrier. "But it's the principle. We've made everything worse. We're assassins, we don't get involved in politics. If the school had any idea what we've been doing, they would defrock us."

"So what?" Morgan demanded. "We all picked the gig to try and do something that matters. This is the most important thing we'll ever do."

Quentin laughed bitterly. "You're totally biased! You're only doing this to save your girlfriend."

"Girlfriend?" Darcy asked.

"You have no idea what you are talking about," Morgan warned.

"Really?" Quentin asked. "Because I'm pretty sure this whole mess started because you wouldn't kill Clara. Do you know how unprofessional that is?"

"Keep talking, and I'll show you just how unprofessional I can be," Morgan threatened.

"Are they dating?" Dan asked Darcy. She hushed him.

Quentin pointed an accusing finger at Morgan. "You should have left her in that vat of toxic waste, and you know it!"

"Shut up!" I shouted.

Quentin abandoned whatever he was planning to say next. He could not look me in the face, but no one else had that problem.

"Both of you stop talking before you say something you really regret," I said. "Quentin, you don't mean any of it. You're just in a bad mood because you think you're about to lose the love of your life."

His brow furrowed in confusion. "Who? Morgan?"

I rolled my eyes. "No, dipshit. You're in love with Darcy. You think she likes Dan, but she's actually in love with you—sorry about that, Dan. She's been in love with you for a long time, she just doesn't know it. Now, I was happy to let you dance around each other for the rest of your pointless existence, but it's starting to get in the way of important matters. So, if you two could just lock yourselves in the broom closet and figure this all out, I would greatly appreciate it because all your yelling is giving me more of a headache than Morgan could ever possibly manage."

I closed my eyes and massaged my temples. I really did have a headache. There were too many people in this room and not enough intelligent thoughts. At least I had managed to bring a bit of quiet. It was a suspiciously profound silence. I opened my eyes. Quentin and Darcy were gaping like they had never seen each other before.

"Are you courting an assassin?" Dan asked.

"Okay, and while we're on it." I raised my voice again. "Courting anyone while hiding out is pretty difficult, and it's also nobody's damn business."

Dan, Darcy, and Quentin had the decency to look sheepish. Craig was looking like a puppy I had just kicked.

"It's all right, Craig, you're not in trouble."

He breathed a sigh of relief.

Darcy cleared her throat awkwardly. "I think I'll go to the Finishing School, try to find out what they are going to do about this. Quentin, would you like to come?" she asked tentatively.

"Sure," he replied, sounding just as uncomfortable.

They both tried to climb out of the window at the same time.

"After you," Quentin said quickly.

"No, you go," Darcy replied.

With a lot more hesitation, they both managed to make it out of the window. Had I just made a terrible mistake? Was awkward Darcy and Quentin going to be worse than oblivious Darcy and Quentin?

I don't know, Morgan said in my head. *I didn't want to witness their thoughts just then. I thought they would be too emotional.*

She was standing, arms crossed, looking furious, but I guessed she was just thinking. I sat on the edge of the bed.

"I'm sorry about the school," I said.

"It's fine."

"No, it's not. Being an assassin means everything to you."

"Yes, it does, but I meant what I said." She crouched on the bed next to me. It was a good thing the mattress was so hard, or she might have struggled to keep her balance. "I believe that stopping the Blythwoods is more important than anything else. If it means that the last seven years of my life come to nothing, so be it."

"Don't be so dramatic."

"You don't think it's worth my career?"

I pretended to think about it. "I would say it is worth sustaining a minor injury at best."

"Broken finger?"

"Maybe sprained."

She gave a small smile. "I can't believe it's come to this."

"What? Trying to save the world with Miss Take?"

"We will succeed. We'll get the Blythwoods, it's just a shame we might destroy the Finishing School in the process."

"Do you think this is the end of assassins?"

"I don't know. It could be. Without trust, the whole thing just falls apart."

"I can't imagine a world without them. What would the upper classes do? Die of old age?"

"I suppose they would have to."

I nudged her. "What would you do? If being an assassin was no longer a viable career option?"

"I don't know. I'm not really qualified to do anything else."

"The Hero Brigade would probably take you if you leave maiming Mr Indestructible off your résumé."

"I told you I don't look good in rubber."

"What about politics? You would get to do loads of public speaking."

"Maybe I'll just emigrate," she said quickly. "I heard Russia could do with some more assassins."

Dan shuffled over to us. "Clara, could I talk to you for a moment?" He nodded to a corner of the room.

"No."

He put his hands on his hips.

I sighed. "Fine."

I followed him to the corner. It was only a few feet from Morgan. We really needed a bigger safe house.

Dan shifted from foot to foot.

"Spit it out," I said.

"We've known each other for a long time now. I've come to think of you as a little sister."

I fixed him with an apathetic stare, making it clear that I did not want to have this conversation. He was not deterred.

"Morgan seems kind of imposing. You said she can read minds. Can she change them too?"

Morgan was trying to act like she could not hear every single word we were saying.

"No Dan, I am not being mind controlled. What mind controller would use their power to make me…" I floundered about for the words.

"Develop feelings?" Dan finished.

"Shut up."

He put his hand on my arm. "You deserve happiness, Clara."

I shrugged him off. "That is where you are wrong. The world doesn't owe me anything."

"Have it your way. Also." He punched my arm. It wasn't much of a hit, but still.

"What was that for?"

"That was a little thank you for the heads-up about Darcy. You're a really great friend."

"I try."

Morgan's head snapped to the window. A moment later, Darcy and Quentin manoeuvred clumsily through it. They were holding hands. I was going to puke.

"That was fast," I noted.

"We didn't have to go far," Darcy said. "The assassins are in uproar. The roofs are simply covered with them."

"Is it good news?" I asked.

They looked at each other and smiled mushily while they nodded.

"From the school?" I clarified.

"The school? Oh, no," Quentin said. "The board is furious. They are threatening to make all their records public, saying it will 'boost confidence.'"

"It's bad," Darcy summarised. "No one will hire an assassin if they know the contract will go public."

And everyone would know Morgan had killed Forgo. It was strange how it had once been my goal to have everyone know Forgo had been killed by an assassin. Now, though, it would lead the Blythwoods straight to Morgan.

Morgan rested her head on her knees. She was crying. No, she was laughing. People grieved in different ways. Maybe this was hysteria. She had just lost her job, after all. She raised her head and smiled at me.

"What?" I asked.

"The Prime Minister will back down," Morgan said.

"How do you know?" I asked.

She said nothing, just flipped up her hood and put on her mask.

"Morgan, how do you know?" I insisted urgently.

"I'll go listen for the news," she replied.

Morgan leapt through the window before I could grab her. I rushed to the sill and stuck my head out, but she was not on the street below or any of the roofs I could see. Damn her. We were going to have a long talk about how unfair it was that she could have secrets and I couldn't. I pulled back inside.

Darcy was waiting for me with open arms. I weighed up the pros and cons of kneeing her in the groin as she hugged me.

"Thank you, thank you," she squealed. "I'm so happy, Clara, and it's all because of you. Quentin and I are together. I still can't believe it."

What I couldn't believe was she had somehow decided I was her confidant.

"I know it's still early days—"

Early minutes more like.

"—but I really think this could be it. How did you know we liked each other? We didn't even know."

"I'm good at observing people." Especially when they slapped me round the head with their repressed emotions.

"Well, thank you, and if you need any relationship advice with Morgan, I would be happy to help."

"How very kind of you." I would rather hug the Dirt Man, and it would probably do me more good. "Now, if you'll excuse me, I need to talk to the kid."

Craig quailed. "What do you need me for?"

I sat on the floor in front of him. "I believe I was teaching you how to play cards."

"Yeah, you were," he said suspiciously.

"How much you got in the bank? Let's raise the stakes."

I was going to make Morgan regret leaving me.

❖ ❖ ❖

When Morgan came back, she was positively beaming. "That took less time than I thought it would. The Prime Minister has backed down. Assassins are free to cover their faces for as long as they want."

"How did you know he would back down?" I asked.

"Because he doesn't want the school's records to go public," she replied.

"Well, that much was fairly obvious. How did you know?" I pressed.

"I did a job for him," she said casually.

I gaped. "You did a job for the Prime Minister?"

Quentin and Darcy looked just as amazed. It was not really a surprise that the Prime Minister had ordered an assassination, but I was shocked he had employed Morgan to do it. I couldn't imagine she would show him the reverence he was used to.

"Who did you kill?" I asked.

"That would be a breach of client confidentiality," she replied.

I couldn't believe this. "We're facing down villains together. We're a team, a band of brothers, misfit heroes. Please tell us who you murdered."

"I will tell you that it was a royal," she said.

I took a moment to process this. Morgan had killed a royal. Why did I find that so attractive? Did I need to join a revolution, or did I just need therapy?

Quentin's brows furrowed. "Wait, you mentioned a contract taking up a lot of your time. This would have been, what, a year ago? Oh my god."

I hit upon the same conclusion. "You killed Prince Albert?"

"I thought he died of typhoid," Dan said.

"Prolonged poisoning of a royal. Might be my finest work," Morgan said with just a hint of smugness.

"How on earth did you get that contract?" Quentin asked jealously. "You were on your placement. You didn't even have your seal. You don't even know which fork to use at dinner."

"The teachers recommended me to him," Morgan replied. "He was traditional, wanted an assassin who he didn't have to make small talk with."

Quentin stared at her in bewilderment. I doubted he could have been more surprised if Morgan suddenly launched into a tap-dancing recital.

"Is anyone else even more scared of her now?" Craig whispered.

"I can't believe you kept this from us," Darcy said. "We would have thrown you a party if we had known."

"Exactly," Morgan said.

It made sense to me now why the Prime Minister didn't want the records going public. Since he had been caught living it up in the middle of a Black Death scare, his popularity had been on a downwards trajectory. People were strangely attached to the royal family. They were kind of like your grandparents—if your grandparents were racist bigots who plundered half the world to make a pretty tiara. If people found out about this, they would tear the Prime Minister apart, if the Queen didn't get to him first.

"Why did he want him dead?" I asked.

She shrugged. "I didn't ask."

"Morgan, you really need to start asking questions," I told her.

She ignored me. "All the same, we should be more careful. The Blythwoods will be looking for assassins now."

My encounter with the hero on the street had slipped my mind.

"I forgot to say—" I broke off at the sound of heavy footfalls on the stairs leading up to our door. A fist hammered as a voice cried out.

"Hero Brigade! Open up!"

Chapter
20

"There are more heroes on the street," Morgan said as she stepped back from the window.

Darcy squared her shoulders. "I guess we'll have to see what they want then. Masks on, everyone."

I hurriedly pulled up my hood and mask. Darcy made sure everyone was covered, then answered the door. Mr Righteous stood on the threshold. Gold lions covered his suit like a spray of patriotic vomit. Miss Fortitude did not seem to be accompanying him, which gave me hope, but it was still an undesirable situation. I wished I could remember what his function was.

He shoots lightning from his hands, Morgan supplied.

Of course. How had I forgotten that? I had heard plenty of stories of unsuspecting bystanders being accidentally barbecued. Apparently, his aim was often a little off.

It was nice of Morgan to be keeping me company in my head, but I did think she would be better off keeping an eye on Mr Righteous. He walked into the room like he owned it, cockiness rolling off him like a second cape. Behind him, a hero I did not know took up position in the doorway, blocking our exit.

"We're looking for Miss Clara Blakely," Mr Righteous said, running his finger along the wall and grimacing at the layer of grime that came away.

"You're looking in the wrong place," Morgan replied with a tone that suggested finality.

Mr Righteous ignored it. "A lot of assassins in here," he observed, letting his eyes travel languidly from person to person.

"Is that illegal now?" Morgan asked coldly.

He returned his attention to Morgan. "We were told there had been an irregular level of assassin activity on this street. What with Miss Take disguising herself as an assassin to break her accomplice out of prison, we thought it best to check it out."

"I admire your diligence." She sounded like she would admire horse muck on his shoe more than him. "But clearly, Miss Blakely is not here."

He took out his pipe and lit it. "You won't mind if I take a look at your seals, will you?"

This was taking a turn for the worse. I was glad Morgan's face was covered because I could feel her gaze flicking nervously towards me. She held out her seal. Mr Righteous spent a long time examining it, puffing smoke up into Morgan's face. I wanted to take the pipe and jam it down his throat. There was no reason for him to dally. The seal showed nothing but the man being impaled by knives. There was no name, no identification number. She might as well have handed him a rock.

Quentin and Darcy received the same scrutiny. Then it was my turn.

"I don't have one," I said casually. "I haven't graduated yet."

"Shouldn't you be in the school, then?" Mr Righteous asked suspiciously.

"I'm on my placement," I answered.

He chewed thoughtfully on his pipe. "I was under the impression that assassins on their placement got a provisional seal."

Did they?

They do, Morgan said in my head.

Damn. I had really thought I was going to get away with it. Oh well, there was only one thing for it. I punched Mr Righteous in the face. Using his surprise as propulsion, I threw him towards the door. He crashed into the hero waiting there, and they both tumbled down the stairs. Morgan slammed the door shut, and Darcy and Quentin pushed the bed over to block it.

"Now what?" Dan asked hysterically. "We've no way out!"

"Yes, we do," Morgan said.

She threw open the window and hauled herself upwards and away from the baying heroes. Quentin and Darcy followed suit. Dan stuck his head out after them.

"How do you expect us to—" He was cut off as two hands grabbed either one of his shoulders and dragged him up.

There was a loud bang against the door. The bed shuddered.

"You, next." I pushed Craig over to the window.

The door strained against its hinges with the next blow.

"Get out of my way," I heard Mr Righteous say.

I threw myself towards the window as the door exploded inwards. Darcy grabbed my hand and pulled me up onto the roof of the house. I tried to find a footing, but the tiles were angled sharply and slick with rain. Darcy had to drag me up to the ridge where the others were waiting.

"We're going to have to jump," Morgan said.

The gap between our building and the next was only a few feet, but altitude must have skewed distance because the space seemed huge. No wonder there was a housing shortage if they left continent-sized gaps between them.

Morgan stood from her crouch, sprinted across the roof, and leapt into the air. She landed with an unnecessary roll and twirled around to face us.

"See you on the other side, babe," Darcy said.

"See you there, babe," Quentin replied, and he sprung after Morgan.

I considered jumping into the open arms of the Hero Brigade.

Dan was next in line. Darcy nudged him, and he crawled forward reluctantly.

"You can do it, Dan," Darcy said encouragingly.

"Oh hell," he muttered, and he jumped. He landed, slipped, and ended up spread-eagled on the roof, but he was safe.

"You all right with this, Craig?" Darcy asked.

Craig nodded hesitantly, and satisfied that he would have no trouble at all, Darcy leapt.

"I can't do this," Craig whispered hoarsely.

I glanced behind us. Mr Righteous was almost on the roof. "I would love to give you another pep talk, Craig, but the heroes are getting worryingly close. Either you jump and possibly die by gravity or you stay and possibly die by Mr Righteous. I know which I would rather do."

He nodded.

"And I'm not jumping till you jump, and if the heroes catch us, I'm going to find a way to pin all the blame on you."

Craig lobbed himself off the roof into Darcy's open arms.

"Hey!"

I turned back. Mr Righteous had made it onto the roof. I gave him a two fingered salute and jumped. Tiles can cut you to shreds if you land on them wrong. Luckily, I landed on Craig.

"Let's go!" Morgan yelled.

I looked back and saw what she was so worried about. Mr Righteous was rubbing his hands together, making sparks crackle between his fingers. I ducked as he shot lightning over our heads. It blasted a chimney apart. Funny how the fear of electrocution could make any fear of heights simply go away. We ran as fast as our balance would allow across the roof.

A blast behind me sent me flying forward. I hit the roof and began to roll down the incline. I scrambled for purchase on the tiles, but my fingers found nothing. The roof stopped, and I didn't. It was like falling into that damn vat all over again. Except this time, there would be nothing but the cold, hard ground to catch me.

I landed with an *oof*. That had been a lot softer than expected. I opened my eyes to find myself lying in a cart of hay. I was going to pretend I had planned that.

"Oi, what are you playing at?" the cart driver called.

I rolled off the cart and landed on the road. Someone knelt on my back, pinning me down. I threw my pain onto them. It wasn't much, but I had just fallen off a roof. They fell back off me.

"It's Miss Take," they cried. "We've got Miss Take!"

I pushed them over and barged through the line of people who had gathered to watch the show. I glanced up at the rooftops. There was no sign of the others. I skidded around a corner, and the smell of the Thames hit me a second before the sight of it did. I ran for the bridge. It had plenty of carts and pedestrians to act as cover. Or, failing that, human shields.

"Miss Take!"

I turned. The pedestrians were scattering, running out of the way as Mr Righteous hurtled towards me, hands glowing and crackling. So much for my cover. A bolt of lightning shot by, close enough to make me fear for my eyebrows. Mr Righteous stopped at the entrance to the bridge. I had no choice but to face him.

"I'm going to make you pay for what you did to Mr Indestructible!" he yelled.

Why did he care? With Mr Indestructible missing, he could step up into his position as top dog.

"Haven't you read the tabloids?" I shouted back. "We've bought a house in Spain together. We're going to settle down, raise a family."

"No, he's recovering from surgery after you and your assassin tried to kill him!"

Unbelievable. "Are you working for the Blythwoods too? How come I was never invited to join the payroll?"

"There are many things you don't know."

"It's not my fault this country's education system is severely lacking."

He did not seem to be in a joking mood if his gnashing teeth were anything to go by. "Give me the name of the assassin."

"I don't know what Mr Indestructible's pain-addled mind told you, but there was no assassin."

"You're lying!"

The fans had got it wrong. It was not Miss Fortitude that had been courting Mr Indestructible, it was Mr Righteous. I knew a broken-hearted mess when I saw one. He rubbed his hands together and they began to glow.

"I can't answer your questions if I'm dead," I reminded him.

"I'll tell you what. I'll hang the charred remains of your body from the Finishing School and see if anyone comes for them."

It was a straight bridge, there was nowhere to go. Well, almost nowhere. I grabbed the balustrade and rolled over it. I heard Mr Righteous roar behind me as I hurtled in freefall, flailing as the brown water came closer. My body pierced the water like an arrow, sinking downwards. I fought against my own momentum, trying desperately to crawl upwards. I told myself not to think about the vat, but it was hard not to think about the vat. I could feel my panic rising a lot faster than I was.

My lungs were burning as I burst through the surface. I ripped the sodden mask from my face and took a gasping breath of air. Above me was the underside of the bridge. I had drifted under it. With an incredible show of strength and determination in the face of exhaustion and leather trousers, I swam over to a giant strut of the bridge. I clutched the concrete and enjoyed breathing. It was an underrated activity, and I did not know how long I was going to be able to enjoy it. In a display of unexpected intelligence, Mr Righteous had not jumped after me, but he was still up there, and my options were just as limited as they had been on the bridge. I could swim for it and see how long it took Mr Righteous' dodgy aim to pick me out, or I could hang onto this lump of concrete until I died of hyperthermia.

I perked up at the sound of an engine chugging closer. A boat was making its leisurely way towards the bridge. I could make out an elderly man steering and a young boy shovelling coal. Neither looked like they belonged to law enforcement. I slapped the mask back on my face and waved at them.

"Any chance of a ride?" I shouted.

"Saw one of them heroes on the bridge. That who you hiding from?" the man shouted back.

The way he sneered the word hero made me go out on a limb and guess he did not like them. "Yes!"

"Hop aboard then. Enemy of my enemy and all that."

He steered the boat close enough for me to leap on. I ducked down next to the pile of coal as we sailed out from under the bridge. Mr Righteous was standing alone on it, staring at the water. He was going to be waiting a long time.

Only when he was a speck in the distance did I make my unsteady way over to the man.

"Thanks," I said.

"Damn functionables." He spat over the side of the boat. "Don't know why they're so proud. Functions are disease."

"Tell me about it," I said.

"I live in constant fear my son is going to get one." He pointed his thumb over his shoulder at the boy shovelling coal. The boy looked like he wouldn't mind a function if that function let him fly away.

"Thought about moving out into the country, but I can't afford it. Wouldn't help anyway. They say more people are getting functions out there too. You can't escape it."

"No, you can't."

"They say it makes more jobs, but I know a lot of unemployed functionables. Most of them are born in slums. They aren't taught how to control their powers, they make stupid mistakes, and they end up dead or thrown in prison. And those are the ones that survive the conditions that give them the functions in the first place."

There was nothing I could say that would console him. He was right, functions had only ever caused more harm.

"What do you think of Clara Blakely's accusations about the Blythwoods and the Dirt Man?" I asked.

"True. All true."

At least I could say that bitter boat man was firmly on our side.

"It's the end of the world. The writing's been on the wall for a while now. It's just that the people who could read it wouldn't translate it for those of us who couldn't. But it's not too late to do something about it. There's going to be a protest at Mundmere. I'll be there. You should too."

Like a little protest would accomplish anything. The people in power didn't care if a few people bunked off work to yell at a fence.

"I'll think about it," I said. "I've got a lot on my plate at the moment."

He nodded grimly, taking this as the "no" that it was. "Where shall I drop you?"

I had no idea. I didn't know where the others were, or if they were even alive. I had nowhere to go.

"If you could drop me off wherever you're going, that would be great, thank you."

"Let's pick up the pace," he called to the boy.

I looked back at the bridge. It was almost out of sight now. The smoke belching from the boat floated out behind us, looking purple in the light of the setting sun. The river glinted like a trail of liquid fire, but the wake we cut through it was dark and cold. I refused to let myself shiver. An assassin wouldn't shiver.

Chapter
21

We reached land as the last pink streaks left the sky.

"Think about the protest, all right?" the man asked me as I clambered ashore. "Things only change when they are too uncomfortable for the people in power to maintain. We need to remind them that there are more of us than there are of them. Every voice counts."

I nodded, not trusting myself to speak. The only way to keep my teeth from chattering was to lock my jaw shut.

The man tilted his hat and then set about helping his son unload the boat's cargo. They had dropped me at a worksite where they were trying to build an embankment to keep back the Thames. I quickly navigated the wooden boards laid down across the marshland for the workers. I didn't want to have to do it in the dark.

Finally, I made it back to solid ground. I had no idea where to go, but I needed to keep moving if I was going to keep my legs from going numb. I hesitated. The Finishing School was upstream, but it was very unlikely the assassins would take Dan and Craig there. Perhaps they had gone to Craig's house to lie low or checked into one of the hundred hotels in the city. The best place to start looking would be downstream where I had last seen them. But that was also where I had last seen Mr Righteous.

Something flew out of the darkness towards my head. I ducked, and it passed over me. I fumbled for Darcy's knife. The thing was swooping around, coming in for another attack. My fingers were shaking too much to get the knife out. I raised my hands to my face and braced for impact. Nothing happened. I peeked through my fingers, but there was nothing there. I dropped my hands to my side. A pigeon was sat on the ground in front of me.

I waved my hand at it. "Shoo."

It cocked its head to one side and disappeared. What the hell? I looked around, but it had vanished. A weight suddenly appeared on my shoulder. I almost fell over in shock. The pigeon on my shoulder cooed.

"Victor?" I asked tentatively.

It cooed again.

I raised a hand to it and carefully felt its legs, but there was no message. Typical, the one time I would have enjoyed getting a letter.

Victor flew off my shoulder. He flapped down the street a little way and perched on a railing. He looked back at me.

"What do you want? Now is not really the time to get porridge."

He flew back, circled me, and went back to his perch.

"I can't read your mind, birdbrain."

He cooed at me impatiently. Morgan had claimed Victor had led her to me at Mundmere Factory. Was it possible that he was trying to take me to Morgan? I shook my head. This was ridiculous. Was I seriously considering following a bird? I was insane. I must have caught some terrible infection in the Thames that was slowly dissolving the last of my sanity.

"You're a flying rat," I told Victor as I stalked past him.

He took off and flapped noisily to a perch farther down the street. I trailed after him, keeping the Thames on my right. We were heading downstream. When we reached Blackfriars, Victor turned away from the river. My footsteps echoed on the cobbles. I could not help looking up at the roofs. I was unnerved. The streets were quieter than they usually were this early in the night. They were darker than usual too. Some of the lamps had not been lit.

I pressed my back against a wall as a duo from the Community Squadron walked past at speed.

"I don't care what time it is, I'm going back," one of them said.

"We're fine. Nothing is coming after us," the other one replied, an octave too high to be reassuring.

"I'm not saying I believe Dirt Man is a pile of mud which is summoned by the Blythwoods every night, but it's a risk I'm not going to take. I only showed up for patrol because it's part of my parole, but if everyone else is going to bunk off, then I am too. There's no one out here anyway. Have you ever seen it this quiet?"

"No, I haven't," the other admitted. "It is pretty pointless, us being out here. I suppose we might as well head back."

They sprinted down the rest of the street and disappeared out of sight. I peeled myself from the wall. Victor was waiting for me on a post box, preening. He took off again as I approached.

"Not one for conversation, are you?"

He swerved suddenly down a side street, and I found myself confronted with a wooden safety fence. There was nothing safe about it. It wouldn't stop anyone, just give those climbing over it splinters. Victor flew over it. I paused. These fences were usually put up for a reason. There could have been an open sewer or something similarly nasty on the other side. Perhaps Victor's navigational system had not registered that this road was closed. I could try and make my own diversion and get inevitably lost, or I could just watch where I was putting my feet.

I climbed over the fence and made my way across the building site, winding through the huge mounds of dirt. Rounding one, I came upon a giant tunnel cut into the earth, surrounded by layers of scaffolding. It was such a weird thing to stumble across in the middle of a city. It had to be the Metropolitan Railway. I had read about it while I was wasting my time kicking around a lord's house. Someone had come up with the brilliant idea to put a railway underground, as though that wasn't just asking for disaster.

Victor flew down and started pecking at the ground in the entrance of the tunnel. Well, it had been a fun adventure, but this was where my loyalty to the strange bird ended. There was no way I was following him into the mouth of hell. Victor looked at me. I sighed. What had happened to my spine? I must have lost it somewhere along the line if I was now letting a pigeon boss me around.

I picked my way down the ramp into the trench and under the scaffolding. I stopped next to Victor.

"If this is an ambush, I will put you in a pie, understand?"

He cooed and flew into the tunnel. I followed at a distance. There was a light up ahead. It could not be the workforce, not at this time, or at any time probably. They just dug trenches and then left. They spent most of their time laying out haybales to close off streets so they could not work in them. I froze as a voice echoed down the tunnel.

"We'll split up. We should cover the school and the Brigade. Someone should go back to the safe house in case she doubled back."

"Morgan, this is ridiculous. She could be anywhere in the city, that is if Mr Righteous didn't turn her into a human-sized kebab. Whoa, whoa, put the knife down."

Someone shrieked. "Did you see that? What the hell is it?"

"It's Victor. He might know where Clara is. Give me a second."

I walked forward. The glow from a fire in a drum silhouetted five people.

"I am not someone to be summoned by your bird," I said. "Next time, send Craig."

There was a chorus of shouts. Morgan reached me first. She stopped a few feet from me and stared.

"You're back."

I smiled. Darcy stepped around Morgan and hugged me. She pulled away, and Dan stepped in. I pushed him off.

"The next person to hug me gets a kick in the groin," I snapped.

"How lovely," Dan said drily. "We were worried sick about you."

"Really? I was kind of hoping you all died. It would absolve me of some responsibility," I said.

Dan punched my arm then wiped his palm against it. "Why are you wet?"

I took off my mask and hood. My hair was still dripping down my neck. I responded as I wrung it out. "I jumped off London Bridge."

"What? Why?" he asked in horror.

"To get away from the angry hero with lightning coming out of his hands," I said, like it was obvious. "It worked a treat."

"I leave you for five minutes, and you jump off a bridge?" Morgan said furiously.

"I'm sorry if I made a decision without your consent, but staying alive was my priority," I said.

"If staying alive was your priority, why did you jump off a bridge?" she asked.

I ignored her and went to their fire. The heat was delicious. It sank down right into the depths of my bones. I shivered as I drank it up.

"Did you have any trouble?" I asked.

"We were chased by a few stray heroes, but we managed to lose them," Quentin said.

"Good," I replied.

"It is the last time I ever go up on a roof," Dan said. "From now on, I'll be hiring someone to clean the gutters."

"At least you didn't fall off a roof like Clara did," Darcy pointed out.

"I didn't fall, I strategically jumped into a pile of hay," I countered.

She patted my shoulder. "Sure you did."

I shuffled even closer to the fire so the bright glare would hide their faces.

"I'm sorry," I said, trying to muster up as much sincerity as I could.

"For what?" Quentin asked. "Being the reason we are currently camped out in a tunnel? I got to see Miss Take deck Mr Righteous. I could live in this tunnel for the rest of my life, and I would say it was worth it to see that. It was beautiful, a masterpiece."

"If the Blythwoods weren't going after assassins before, they certainly are now," I pointed out.

Darcy sat down beside me. As she was holding Quentin's hand, it meant he sat down too. All that sweaty palm contact was just asking for a fungal infection.

"It's okay," Darcy said. "It's just a shame that our cover isn't going to work anymore. We already asked Craig, and he can't fake a leather seal. You're going to have to stay out of sight."

How thrilling. My role in the Blythwood sabotage was over. I was going to have to sit the rest of the fight out and leave it in their capable hands. That was if the Finishing School didn't revoke their seals.

"Will the school take your seals?" I asked.

What happened to disavowed assassins? Were they given a reference and sent on their way, or did they get dropped into a bottomless pit?

Quentin waved it off. "The school may suspect assassins are harbouring you, but they don't know which ones. They pretend to be omniscient, but they don't really know anything about anyone. They're killers, not spies."

Morgan would make a terrible spy. She could do the gathering information bit, but eventually, she would have to pass it on, and that would mean talking. She was skulking out of range of the light. I wondered if she was still annoyed at me for jumping off a bridge. I bet if she had been there, she would have done the exact same thing.

"What are we supposed to do now?" Dan asked.

"I don't know," I admitted.

The Blythwoods were trying to kill me, the Hero Brigade was trying to kill me, the police wanted to catch and probably maim me. I wouldn't be surprised if the Finishing School wanted to kill me for damaging their integrity. What had we accomplished so far? Some people, including bitter man on a boat, believed us. People were scared, sure, but they weren't doing anything about it. A stupid protest was not going to fix everything.

"What protest?" Morgan asked.

Great. Now I had to explain before anyone got too hopeful.

"I met a boatman who was part radical socialist, part bigoted anti-functionable," I said. "He told me there's going to be a protest tomorrow against the Blythwoods at Mundmere Common."

"That's great!" Darcy exclaimed.

I held up my hand. "Hold your horses. It's not going to accomplish anything. People will wake up tomorrow and decide that the sun is shining, and they have better things to do, like keep their jobs. I bet there will be five people with a couple of placards."

"You don't know that," Quentin said.

"Yeah, I do," I countered.

"Are you willing to put your money where your mouth is?" Craig asked.

I grinned. "You're on, kid."

Morgan folded her arms disapprovingly.

"What? We're bonding. Isn't that what you wanted?" I pulled off my boots. Running from Mr Righteous had given me blisters. I wondered if I could pass the pain to Quentin without him noticing. "Does anyone have any food? I'm starving."

"Yeah, we just stopped while we were running for our lives to pick up a couple of jellied eels," Quentin said.

"The sarcasm was unnecessary," I replied.

"Oh, I wasn't being sarcastic. We really did stop to pick up some jellied eels." He reached behind him for a jar.

"Craig needed food. He looked like he was going to faint," Darcy explained.

Craig made a noise of protest. "Men don't faint."

"Of course they do," Quentin said. "In our first dissection session, I fainted right onto the corpse."

I grabbed the jar of jellied eels from him and unscrewed the top. Never had something with the consistency of a slug tasted so good. I didn't even care that these were the highly suspect fish that were able to live in the putrid waters of the Thames.

"Okay, maybe you should slow down on the eels," Dan said, taking the jar from me.

I tried to grab it back, but he was faster. That was unusual. Come to think of it, I was struggling to remain upright.

"I'm going to see if my subconscious can come up with a masterful plan," I yawned.

"There are some empty cement sacks by the wall," Morgan said.

I leant over and dragged one towards to the fire. Morgan pushed it back.

"Morgan," I whined.

"Any closer, and you will set yourself on fire," she said.

Fire could not burn what was already hot.

You are unbelievable. "Here," Morgan said aloud, grabbing a couple more empty sacks and piling them on top of me. "Better?"

I hummed and closed my eyes. I felt like I was cocooned in a little nest.

"She's almost sweet when she's asleep," Quentin said.

I couldn't be bothered to kill him. I was too busy employing my second, secret function: my amazing ability to sleep anywhere.

Chapter
22

I woke myself up coughing. Sleeping in cement dust did wonders for the lungs. It felt like someone was constructing a house in my chest cavity. A slither of cold, flat light crept in from the tunnel's entrance.

"Aren't we missing some people?" I asked, rubbing my eyes.

"Morgan has gone to check on the state of the protest," Quentin said. He was standing by the mouth of the tunnel. "Darcy is keeping watch outside." He waved to someone out of sight and blew them a kiss.

"Here," Dan handed me a bowl of porridge. "You slept through breakfast."

"Never waste an opportunity to sleep," I said, punctuating the sentence with a yawn.

Victor sidled up to me, eyeing my bowl. I turned my back on him, but he just reappeared in front of me. I threw a spoonful on the floor for him.

"Fancy another game?" Craig asked. He was sitting against the side of the tunnel, failing to throw playing cards.

I shook my head. "Our days of games are over now that we know your function extends to cards."

He smiled sheepishly. "You know what amazes me? This time last week, I was living in a comfortable house with a well-paying job and three meals a day, and now, I'm on the run and sleeping in a railway tunnel with a bunch of assassins."

"You and me both," Dan said, sitting down beside him.

"It's different. You chose to be friends with her," Craig complained.

"You chose to work for the Blythwoods," I retorted.

"I had to pay the bills," he said defensively.

I snorted. "Don't try and pass off your ambition as necessity."

"Morgan's back," Quentin called.

I looked up as Morgan appeared in the tunnel's entrance. Darcy skipped in behind her and threw her arms around Quentin.

"I missed you," she said.

"I missed you too," Quentin replied.

Gross. Right in front of my porridge. I gave the bowl to Victor and tried to gauge Morgan's level of disappointment. She was inscrutable.

"So, what's the verdict?" I asked her.

"The protest is starting to gather outside Mundmere Common. It's a few more than five people with a couple of placards," she replied.

This was unexpected. "How many?"

"Hard to tell," she said casually. "A couple of hundred, more on their way."

Craig laughed and high-fived Dan. I was shocked. Had we found a cause that people were willing to sacrifice the drudgery of their routine for?

"You just lost your lifesavings, Clara!" Craig hollered.

The joke was on him. I didn't have any lifesavings.

"And the Blythwoods have shown their hand by calling in Miss Fortitude to protect the common," Morgan continued. "It's obvious she is working for them, and that has damaged the credibility of the Brigade. I wouldn't be surprised if there's an investigation."

"This is great," Quentin gushed. "The protest will storm the gates and see the Dirt Man for themselves."

His optimism really was astounding. "No, they won't. Miss Fortitude is the most powerful functionable in the Brigade. Her kill count is almost as high as Dirt Man's. If anyone even so much as thinks about storming the common, they'll be dead."

"She's the teleporter, isn't she?" Dan asked.

"Yes," I replied. "For the protest to accomplish anything, she would need to be taken out of the picture, but we can't help with that if you want to keep your jobs as assassins. Not unless she decides to leave the common."

"I have an idea," Quentin said.

"No," Morgan interrupted.

"I hadn't said it," he protested.

"You thought it, and that was bad enough. Unthink it," Morgan commanded.

"What were you thinking?" I asked.

"We use you as bait," he said cheerfully.

I sighed. "Fabulous."

"We are not using Clara as bait," Morgan said with determination.

"I want to hear his plan," I told her.

Quentin was a brave soul to soldier on under the withering power of Morgan's glare.

"You appear somewhere near Mundmere Common," he explained. "A runner goes down the street, shouting that Clara Mabel Evangeline Blakely is nearby doing some nefarious deed."

It was unnerving that he knew my whole name.

"Miss Fortitude, who was Mr Indestructible's lover—" Quentin said.

"No, she was not," I argued wearily.

Quentin ploughed on regardless. "—is very angry and goes rushing out to apprehend her beloved's maimer—"

"I didn't maim him," I said.

"—and we are waiting to ambush her. We kill her, and the masses go right ahead into Mundmere," Quentin finished with a smile.

"And what happens when she doesn't leave her post like an idiot?" Morgan demanded. "What happens when the police turn up instead?"

Quentin waved her off. "Then we get Clara out of there."

"What happens if she does get there, and she kills her?" Morgan asked.

"She won't," Quentin replied.

"I'm in," I said.

"No," Morgan countered.

"Morgan, we need everyone to see what the Blythwoods are doing at Mundmere," I argued. "They will never truly believe if they don't see, and if we don't act fast, they will have no choice but to move on with their lives and ignore whatever is happening at that lake. No one can protest forever. We need to use this unexpected support to our advantage. This is as good a plan as any. I'm not some self-sacrificing fool. I wouldn't do this if I didn't trust you all to keep me safe."

"But you were the one who took out Mrs Grace," Morgan pointed out.

"You know you can't rely on us to beat a hero."

"Okay, so I have had more experience dealing with these ratbags, but that just means I'm less likely to have to rely on you," I replied.

Dan raised his hand. "From experience, I would suggest you stop wasting time arguing. Clara is stubborn. If she's got her mind set on this plan, she'll do it with or without you. Short of tying her to a chair, I don't think you'll stop her."

"We have rope," Morgan said menacingly.

How kinky.

Morgan scowled. "Clara, this is serious."

"I am taking it very seriously," I said innocently. "Will you trust me? Pretty please."

I batted my eyelashes at her. She glared back at me.

"Fine," she said, in a way that made it clear it was not fine at all.

I would take what I could get. "Okay. I don't want to implicate you assassins any more than strictly necessary, so could someone go buy me some clothes?"

"I'm on it," Darcy said.

"I want a blouse and a pair of trousers. Something bright. Can you manage that?" I asked.

"Sure," she answered with a smile.

"I'll come too, babe," Quentin said.

"Thanks, babe," Darcy replied, giving him a great big slobbering kiss on his cheek. I fought down a mouthful of bile.

"I'm guessing Craig and I aren't needed for this bit," Dan said.

"You're coming with me, obviously," I said.

Craig's eyes bugged out of his head.

I chuckled. "I'm kidding."

Morgan approached Craig. "If I showed you what an assassination contract looked like, would you be able to forge one for Miss Fortitude? We might as well try and make this legitimate."

"Why don't you just get one of us to sign a contract?" I asked.

"Because everyone in this tunnel is disreputable and/or broke," she explained.

"Fair enough," I replied.

"I can do it," Craig said.

"While we are all occupied, Clara, you might want to freshen up," Quentin suggested.

I levelled him with my most unimpressed glare. "Seriously?"

He held his hands up in defence. "I'm just saying you look more like Dirt Man than Miss Take."

"Fine, I'll go hunt down a bucket of water because, apparently, even fugitives have beauty standards." I stalked off towards the entrance of the tunnel, then stopped and turned back to Craig. "If you need a name for the contract, what about Lord Begrudd?"

Craig grinned and nodded.

"Who's he?" Dan asked.

I walked on. "Well, he's not broke." Not yet anyway. It would take him a couple of years to blow through Forgo's fortune.

I walked out into the grey light. The clouds were building, threatening rain. I noticed a bucket on a lower level of scaffolding and hauled myself up to it. The water in it looked clean enough. I stuck my hands in and watched it turn a milky grey. I hated to admit it, but maybe Quentin had a point.

"Be careful up there," Darcy said as she and Quentin emerged from the tunnel. "Don't get seen."

I knocked on the bit of scaffolding over my head. "I think I'm safe."

They darted up the ramp and disappeared amongst the mounds of earth. If they came back with something black, I was going to skin them and wear their flesh instead.

"I thought you might want this."

I jumped. Morgan was crouching beside me. She held out a comb. I should have guessed she had one. No one's centre parting could be that straight naturally.

"Give me a minute to finish this." I commenced scrubbing my face. It was a lot more pleasant than swimming in the Thames, that was for sure.

Morgan remained as still as stone beside me. It was obvious she had something on her mind. If I waited for her to say it, we would be there all day.

"You don't like this plan."

"Dropping you in the middle of the street and hoping for the best is barely a plan."

"It's not *not* a plan."

"Couldn't we at least wait until it's dark? I work best in the dark."

"This is good for you, Morgan. We need to get you out of your comfort zone."

"I left that a long time ago."

"Look, we'll give it go, and when it doesn't work, we'll regroup and think of something else."

We couldn't keep hiding away like frightened rabbits down a hole. Even if the hole was three-and-a-half miles long. Who came up with this stuff? The only thing worse than a railway was one underground.

"You don't think it's an amazing feat of human strength?" Morgan asked.

"No. Do you trust the people who made this to put their all into it? Do you think they came into work and said, 'You know what, today I am going to do the best job I can do?' Or do you think the engineers looked at a blueprint and went, 'That's good enough,' and the construction workers came in, did the bare minimum, and went home? In another year, there will be a marker on this very spot saying, 'Sorry we buried all those people alive, that's our bad.'"

Morgan smiled.

"You think that's funny?"

"No, I just think I could show you paradise and you would still find fault with it."

"Complaining is a skill. Some people get paid to do it. It's called being a critic."

I pushed the bucket aside. It was a shame about Mr Indestructible's gift of bruising, but the slight swelling might make me look more like that wildly inaccurate cartoon. I picked up the comb and started gathering my hair at the base of my neck.

"I'm surprised you're still helping me now that I'm no longer a pretty face." I gestured to the bruises.

"Now you have the face to match your soul."

I gasped, putting a hand to my heart in mock outrage. "Morgan Murdur! I am shocked and horrified that you could be so cruel. You think you know someone—"

"You don't," she snapped.

I could feel the confusion written plainly on my face. It had just been a joke.

"I'm sorry. That's not what I… I didn't mean…" She was angry. The words weren't coming out right.

"It's okay, Morgan. Speak to me in whatever way you need."

There was a pause. She took a deep breath.

You don't know me. You can never know me the way I know you. I see inside your head, into the most intimate part of you. You can't do the same and it's not fair, not on you or me. Maybe this is my curse, to know everyone and never have anyone know me.

It was such a lonely thought, and I was the wrong one to console her. I was possibly the most self-absorbed person on the planet. Not only did I not have the patience to properly know anyone, but I didn't care enough to try. And yet, when I thought about it, I did want to know Morgan. I wanted to know what each tiny change to her face meant, and I wanted to know what I had to say or do to bring out my favourites. Maybe it didn't matter that I would never truly know her, because I reckoned, out of everyone on the planet, I was the one who wanted to know her the most.

"Maybe I just need more time to know you," I said. "I'm thinking forty years should do it."

There it was, that little crinkle of a smile. "Live in that cottage in the woods?"

"Wouldn't want any distractions to keep me from the very important task of getting to know you."

"Except maybe making jam."

"Except the jam."

"Hello!" The shout had come from below.

I looked over the edge. Quentin and Darcy were standing by the entrance to the tunnel.

"I don't want to interrupt your budding new relationship," Quentin said, "but we've got your clothes, and I thought maybe we should prioritise saving the world?"

I kicked the bucket over the edge. Quentin jumped backwards as it hit the ground in front of him, sloshing water all over his feet. I clambered down with Morgan, and Darcy threw me a parcel. I opened it and pulled out a red jumpsuit.

"What is this?" I asked.

"It's brightly coloured," Darcy pointed out unnecessarily. It was so bright it hurt my eyes.

"Is this that fake Miss Take costume from that music hall?" I asked.

"Maybe," she said, bouncing on the balls of her feet.

There was a special place in hell reserved for these two.

"Is this wool?" I asked, rubbing the material between my fingers. How had the performer not sweated her liver out in it?

"You want people to recognise you as Miss Take, don't you?" Quentin asked.

"I also want to get through this day with a shred of my dignity intact," I explained.

"Come on, it will be so cool: the grand return of Clara Blakely," Quentin said.

"Clara Blakely never left," I reminded him. "Besides, I am actually trying to convince everyone I'm innocent. I don't think readopting my villain persona will help my case."

"But it will be so cool," he reiterated, looking like a schoolboy that had been told off for dressing up his puppy.

"I give up." I stuffed it back into the bag while imagining it was Quentin's intestines. With that done, I hitched the bag over my shoulder, slipped on the mask, and pulled up the hood.

"We need to be careful," Darcy said. "We got stopped twice on our way and had to show our seals. They are all over assassins."

I looked at Morgan.

"I can get us there undetected," she said.

"Another rooftop escapade?" I asked.

"Not exactly," she mumbled.

"Good luck," Dan said.

"Don't let the kid stay up after his bedtime," I ordered.

Craig stuck his tongue out at me and passed Morgan the forged contract. Darcy hugged him and Dan.

"We'll see you soon. Stay out of trouble," Darcy told them.

Dan smiled at her and tilted his head towards me. "You're taking all the trouble with you."

Chapter
23

Morgan lifted the manhole cover. Quentin clamped the hand that was holding Darcy's over his mouth. I didn't think it smelt any worse than the Thames.

"This is one of the main sewers," Morgan said. "It leads towards the East End. We can get close without anyone noticing."

"Come to think of it, my plan is stupid," Quentin said, backing away. "Let's retreat to the tunnel and come up with another one."

Darcy pulled him back to the hole. "Come on. Where's your sense of adventure?"

"It just died with my sense of smell," he choked out.

"I could push him in if that would help," I offered.

Quentin swung himself onto the ladder and climbed down. Darcy followed him. I looked at Morgan.

"We could just put the lid back on," I suggested.

"Is Clara saying something mean again?" Darcy yelled.

"No," we shouted in unison.

"After you," Morgan said.

I tutted. "O ye of little faith."

I descended the ladder into the tunnel. I took back what I had said about underground trains; this was much worse. I had to bend myself in half to fit. The sewage slopped around my shins. Morgan pulled the cover back into place, and we were consumed by darkness. She struck a match and lit the two lanterns she had brought with her. The light accentuated the darkness of her eyes and sharpness of her face, making her look more terrifying than usual. I noticed her shoulder was pigeon-free.

"What happened to Victor?" I asked.

"I left him up there. He'll find us if he needs to." Morgan passed the spare lantern to Quentin, who still had a hand over his nose. "That way." She pointed the light down the tunnel.

Quentin and Darcy shuffled forward. At least the space was too narrow for them to hold hands. I brought up the rear. Morgan's body looked like a shadow, silhouetted as it was by her lantern. I was afraid she would vanish. The darkness pressed in behind me, keeping pace as we moved upstream. The detritus flowed past us on its way to the river. What was the point in cleaning myself if I was going to wade through human excrement?

"Question, Morgan," Quentin asked from the front. "That time we played hide and seek and I couldn't find you for three days, was this where you were?"

"No, I hid behind the clock face of Big Ben," she replied.

"And you call me flamboyant," he muttered under his breath.

"What do we need to know about Miss Fortitude's function, Clara?" Darcy asked.

"I know this," Quentin gushed. "She can only teleport to places she has already been or that are within her line of sight."

"Five points to Quentin," I said. "She normally appears behind her victim so she can stab them in the back, but she'll have to get me in her line of sight first. As soon as you see her appear, aim your crossbows at me."

I didn't have to be able to see Morgan's expression to know she was liking this plan less and less by the minute.

"Her reflexes are no faster than those of an average human, so you'll have plenty of time to take her down," I said to try and cheer her up.

"Morgan, do you really know where we are?" Darcy asked. "It's not that I don't trust you, but the thought that we might wander in here until our lanterns go out and man-eating rats find us did cross my mind."

"I know where we are. We need to pass three manholes," Morgan said.

"There's one!" Quentin cried.

"I saw it first!" Darcy objected. "I'm going to get the next one!"

They ran off, giggling manically.

"I thought we left the children behind," I said.

Morgan huffed out a laugh.

We walked on. The only sounds were Quentin and Darcy shoving each other up ahead, the sloshing around our feet, and the far-off scuttling of rats as they ran from the light.

"Why do you know the sewers so well?" I asked.

Morgan's silhouette shrugged. "They can be useful for travel, but I prefer roofs."

"Does it remind you of your days hiding in mines?"

"I guess a bit, but the mines were more likely to have bats than rats."

"That's number two!" came a shout up ahead followed by a cackle of laughter.

"Remind me, is mania a symptom of cholera?" I asked.

"No, but I think irritability is." Morgan shone the lantern down a smaller tunnel that joined ours. "I once bumped into some people cleaning. It's an awful inconvenience trying to fit past anyone down here."

"Fortunately, I never encountered that particular problem. If anyone ever caught sight of me in a sewer, they turned tail and ran."

"You've been in a sewer before?" She sounded surprised. I supposed that was a compliment.

"I used them a couple of times in my days as a villain. My parents did have to do a certain amount of skulking around. Contrary to popular belief, they did actually have secret identities."

"The Faceless Family."

"Indeed."

"Miss Take."

"Please stop."

"That's number three!" Darcy shouted.

"I was just about to say it!" Quentin called back.

"Come on, it's the next one," Morgan said.

We picked up our pace. Quentin and Darcy were waiting for us under a manhole cover.

"This is the one," Morgan said.

Darcy climbed up the ladder and pushed the lid. "It's stuck."

Quentin joined her, and together, they hefted it up and out of the way. The person who had been standing on it let out a yell and fell over.

"I am so sorry," Darcy said, sticking her head out.

"That's all right, I should have been watching my feet. Do you need a hand?" the random bystander offered.

"Thank you, that would be wonderful," Darcy replied.

The man helped Darcy up. Quentin went next, then Morgan, who refused the hand offered her. I was last to emerge into the street. I rotated on the spot. The smoking chimneys of Mundmere Factory reached up like skeletal fingers. People were passing us, funnelling around our immobile group like a river around a rock. Were they all part of the protest? Perhaps some of them were just spectators. Roll up, roll up, come see the social anarchists. Watch as they make their outlandish demands for the right to live. I could hear the protest from where we stood. The indistinct chant was joined by tuneless whistles and shouts. One wrong move, and this day would end in a massacre.

"We shouldn't hang around too long," Morgan said.

I noticed writing on a building. "How close are we to Mundmere?"

"Two streets," Morgan said. "It would take two to three minutes for a runner to get to the common, depending on their stamina."

"Where's the nearest police station?" I asked.

She pointed towards the common. "That way. About ten minutes."

I hummed thoughtfully. "So, in theory, Miss Fortitude would hear the news before the police?"

"You want to do it here. Why?" Morgan asked.

I nodded to the building, where the word "Bank" was engraved in large letters. "We need to give them all a believable reason as to why I'm here so they don't get suspicious. I'll even have the outfit."

Quentin tapped his chin thoughtfully. "Coverable exits, lots of hiding places. It could work."

"You two find positions," Morgan said. "I'll stay with Clara till she's ready."

Darcy and Quentin disappeared into the bank. I dragged Morgan down a narrow gap between the bank and the next-door funeral parlour.

"Keep a lookout," I told her. "I don't want to have to fight anyone in the nude."

Making sure there were no windows above me out of which peeping Toms or buckets of excrement could appear, I peeled off the leathers and pulled on the hideous red jumpsuit. It was saggy around the shoulders, chest, and hips, and the ruffles were large enough to act as wings. It was truly awful. At least I would smell less like a sewer now. I strapped Darcy's knife to my thigh.

"I'm ready," I said reluctantly.

Morgan turned around. I could see her trying not to laugh. "I think it looks good."

I pointed my finger at her. "Not another word. Let's just get on with it."

I walked into the bank, trying my best not to pull at the costume. I had never felt more self-conscious in my life. The humiliation of working with my parents was all coming back. I had kicked open many a bank door with a gun and a cheesy catchphrase.

I shook myself. This was not the time for self-doubt. It was a go-big-or-go-home moment. I climbed on top of the nearest clerk's desk.

"Your attention please! For those of you who don't know me, my name is Clara Blakely. I am here to make a withdrawal."

The thirty or so people in the bank were frozen in place, staring at me in horror.

"Go on then. Run for your life," I told them.

No one moved.

"Go!" I shouted.

Thirty pairs of shoes squeaked on tiles as everyone raced for the exit. People pushed each other over and stepped on each other in their mad rush to escape. I could hear them screaming as they ran down the street. So far, so good.

I jumped down from the desk and found the clerk who belonged to it still sitting there. I grabbed him by his tie and dragged him towards the back of the bank. I shoved him forward, sending him sprawling.

"Go get some money or something," I said. "Take as long as you want."

He nodded vigorously and stumbled off in the direction of the vault.

There was nothing to do now but wait. I picked up a ledger and started snooping through people's accounts. I memorised a few potential clients and then realised I was being terribly optimistic about my chances of survival. I threw down the ledger and began playing with the abacus. The huge clock that hung over the work floor ticked on, reminding everyone of the precious commodity that was time. Miss Fortitude should have been there by now. Even the police should have been there by now. They knew it was a trap.

"It's a bust," I said to the rafters.

I heard the sound of the door opening. I turned, but it was swinging shut on nobody. That was strange.

Suddenly, a strong breeze whipped past me, making me stagger sideways. A hand grabbed my shoulder and yanked me forward. I closed my eyes instinctively. I knew that feeling. Every muscle in my body was stretching beyond what it should. My stomach had been left somewhere far behind.

The sensation stopped. I leant forward, hands on my knees, and vomited. Straightening up, I wiped my mouth and faced the two people in front of me.

"Mother. Father. Good to see you again."

Chapter
24

I had thought testifying in court would top the list as the most awkward interaction I would ever have with my parents, but this made the tribunal look like Sunday lunch.

"How was Botany Bay?" I asked, because when in doubt, make small talk. "I heard Australia's beaches are lovely. Fresh air, physical exercise, I was almost jealous. It sounded like the ideal retirement."

Together, they took a step towards me. I took a quick step back. I was in a rather ornate hall. The wall panels were lovely, I noted as I sought fervently for an exit, and the marble floor I had thrown up on really was splendid. My parents looked out of place in such smart surroundings. They were older and more haggard than when I had last seen them. It was not a surprise given where they had spent the last four years. They looked angry. This too, was to be expected.

I held up my hands. "Before you do anything you'll regret, like kill your only daughter, just remember that it's your own fault I betrayed you. You taught me to be utterly selfish. It was a lesson I took to heart."

Another step towards me. At least my death would be quick. They knew not to mess around with trying to cause me pain.

"What are you doing here? You're not supposed to be here." I recognised the indignant tones of Mr Righteous.

My parents turned in the direction of the voice. He was still hidden from my sight.

"We were employed by Lady Blythwood to find Clara," my mother said. "Well, we found her."

They stepped aside, and I was left in direct view of Mr Righteous. Surely, he wouldn't risk setting fire to such a posh house. He brought his hands together.

"Let them in," said another, much more tired voice.

"They shouldn't see you," Mr Righteous told the person out of sight.

"It doesn't matter now," the other voice replied.

Reluctantly, Mr Righteous stepped aside. My parents looked at me pointedly. I sidestepped my pile of vomit and approached Mr Righteous. My parents followed behind me, practically breathing down my neck. I had to turn sideways to pass Mr Righteous. He smelt like burning toast.

I found myself in a sitting room. It was lovely if you were into showing off. Through a gap in the silk curtains, I could see a street lined with maple trees. I wasn't in the East End anymore. Above a fireplace hung a portrait of the original John Blythwood. Next to it was a slightly larger portrait of the current Blythwoods, John and Edith. Someone was a fan.

My suspicions growing, I navigated around the sofa on which a person was sitting with their back to me. As soon as their face came into view, my feet forgot how to walk. The shock was great enough to make me stumble. I had been correct and also completely wrong. The man lounging on the sofa in a green dressing gown was definitely John Blythwood III. He looked exactly like his portrait except for one crucial difference.

He only had one eye.

"Miss Blakely," he greeted frostily.

"Lord Blythwood," I replied. "Or should I call you Mr Indestructible?"

My parents exchanged a glance. This was news to them. They must have been unaware that the man who hired them was the same one who had tried to put them behind bars.

"Either is fine," John told me.

"Johnny it is," I said.

He scowled. I went to take a seat in a cream-coloured armchair.

"Please don't," he said. "They are difficult to clean."

I sat. Mr Righteous stepped towards me. John placed a hold on his arm, keeping him back.

"Leave it," John said, curling his lip at me like I was a rather repulsive earwig. I hoped he would feel the need to burn the room after I was gone.

My parents circled around so they were standing behind me. The whole situation had me completely wrong-footed, so I did what I did best: faked it. Leaning back in the chair, I grinned at John like finding out he was the hero who wanted me dead was the best fun in the world.

"Tell me, on a scale of one to ten, how disappointed were your parents when you developed a function?" I asked. "I know the Blythwoods try to present themselves as the champions of functionables, but it's no secret your family considers them a working-class phenomenon. You must have felt like a carthorse growing up amongst stallions. Is that why you've gone through so much trouble to keep your identity secret? Embarrassment?"

Mr Righteous twitched forward. Once again, John held him back. It was far more restraint than he had showed in our previous encounters. Morgan must have really done a number on him.

"I had company," he said.

I chuckled. "Don't tell me your sister has a function too? Who is she in this grand charade? Miss Fortitude?"

John kept his face neutral, but this was an answer in itself.

"No way. Edith Blythwood is Miss Fortitude?" I asked in amazement.

I looked at the portrait of brother and sister. Edith stared out of the frame with the same dead-eyed gaze I had found myself subject to in Mundmere Factory. They were both living extremely stressful double lives. The violent outbursts were starting to make sense.

"Are you done playing detective?" Mr Righteous asked condescendingly.

"All we need is for you to be the Prime Minister and for Mrs Grace to have been the Queen." I was suddenly worried by the prospect. "She wasn't the Queen, was she?"

"No, she was not," John said wearily.

I breathed a sigh of relief. "She was part of your team though, right? Because no one seems particularly concerned that I killed her." I pointed to Mr Righteous. "This guy tried to explode me because I was simply in the area when you had your eye gouged out. Yet, Mrs Grace suffers blunt-force trauma to the head, and no one bothers lifting so much as one avenging finger."

John cleared his throat a little awkwardly. "Mrs Grace was the odd one out in our group."

I nodded. "I get it. You and Miss Fortitude are siblings, Mr Righteous here is your boyfriend. Mrs Grace was the interloper."

John and Mr Righteous looked like they would quite enjoy taking one of my arms each and running in opposite directions.

"I would watch your tongue if I were you," John said through gritted teeth.

"Why? You're going to kill me anyway," I reminded him.

"Perhaps," he replied.

Was he suggesting there was a way I could survive this? "Please feel free to elaborate."

John shrugged off his dressing gown and picked up a walking stick. I had heard rumours that heroes always wore their Brigade uniforms under their clothes, but I had not wanted to believe it. It sounded sweaty to me. The red, white, and blue of his uniform hurt my eyes. I did not know how Mr Righteous could bear to be so close to it, but he made sure to hover nervously while John walked slowly over to the portrait of the original John Blythwood. It was a remarkably dull painting. I could not blame the artist; John Blythwood was, most likely, a remarkably dull man.

"My grandfather was a brilliant man," John said. "He foresaw what damage the anti-function movement would have on our economy, and he stopped it. Not with inventions or force, but with words. With the right words, he changed the way people thought."

So could a bottle of milk with the right advertisement. John Blythwood had not invented propaganda. "He was only successful because he came up with a way everything could carry on as normal, business as usual. We hate change, we like comfort. Offer us a way to keep pretending everything is fine, and we'll take it."

John turned his gaze on me. "Then why won't you take it? Why are you choosing the road that ends in panic? If people find out about the *Lutum gigantos* before we can control it, functions will be seen as dangerous and functionables as monstrosities. As a functionable yourself, surely you don't want that."

I shrugged. "People already see me as a monster. It won't really affect me."

"But do you know what will affect you? The collapse of our economy. Calls to end pollution to avoid cases of more functionables would break this country. By keeping *Lutum gigantos* a secret, we are allowing people to live their lives the way they want to."

"No, you're not. You're protecting your pockets and dooming the next generation."

"We're not dooming anyone. We are searching for a way to control it."

"And not finding one."

"Do you have so little faith in science? We have seen technological achievements in the last few years that people could only dream of. We will find a way."

"And then you'll sell it as a weapon, which will still mean a world terrorised by the Dirt Man."

John laughed. "You delude yourself. You do not care about the world. You only stand against us out of some petty rebellious streak left over from your criminal youth."

"You people," I scoffed. "I do care about the world. I have to because, much to my dismay, I am in it. I don't want to die by your *Lutum ridiculous*, and you have proved that you don't care who this thing kills so long as it's not yourself. That makes it pretty hard for me to trust you."

"Luckily for you, trust is not required to negotiate."

"What are we negotiating?"

"You're not working alone. We know Craig Little is involved. Who else? Which assassins are working with you?"

I laughed. "Working with me? They're working for me. I hired them to do a job, they did it. I don't make a habit of associating myself with assassins."

"I struggle to believe that. You were seen at the latest graduation at the Finishing School. Craig came to us after he had hired an assassin to kill you and they refused. You seem to be very friendly with them. Tell me who and where to find them, and I will let you live."

I considered him carefully, then shook my head. "Pull the other one."

"What other option do we have? To get the information we need, we must give you a choice. I would rather the choice be between a quick or a painful death, but that is not an option with you."

He had a point.

"You think they will let me walk away unharmed?" I nodded to my looming parents.

"We have an arrangement. They are going to tell everyone that you were just pretending to be a pain reliever and your real function is controlling dirt."

I was confused. "You're going to make me into Dirt Man? No one will believe it."

"On the contrary, the public will eat this up. It's a far better story than your corporate corruption idea."

"Personally, I think living dirt is more interesting."

"Let's agree to disagree."

This was making my head hurt. "I'm guessing you broke my parents out of prison to give your crazy story a touch of credibility, but have you considered that they are well-established liars?"

John waved it off. "Perhaps prison changed them. Edith thought they would be highly motivated to find you, and she was right. Besides, it was an easy breakout. We have good connections."

"I bet you do. And I bet Edith came up with this whole plan. It's far too complicated to be your doing."

John bristled. Goading him was all well and good, but I needed answers.

"I'm still not seeing why my parents would let me go."

"If you give me the names of your accomplices, your parents have agreed to give you a one-month head start."

I raised my eyebrows. "They said that?"

He nodded.

"And you believed them?"

"It doesn't really matter if they're telling the truth or not. It's still the best chance you've got. Because if you don't tell me, they are going to kill you. Right here, right now."

I saw a flaw in the plan and leapt on it. "Won't people get suspicious if the supposed Dirt Man is dead, yet people are still dying from attacks?"

"We're not going to tell anyone you're dead. They'll think you got away and are still stalking the streets of London. Your parents assured Edith that they will have no difficulty disposing of your body quietly."

A sudden bang made me jump. I thought for a moment my parents had decided to cut the negotiations short, but then I realised the knock had come from the window. I looked over to see a pigeon tapping its beak against the glass. John left his post by the portrait and banged on the frame until the bird flew away. Could it have been Victor? These damn birds all looked the same. But if it was, that was both wonderful and frightening news. That pigeon was the best and most terrifying thing that had ever happened to me.

"Give me the names of the assassins," John said.

"No."

"Take a moment to consider—"

I cut him off. "Don't try and tempt me out of my one selfless act. I'm protecting my friends. This is my heroic redemption moment."

John's scowl deepened. "I'm not buying it."

I smiled at him. "And you shouldn't. I don't have a single selfless bone in my body. But do you know what I do have? A surplus of spite. If you wanted to work with me, you should have thought of that before you tied me to a chair and ruined my complexion. You should have thought of that before you put an unfixable dent in my reputation by blaming me for your own disappearance. If there is one thing I can do, it's hold a grudge. So go ahead and kill me. You won't last long. My assassin friends will finish the job. They will expose you, and then they will kill you. And in your final moments, you will wish I was there, because I can promise you, it will hurt."

John looked down on me with the happiest expression I had seen on him yet. "Edith will be disappointed with your decision, but I must say, I was hoping you would choose this." He spoke to my parents. "She's all yours. But if you don't mind, I would like to watch."

It was nice to think that my parents had found something to work together for. It was almost heartening to know that because of me, they were putting aside their differences. It was just a shame they were bonding over my death rather than my life.

I could feel my parents moving in, but I refused to look around. I had precious few moments left on this Earth, and I would not be spending them blubbering and begging for my life. A hand came to rest on my shoulder. It was my mother's. This was it, then. I had seen her separate someone's head from their neck with all the difficulty of plucking an orange from a tree. She patted my shoulder.

"No, Lord Blythwood, I do mind," she said.

My confusion was mirrored in John's face. I looked up at my mother.

She smiled at me in a way I found difficult to analyse. It looked almost warm. She squeezed my shoulder gently and let go, walking around the armchair to approach the heroes.

"What are you doing?" John asked. "Stop this at once."

My mother grabbed him and threw him across the room. The poor bookcase faired far worse than him. While the splinters of wood and glass were still falling to the ground, John was getting back to his feet. My father sped behind him and pushed him back up against the bookcase while he tied his hands.

"How dare you!" Mr Righteous shouted.

Before he could get his hands together, my mother had grabbed his arms and forced them apart. My father came up behind him and secured his arms to his sides with material I now recognised as once belonging to the curtains. He struggled against his binds helplessly.

"We had a deal!" John yelled. He tried to lunge for my parents and fell over.

"We're changing the deal," my mother replied.

Mr Righteous tried to reach for John and fell over too.

My mother turned back to me. I was still sitting in the armchair, frozen in place. She walked towards me and placed her hands on my shoulders. She was pulling me up and towards her. Here came the decapitation. No, her arms were tightening around me. She was clearly planning on squeezing the life out of me like a python. Yet, she was doing so very softly. It almost felt like a hug. It was a hug. I was being hugged by my mother. What a novel experience. I felt like I should do something. I patted her awkwardly on the back.

She pulled away and wiped a tear from her eye. "We are so proud of you."

"That's horrifying," I said without thinking.

She laughed. My father slung an arm over her shoulder.

"I'm sorry, but I'm confused," I said.

"Look at what you have accomplished when not living in our shadow," she said. "You found a use for your function, took on one of the most powerful families in Britain, and killed Mrs Grace. It's more than we could have hoped."

It was a lot to process. I focused on what I thought to be the most pressing problem. "Don't you hate me?"

"We did for a long time. We would spend nights plotting how we would get our revenge. Do you remember that, Wyatt?"

He laughed. "I sure do."

"But then the reports started coming in about you being arrested for murdering a lord, bribing your way out of prison, making heroes disappear. Suddenly, we saw you in a new light. We talked it over and realised that we would have done the same thing to you that you did to us if it would have prevented us from going to prison."

I honestly didn't know whether to feel grateful or insulted.

"We know that things have been rocky between us," my mother continued. "We weren't always the most affectionate parents, and you weren't always the easiest daughter. But we were hoping that maybe we could start fresh, figure out how to be a family again."

I could not form any words. My parents were proud of me? They understood the reasons behind my actions and forgave me for all the ways I had wronged them? They were willing to accept part of the blame? Prison really did change people.

They were waiting for me to say something.

"Sure," I said slowly.

The window exploded with a crash, and I dropped to the floor instinctively. When I looked up, the room was littered with glass, and my father was pinning someone to the floor. He let go with a yelp, and the figure rolled out from underneath him. My father crawled away with a knife in his leg.

"You will not touch her," Morgan said with deadly venom. She had another knife in her hand, and it was pointing at my mother.

I quickly stepped between them with my hands held out placatingly. "All right, let's just everyone calm down."

Morgan looked at me like I had lost my mind.

"They're on our side," I said, barely believing the words myself.

She did not lower the knife, but she had not yet stabbed anyone else, so I was taking that as a sign that the truce would hold.

"Mother, Father, this is Morgan Murdur, the best assassin of her class and my extremely close, yet purely platonic, friend," I said.

"If you even think about hurting her, I will skin you," Morgan spat.

"She's not the most socially inclined. That basically means, 'Hello, it's nice to meet you,'" I explained.

"You really are close with assassins," Mother said approvingly.

She held out her hand. Morgan looked at it suspiciously. Mother withdrew her hand, seemingly unoffended.

"I'm Marie Blakely," Mother said. "That is my husband, Wyatt."

My father paused in extracting the knife and waved.

What's going on? Morgan asked.

Truthfully, I had no idea.

"Darling, would you mind taking my pain?" Father asked.

I took the pain of his stab wound and passed it to John. He cried out, and Mr Righteous yelled profanities at me. My mother went to wrap my father's leg with another strip of curtain.

"Not too tight, dear," he warned.

Morgan edged closer to me, keeping my parents in her sight at all times.

"They aren't what I was expecting," she whispered.

"Me neither," I admitted. I cleared my throat and raised my voice. "Look, the thing is, I'm kind of in the middle of trying to expose the Blythwoods."

"We gathered that much," Father said.

"So, you don't mind if I just go off and finish that?" I asked.

"Would you like help?" Mother offered.

"You want to help?" I asked, surprised.

"Of course we would like to help bring down the Blythwoods," Father said cheerfully. "It will be the criminal act of the century."

"I guess so," I said slowly. "Okay, then. We should probably go."

"What about them?" Morgan asked, scowling at John and Mr Righteous.

I made my way over to John's corner. He was lying where he had fallen, looking pale and furious. I smiled down at him smugly.

"They're coming with us," I said. "I'm sure the crowd will want to meet the real Mr Indestructible."

I had not thought it was possible for John to look angrier. He was full of surprises.

"You will pay for this!" Mr Righteous cried, attracting my attention.

I carefully reached down and took off his mask. I squinted. "Does anyone recognise him?"

Mother and Father shook their heads.

He's John Blythwood's assistant, Morgan supplied.

They worked together when they were heroes, and they worked together as Blythwood and his assistant, and they were in a romantic relationship. How could anyone stand to spend that much time with another human being? It was baffling.

"I should probably keep my weight off the leg until absolutely necessary," Father said.

"Sorry about that." Morgan didn't sound sorry.

My father waved her off. "Nonsense, my dear. I would have done the same."

"I'll carry the prisoners," Mother offered. "I like the outfit by the way," she said to me. "It's a shame we don't have ours anymore."

"Real shame," I muttered. I turned to Morgan. "Where are Quentin and Darcy?"

"I left them watching the protest," she said. "It's grown. There's police and a few minor heroes trying to break it up but, so far, no bloodshed."

"You should go make sure Dan and Craig are okay," I told her.

"You're putting me on babysitting duty?" she asked scornfully.

"You can't do any more, but don't worry, I've got backup." I glanced over at my parents. It was still seriously weird.

"Be careful," Morgan said. She made it sound like an order.

"You know me, no undue risks," I joked. As reassurances went, it was not my best.

She reached into her boot and pulled out her tiny knife. She pressed it into my palm.

"In case anyone gets too close," she whispered.

"How sweet," Father said.

I spun around. My parents were watching us with their arms around each other.

"Miss Take has become Miss Taken. Clara's going to marry an assassin," Mother said.

"Marry?" I stuttered. "Let's cut the engine on that thought right away."

Mother raised her hands in surrender. "All right. We'll discuss it later. It was simply marvellous meeting you, Morgan. You must come over for tea sometime. Perhaps when we are not in prison."

Morgan nodded stiffly. *Are you sure you're okay with this?* she asked in my head.

"Just go. I'll be fine," I said.

With a final worried look, she clambered through the broken window and disappeared onto the street.

"Let's do this as a family," Mother said, holding out her hand.

"As a family," Father agreed, clasping hers.

They looked at me expectantly. I searched for that inner strength that had got me through sixteen years of their company.

"As a family," I said, placing my hand on theirs.

Chapter
25

My mother stepped out into the road in front of a carriage. The horses skidded to a stop.

"What are you doing?" the driver cried. "You trying to die or something?"

Mother grabbed the horses' bridles and held them still.

"Get down from the carriage," Father ordered.

The man laughed. He looked at me. "Nice costume. Halloween isn't for a few weeks yet."

I didn't wear this stupid thing for people to think I was dressing up. Mother reached up, pulled the driver off the seat, and threw him into the street. I opened the door of the carriage.

"If you wouldn't mind stepping out," I said to the well-dressed couple inside.

They fell out, looking like two brightly coloured, flightless birds running for their lives. Mother dumped John and Mr Righteous on the floor and climbed onto the box beside my father.

"Can you drive a carriage?" I asked them.

"Of course," Father replied offhandedly. "Remember the chase after the diamond heist in fifty-six?"

Yes, I did, which was why I was worried. That had not been driving. The carriage had ended up upside-down in an ornamental fountain with me still inside.

I got into the carriage and held onto the door handle, ready for a quick getaway.

"This isn't going to end well for you," John said as we hurtled forward.

"No, nothing tends to." It was the truth, but I still felt like John should not be lecturing me about my life choices when I was sitting on a velvet-clad bench while he was lying on the floor.

"Untie us," Mr Righteous demanded. "Help us escape, and we will renegotiate our terms."

I laughed. "No, thanks. I may hate my parents, but I hate you a lot more. I would lay down on hot coals if it meant it would burn you too."

I leant back and tried to focus on the sound of the wheels rumbling over the cobbles. This was it. The day would end with prison, death, or exoneration. One seemed less likely than the others. I knew how it would look, marching up to Mundmere in this ridiculous costume with my parents in tow, but the truth was I could turn up in a tutu with the tooth fairy and people would still see nothing but a criminal. All these years, I had painstakingly built my reputation up with my bare hands, one brick at a time, but its foundations were weak. One push, one tiny accusation of murder, and it came tumbling down. If I was honest with myself, I had done a fantastic job at rigging it to fall.

❖ ❖ ❖

The carriage came to an abrupt stop. There was shouting. It took me a moment to pick out the chant from the cacophony of other sounds.

"Let us in! Let us in!"

Were they trying to get into the carriage? I pulled back the curtain and peeked out. We were surrounded by a crowd, but they were not focused on us. I pressed my face right against the glass. Over the tops of their heads, I could see the fence of Mundmere Common.

"We're going to have to walk from here," Mother called from the front.

"You can't expect us to get out in that. It's a mob," Mr Righteous objected.

"Why would they hurt you?" I asked innocently. "They'll recognise you as their betters, won't they? Surely, they will lie down and let you use them as a carpet."

I pushed open the door and stepped down. The crush of so many bodies was sickening. The smell of fear and anger rose in great clouds of sweat. People around me tried to drop back, but they were fighting against the push of hundreds of other bodies. Whispers of my name floated out like oil on water.

"Clara!" someone shouted.

Two assassins were pushing through the crowd towards me.

"Clara, you're all right," Quentin said in relief as he reached me. "One second, you were in the bank, next, you were gone. We didn't see Miss Fortitude. They are saying she's still in Mundmere. What happened? Is Morgan okay? She took off."

"No, she's hurt," I lied. "She was heading back to the safe house. You should go make sure she's okay."

"We're on it," Darcy said grimly. She tugged on Quentin's hand. "Quentin, are you coming?"

Quentin seemed to have forgotten her. He was watching my parents climb off the box. If not for his mask, I suspected his jaw would have been on the floor.

"Is that…" he trailed off, as though voicing it would break the illusion.

"Oh, right. Mother, Father, this is Quentin Shadow. He's a big fan," I said.

My parents smiled at him.

"A friend of Clara's is a friend of ours," Mother said.

I thought Quentin might be about to go full Labrador and lick their hands.

"Mr and Mrs Blakely," he gushed. "It is a such an honour. I'm a huge admirer of your work."

My father clasped Quentin's hand and shook it vigorously. "It's always nice to meet a fan."

"I don't suppose I could ask for an autograph, could I?" Quentin asked.

"We would be delighted," Father replied.

Quentin patted himself down. He pulled out his apology to his victims and passed it to my parents. They scribbled their signatures next to the sad face. Quentin took the paper back and held it to his chest.

"Thank you so much," Quentin said gratefully. "You guys are my heroes, well not heroes, but villains."

"Morgan. Injured," I reminded him.

Quentin seemed to snap out of a daze. "Right. Got to dash."

With a final wave to my parents, he let Darcy drag him into the crowd. That had got rid of them. I did not want them hanging around and doing something stupid, like joining in a fight on a conservation site.

My mother reached into the carriage and slung John over one shoulder and Mr Righteous over the other. She led the way, pushing through the people, towards the main gates of Mundmere. The whispers of my name grew louder, and with them came murmurs of "Marie and Wyatt Blakely," "John Blythwood," "Mr Indestructible," and "Mr Righteous." We made a rather noticeable group. The crowd began to part, and the chants died out. All except one. As we stopped in front of the gates, I noticed one person was still absorbed in their own rallying call.

"What do we want? A recognition of our right for free and easy access to nature! When do we want it? Now!"

"William?" I asked, identifying him as the man I had shared a cell with.

He broke off. "Miss Blakely. I didn't recognise you."

"What are you doing here?"

"Protesting their illegal enclosure of Mundmere Common and demanding an end to the constant land-grabbing by the upper classes. You?"

"I guess I'm demanding that the companies that pose a risk to our safety through damaging our environment be held to account."

He nodded approvingly. "I wish you the best of luck."

"Thanks. Same to you."

"We can't get in. They've got the common all locked up. There's them," he nodded to the line of police and heroes guarding the gate, "and word has it Miss Fortitude is inside."

"You can't beat a hero," I agreed. "Not without villains anyway. Luckily for you, we're here."

My mother put down her captives. They stumbled towards the line of law enforcement.

"I don't think so," she said, grabbing them by their collars and holding them in place.

"Let them go!" one of the policemen shouted.

It was nice to see the police working with the Hero Brigade for once. Mother and Father stepped forward, pushing John and Mr Righteous in front of them. I stayed just behind my parents. The line quailed under their looming presence. As though on command, all but one of them stepped aside. The person left was dressed in a newly starched Community Squadron uniform.

"Stop," Miss Thomas commanded.

"Stand aside, Miss Thomas," I said. "We are not the enemy here."

"You seriously expect me to believe that you are the good person here? You have broken your parents out of prison and kidnapped…some people," Miss Thomas said.

I was delighted to clear up her confusion. "These people are John Blythwood and John Blythwood's assistant, otherwise known as Mr Indestructible and Mr Righteous."

There were murmurs amongst the crowd. Miss Thomas flicked her hair over her shoulder as she looked John up and down. She didn't seem disappointed by the revelation. Perhaps it had something to do with him being rich and aristocratic.

"The Blythwoods have been manipulating the Hero Brigade to accomplish their own aims," I said loudly, more for the crowd's benefit than Miss Thomas's.

"Might I add," Father put in, "that it was Lord and Lady Blythwood who broke us out of prison. They wanted us to work for them, but that didn't really pan out."

Mother took another step forward. Miss Thomas held her chin up high.

"I want it to go on my CV that I stood my ground against the Blakelys," Miss Thomas said.

"If you stand your ground against Mr Swift and Mrs Sturdy, you won't have a CV," I told her. "You can't go to the Brigade Ball if you're dead."

Miss Thomas chewed on her lip nervously. I could almost see the glitter and gowns flashing before her eyes.

"Maybe you're right," she said. "Maybe you're right about the Dirt Man, the Blythwoods, all of it. But no friend of Miss Take will ever be going to the ball."

I realised my mistake a second too late.

With a flick of Miss Thomas's fingers, the silk restraints holding the heroes fell away. Her useless function had finally found a use. I would have been proud of her if she had not just ruined my plan. Mr Righteous turned, hands up. Father grabbed Mother, and they were gone.

"You have got to be kidding me," I said.

The lightning knocked me backwards into the crowd. I must have blacked out, because suddenly, I was on the ground a few feet from where I had been before, being trampled as the crowd scattered. Something smelt like it was burning; I wondered if it was me.

Pushing myself up on my elbows, I watched John and Mr Righteous shutting the gates of Mundmere Common behind them.

My parents reappeared.

"Are you all right?" Father asked.

"Fantastic," I replied as I staggered to my feet.

The police and heroes had reformed their line, but they still looked nervous. I put my pain on Miss Thomas. The snake deserved it. The rest of the enforcers fled as Miss Thomas went down. Mother ripped the gates off their hinges and dumped them in a twisted heap. Miss Fortitude, otherwise known as Edith Blythwood, was standing at the edge of the forest, yelling at her brother.

"What were you thinking?" she fumed. "The last time you faced Clara Blakely without me you lost an eye! You should have sent for me!"

John had his head bowed guiltily. Mr Righteous looked embarrassed. Next to him, about twenty guards were trying to melt into the background.

"We will talk about this later. But first, let me finish this," Edith said, and vanished.

Something cracked against my head, and I fell forward onto my knees. Head injuries were the worst. I was too dizzy to pass the pain on. Through half-closed eyes, I saw Edith reappear amongst the trees. My father was hot on her heels.

John was charging forward. Mother ran to meet him. Her hit sent him flying through a tree. The trunk split in half from the force of the impact.

Someone grabbed my hair and pulled me up roughly. My head was tipped back, and I found myself staring up at Mr Righteous. I put my pain on him, and he let go. I rolled away and got to my feet. Lightning shot towards me, and I bent over backwards to avoid it, then I righted myself.

"What the hell is your problem?" I demanded. "Are you jealous because of that rumour that Mr Indestructible and I are a couple? Because I can assure you, there is no truth in that whatsoever. I pity the fool who ends up with that guy."

Mr Righteous raised his hands. "I'm going to kill you."

"Then get on with it already."

He fired lightning at me. I sidestepped it easily. Another bolt came towards me, but I dived into a roll. Perhaps I would have done well as an assassin after all. I tore Darcy's knife from my thigh and jabbed it up towards Mr Righteous. His hand came out to stop me. I felt the knife meet flesh just as the lightning hit me. I skidded backwards; it felt like I was spending most of this fight staring at the sky. I looked down at the remains of Darcy's knife. The handle was intact, but the blade had shattered. I chucked it aside.

Mr Righteous was trying to stop the blood pumping merrily from the hole in his side.

"You seem a tad worked up," I told him. "Perhaps we should take a short break and resume this when you're less emotional."

He roared as he charged. I put my pain on him, and he missed his step, landing on his face. Swinging my leg over him, I used my weight to pin him down. He struggled beneath me. Keeping him restrained took all my strength. I knew I could not reach Morgan's knife without letting him go.

Across the clearing, Edith and my father were almost too fast to see. Every time he got close, Edith would vanish. It made me feel sick just watching it.

Edith appeared behind my mother. Father arrived a second too late to prevent Edith from stabbing her in the back. Mother was fast enough to give her a kick that sent her flying. She vanished mid-air.

I took Mother's pain and put it on Mr Righteous.

"Thanks, darling," Mother called.

Mr Righteous tried to choke down a sob.

"It's okay," I said comfortingly. "Mr Indestructible wasn't that good at handling pain either. You should have seen him when he got stabbed in the eye. He cried like a baby."

The next sob that broke through was more like a scream. He was vibrating. My hands started tingling, making all my hairs stand on end. There was a feeling, like the moment before a storm hits. The air was tense with it. I scrambled off him, but it was too late. Mr Righteous exploded. I went spinning through the air, hit the ground, and kept rolling. I finally came to a stop with a mouthful of grass. I spat it out and rolled onto my back. It was nice that the sky was excited to see me, but did it have to spin quite so fast?

I had not known Mr Righteous could do that. I suspected that he, too, had been none the wiser. I wondered if he would be so pleased that his grief was unlocking more of his function that he would let bygones be bygones.

A face appeared in the sky. Mr Righteous did not look like he had reconciliation on his mind.

"This is for John," he said.

"You mean Johnny?"

Mr Righteous spread his hand, aiming it at my face. Not even he could miss me at this range. His body jerked. He looked down at the arrow tip sticking out of his chest. A bloodstain blossomed out, drowning the little lions on his suit. He fell to his knees.

"You're not supposed to be here!" I yelled in the general direction the shot had come from.

I put my pain on Mr Righteous and got up. He did not seem to notice the added agony. I lifted his chin so he could look me in the eyes. A trickle of blood ran from the corner of his mouth.

"You can reunite yourself with John's eye now," I said, and I let go of his face. He toppled forward, lifeless.

"You murderer!"

I turned. John was running towards me. He did not look thrilled that we had just killed his boyfriend. In fact, he looked like he was planning on ripping me apart with his bare hands.

My mother tackled him from behind. She grabbed him by the ankles and lobbed him as far as she could. He crashed through the trees and landed in Mundmere Lake with a splash. She dusted off her hands.

"He's very difficult to kill," she said. "But that should keep him occupied for now. Do you think you can handle them?"

I looked to where she was pointing. A pack of guards was heading towards me.

"Yeah, I've got this."

The first guard swung his machete at me. I ducked, grabbed him, and used him as a human shield against the man who had brought a gun. It felt like cheating, bringing a gun to a function fight. I pushed the now-deceased human shield onto him, crushing him. I took his gun. Waste not, want not, and all that.

Morgan was suddenly by my side.

"What are you doing here?" I asked, shooting someone.

"You really thought I would sit this one out?"

"I must have thought you were smarter than you are." I ducked, and she fired her crossbow at the person running towards us. I took their pain and passed it on. "If you were here the whole time, why did you watch me having my arse handed to me by Mr Righteous?"

She fired her last bolt and then threw the crossbow at someone. It hit them on the head.

"I was making sure none of the protestors got caught in the crossfire. I thought you could take care of yourself. Clearly, I thought wrong."

"I handled myself fine."

"How many times did you get electrocuted?"

"Lost count," I admitted as I let Morgan twirl me out of the way of a guard's bat.

There was a scream. Edith was standing over my father, who's leg was not at an angle it was supposed to be. My mother made a grab for her, but she disappeared, reappearing behind my mother and taking hold of the knife still lodged in Mother's back. She twisted it and then pulled it out with a spurt of blood. Mother tried to reach her, but Edith vanished.

Something knocked my gun from my hand and grabbed me from behind. I twisted and managed to block Edith's knife before she buried it in my back. I headbutted her. She stumbled back and disappeared. Something whacked me around the back of the head. Before I knew it, she had her knife pressed to my throat.

"You Blakelys are a disease," she hissed close to my ear. "I will enjoy extinguishing your bloodline."

"Then I should probably give you the address of my cousin, Derek. He works in a grocery store. Nice man."

She pressed the knife harder. Then, she let me go with a scream. I staggered away to find a fury of feathers attacking her. Huge scratches ran down her face. Had I mentioned how much I loved that pigeon? Edith lashed out with her knife, and Victor fell to the ground. She went to stamp on him, but he vanished. She stared bemusedly at the place he had been. She did not seem to enjoy it as much when it happened to her.

Morgan barrelled into Edith and landed in a crouch, a knife in each hand. Edith picked herself up and flicked blood out of her eye.

"Are you the assassin who stabbed my brother?" she asked.

Morgan rose slowly from her crouch.

"All right," Edith said. "I suppose it doesn't matter. One assassin is as good as the next."

She vanished and Morgan spun around. Her knife was already moving before Edith had appeared. It was as though she had anticipated where she would be. Or, more likely, she had seen her think ahead.

"Clara!"

The shout had come from Mother. She was protecting Father from a handful of guards. She should have been able to deal with them easily, but the blood loss was clearly getting to her. I considered leaving them to it. They had left me to get electrocuted by Mr Righteous, after all. But they had also come to this fight willingly, and earlier, they had said some pretty nice things to me.

I picked up my gun from where it had fallen and sprinted through the trees towards them. I shot three guards, then the gun jammed. I reached out for my father's pain. The guard stumbled as he clutched his leg. I brought over my mother's pain. He fell over. I hit him on the head with the handle of the gun and chucked it aside.

Mother tutted. "I wouldn't have done it like that."

"No, I would have gone for the knees," Father said.

"You always go for the knees," Mother pointed out.

"And you always go for the testicles," Father countered.

She shrugged. "It's effective."

I turned on them. "You know, it's hard to kill people when you're criticising my methods."

"We were just trying to help, darling," Mother said innocently.

I looked back to where Morgan had been fighting Edith. I started running, but even as I did, I knew I would not get there in time.

Edith had Morgan pinned to the ground, her hands around her neck.

Chapter 26

As I ran, I reached out for someone's pain, but everyone who had been hurting was now dead. The only thing I had was Morgan's. I took it from her and threw it at Edith. I saw her flinch, but her hands remained around Morgan's neck. I needed more.

With my next step, I reached down and pulled Morgan's knife from my boot. Imagining it was Edith's face, I stabbed it into my hand. I took the pain and chucked it at her. Her hand loosened instinctively. Morgan punched her in the gut and rolled over, reversing their positions and pinning Edith to the ground. Edith vanished, taking Morgan with her.

I rotated on the spot. I couldn't see them anywhere.

"Morgan!" I shouted desperately.

They reappeared a few feet away from where they had disappeared. They were standing close together, but I could see blood. It was a lot of blood, and I couldn't tell who it was coming from. I was running again. Morgan took an unsteady step back. Edith crumpled to the floor.

I reached Morgan just as she doubled over.

"Are you hurt? Where is it?" I ran my hand over her abdomen, searching for an injury.

"I don't feel so good," she groaned.

"Did she stab you?"

She shook her head slowly. "Feel dizzy."

I didn't know whether I wanted to kill Morgan or kiss her. There I was, thinking she was about to die on me, and she was just suffering from a bit of motion sickness.

I glanced over at Edith. She was dead.

Morgan groaned, and I patted her on the back, then realised I was dripping more blood on her. I ripped one of the ruffles off my suit and wrapped it around the wound on my palm. Morgan straightened up and took my hand in hers. She pulled the makeshift bandage tight and tied it off for me.

"About that," she said, her voice sounding even scratchier than usual.

"It was really heroic, wasn't it?"

"It was the stupidest thing I have ever seen."

"I believe that's twice I've saved your life now. Maybe I really am a hero."

"Glad to see you didn't stab your ego."

I grinned and looked around at the carnage we had caused. Protestors were beginning to edge their way into the common, a little daunted by all the bodies.

"You should go," I told Morgan. "You're going to be in enough trouble as it is."

"What happens when I let you out of my sight? You jump off London Bridge, almost die fighting Mr Righteous, and stab yourself. I can't trust you to keep yourself safe. I'm here until the end."

"Then let's end this."

I set off running towards the lake. Morgan ran beside me, even though she could have outpaced me easily.

It was the first time I had seen the lake in daylight. Without the cloak of darkness, its motion was even harder to ignore. It was as wild as the ocean, battering the banks as though it could break free. John was trying to swim out of it, but it was as though the lake was fighting his every move. He managed to pull himself up onto the bank just as we arrived.

I kicked a barrel of chemicals and it fell over, tipping a white powder into the lake.

"Whoops," I deadpanned.

John looked up at me. He was soaked and streaked with mud.

"Edith is dead," I told him. "Mr Righteous is dead. Your secret is out, and your reputation is in ruins. How does it feel to have been bested by the nagging little thorn in your side?"

He spat out a mouthful of gunk. "You think anyone will thank you for this? You think the factories, the Brigade, the functionables will thank you?

You doomed them all."

"No, Johnny, you did the very moment you saw that and saw something you could control."

John followed my gaze over his shoulder. A huge clump of dirt was rising out of the lake. He began crawling as fast as he could away from it. I waited for it to shoot off, go kill some poor, hapless pedestrian, but it didn't. It was coming towards us. I pushed Morgan behind me and reached out with my function.

The dirt wrapped a tendril around John's ankle. He screamed as it spiralled up his body, wrapping him up in a thick layer of mud. It reached up over his face, pushing its way into his nose and mouth. He spasmed once, twice, then lay still. Another husk, just like all those other victims.

For the first, and probably last time in my life, I wished Quentin was there. I would have loved him to tell me how John looked post-death.

"Not so indestructible on the inside," I said.

A scream sounded behind me. Some of the protestors had made it to the lake. I thought it was me they were frightened of or perhaps the corpse at my feet, but then I realised their attention was fixed on something else. Another dirt monster was growing out of the lake.

I had to act fast. I could take its pain and stop it from killing anyone else, then siphon the pain amongst the crowd to make it more manageable.

The sucking sound began again, and another monster appeared. Maybe I had overdone it with the chemicals.

"Give me its pain," Morgan said.

"No."

"We don't have time for an argument, Clara."

The people were turning tail and running. One of the manifestations flew after them, the other shot up into the air. Before it had even disappeared from sight, another three had risen from the lake.

"Morgan, you know how you said you were here until the end? I think it's the end."

"No," she replied. "Not that."

"I just killed John Blythwood and unleashed a whole lot of monsters. If I don't do something very heroic right now, I'm going to jail for, like, ever."

"We don't know if it will work, or if it does, what it will do to you. You're not a self-sacrificing fool, remember?"

"Don't worry, I have enough spite to survive anything."

She reached out, looped an arm around my waist, grabbed me by the collar of my stupid costume, and pulled my face to hers. My lips pressed against her mask.

She pulled away. Around us, people were running and screaming as dirt creatures flew in every direction.

"Remember, if I can't kill you, no one can," Morgan said softly.

"You always say the sweetest things," I murmured back.

She took a step away, and I realised I had just engaged in a public display of affection. Even if everyone was a tad preoccupied with running for their lives, I still wanted to throw myself into the lake.

"I've got it," Morgan said, pointing to a part of the lake that looked just as turbulent as the rest of it. I reached out with my function.

Left a bit, Morgan said in my head. She steered me to a singular pain that felt no different from the rest.

There. Can you feel it?

No. I hoped she was right, because one of the manifestations was coming towards us. I started backing up instinctively.

"Hi Dirt Man, it's me, your good friend Clara. How are you feeling today? Headaches, nausea, the endless pain of being alive? Same."

Of all the stupid things I had ever done, this beat them all by a mile. Claiming I had murdered a lord to attract the attention of an assassin seemed like something someone with a strong sense of self-preservation would do compared to this.

Morgan reached out and squeezed my hand.

We had something in common, the Dirt Man and I. The world thought we were villains, but we weren't really. We had just been dealt a pretty bad hand. I hoped against hope that the Dirt Man would do me a favour as a friend and not kill me.

I took a deep breath and latched onto the pain. It was difficult to get a grip on it. It was like a fish, wriggling and slipping through my fingers. The manifestation was still coming for us, and every instinct was telling me to deal with the threat. I increased my focus, pulling hard enough to feel the strain in my muscles. Then suddenly, I had it. Morgan was right; it was the mind. I could feel the entire lake, the tentacles of *Lutum gigantos* spreading through it like a web. This was no little fish I had caught.

The pain stole my breath away. I was drowning in it, suffocating under its smothering weight. Nothing could live with this. It was forty years' worth of hazardous chemicals dumped arbitrarily. It was forty years' worth of abuse. I understood why the Dirt Man killed people. The Blythwoods could spout scientific jargon about it not having motivation until they were blue in the face. I felt what it felt, and I was about ready to murder everyone. The lake had changed from dazzling clear water to something rotten. *Lutum gigantos* had grown stronger, but at what cost? The sheer stupidity of it was staggering. This was what was happening inside us. If we carried on down this path, one day, we would all feel like this.

The lake and sky seemed to come together, which seemed strange, until my face hit the ground and I realised I had fallen. There was a strange mewling sound, like Mrs Winow's cat made that time I purposefully locked it outside. It was the kind of noise that made you pick up a sack and plan the route to the nearest river. It took an embarrassingly long time to figure out it was coming from me, and even then, I could not stop it. I had to hope no one had a sack large enough to fit me in.

"What's wrong with her?" I heard my father ask.

Morgan replied, but it was too low for me to understand. It was probably something threatening.

"She's just being dramatic," my mother said. "If you're going to marry her, you're going to have to get used to her theatrics. Did you see her stabbing her own hand back there? Classic Clara. Always trying to be the centre of attention."

Oh, to be released into the non-judgemental arms of death. I tried to do one good deed, and this was where it got me, lying on the ground in agony while my parents critiqued my decisions.

"The police are coming," Mother said.

"And that's our cue," Father replied. "Do give Clara our best when she comes around. Where do you fancy going, love?"

"I wouldn't mind a jaunt to Italy."

"Sounds delightful. It was a pleasure meeting you, Morgan."

I wanted to make the pain stop, but I couldn't pull away. It gnawed into my bones, dropping a match at the centre of my being, and burning away everything that I was. I could not pass it on. I could not even feel my function anymore. It was killing me. It was killing my mind.

No, it was not real. It was not my pain. I needed to focus on what was real. The ground beneath me was real. I was lying on my side, hands clawing in the mud. I could smell the earth mixed in with my own blood and sweat. I could see. My eyes were open, and the lake was in front of me. It was flat and still, without a single ripple to disturb it. I had to hope that was real. There was a hand on my shoulder.

"Clara, can you hear me?" It was Morgan. She sounded furious. "You need to calm your thoughts, Clara. You're spiralling."

I tried to respond, to tell her she had a terrible bedside manner, but words eluded me. There was a black fog growing in the corners of my vision, but I fought it off. I had to stay awake, because if I didn't, I might never return to the land of the living. And as tempting as that sounded, there was every possibility I would have to see Quentin holding some stupid sign that said, Sorry You Died, before I was released into the void. I would be forced to stare at that sign, to rage at him silently, and I would not even be able to punch him in the face. Of all the useless functions in the world, his had to top them. Although given the option, I would have traded with him in a heartbeat.

Function; what a stupid term. As though it was my duty to use the curse I had been lumped with, as though sparing myself this pain would make me an inadequate member of our society. To hell with them all. I was going to live through this, and then I was going to burn their city down. Or perhaps nap. Maybe both.

The blackness was nearing the centre of my vision, leaving only pinpricks of light. It seemed fitting that it looked like the light at the end of the tunnel. Maybe I really was dramatic.

There were more voices now, and the familiar sounds of excessive use of truncheons. The police were here. Morgan needed to leave. There was nothing she could do but make it worse. The police would try to arrest her, she would probably stab them, and I would have a harder time convincing everyone we were the innocent party in all of this. I could not speak it, so I tried to think it, but my thoughts were burning up partly formed, crumbling to ash in a mind all aflame. I could not feel her hand anymore. I didn't know if that was because she had left or because I was leaving my body for dead.

Then there were hands on me, moving me, prodding me. They might have been trying to find where I was hurt, or they might have just been beating me up. I tried again to pass on the pain, but everything was fuzzy. I wondered vaguely if I was still screaming, or whether my voice had finally given up. I could feel my muscles starting to relax as unconsciousness loomed closer. I fought to stay awake. My refusal to interact with Quentin was strong. I was strong.

But in the end, the darkness was stronger.

Chapter 27

People were talking. If I was dead, why were there people? If there really was an afterlife, I was going to be livid. All I wanted was some damn peace and quiet. My idea of heaven did not involve engaging with anybody, cosmic or not. Yet again, if I was truly dead, why did everything hurt? I was burning up. Huge tremors were surging through muscles that already felt bruised and battered. Yes, I would agree, all signs did seem to be pointing to hell.

I threw my pain out. Someone screamed, and there was a clatter, but I didn't care. The relief was euphoric. Either I wasn't in hell, or hell was not prepared for me.

I opened my eyes and found I was in a small, windowless room lit by gaslights. The only bed was mine, and I was handcuffed to it. I tugged on the cuffs. They rattled on the metal frame but remained secured. One of my hands was bandaged. My instinct was saying this was not hell. I was sure eternal damnation would involve more chains hanging from the ceiling and blood splatters on the wall. Still, it was giving off a sanitary-dungeon vibe.

The door opened and a man entered the room. He was wearing a lab coat and a frown. A doctor, I presumed.

"Miss Blakely, you are awake."

I reached out with my function. It was not him I had given my pain to. The only thing he was suffering from was shin splints.

"How are you feeling? Much better now I assume. I am afraid the same cannot be said for your nurse. You gave her quite a fright just now."

If I could have aimed for him, I would have. He placed a stethoscope against my chest. I noticed I was wearing a white linen nightdress, the kind they dished out in hospitals.

"How long was I out?" I asked. A long time, judging by the hoarseness of my throat.

"It has been four days since you were brought here from Mundmere. You were in a coma."

I couldn't believe it; the longest sleep of my life, and I didn't feel rested at all.

"Am I under arrest?"

He chuckled. "Oh yes."

"What about my parents?"

"Fled the scene. Left you for dead."

That was not surprising at all. "The assassin who was with me?" I asked, hoping that my heart was not speeding up.

"Also left. You don't have very good friends."

On the contrary, I had one smart friend. It was obvious whoever had put me here thought the same. The room was windowless for a reason. It was assassin-proof.

"What happened to the Dirt Man?" I asked.

"There have been no more attacks for the last four days."

I breathed a sigh of relief. I had done it, I had stopped the Dirt Man. They should have given me a medal, not handcuffed me to a bed. The ingratitude was almost hurtful.

The doctor wrapped up his stethoscope.

"How's my health?" I asked.

"Your heart is weak. I would recommend a period of convalescence by the sea, but unfortunately, I do not think prison organises such outings."

"When's my trial?"

"You'll have to wait for that, but there are some people who have been waiting to see you at your earliest possible convenience. I shall bring them in now." He headed for the door.

"Any chance you could uncuff me?" I called after him.

The door swung shut behind him. Of course, they would leave me cuffed. They wanted to make me feel as vulnerable as possible.

The door opened and three men walked in, unaccompanied by the doctor. They were dressed in smart suits that reeked of self-importance.

"Miss Blakely, I am the Chief Inspector of the Metropolitan Police," one of the men said. "This is the regional commander of the Hero Brigade and the lead scientist who has been assigned to Mundmere."

Incredible, three men I had never had any desire to meet.

"We find ourselves in a difficult situation," the chief inspector continued. "You are a criminal. Off the top of my head, we could charge you with murder, inciting a riot, and trespassing. However, the service you can provide is a unique one."

"We predict that *Lutum gigantos* will return," the scientist put in. "We have examined the work that, until recently, was being carried out in Mundmere, and we are, at this point, unsure how to prevent future attacks. So far, only your function has been successful against it."

The chief inspector cleared his throat. "In light of your function, we are willing to forgo your execution and settle on life imprisonment. In return for our leniency, every time there is an issue with the Dirt Man, you will be escorted to Mundmere to deal with it."

"No," I said.

Disbelief washed over their faces like a cascading waterfall. It was beautiful to watch.

"What do you mean, 'no?'" the Brigade commander demanded.

"I don't think you realise quite what a difficult situation you are in," I said. It was hard to seem cocky when lying handcuffed to a bed, but I rose to the challenge.

"The Dirt Man will come back, and unless I stop it, people will die. The protest at Mundmere proved how passionately this country feels about this particular problem. If you don't act fast, you could be looking at revolution." I waited patiently as I let my words sink in.

The men squirmed uncomfortably as they exchanged nervous looks.

"Of course, as a patriotic citizen, I am perfectly willing to help, but I have some conditions," I said, keeping my tone polite. "Firstly, I want a full pardon. All my previous misdemeanours must be wiped from the record. No more fines, no more community service, and certainly, no prison. Make me a hero. It shouldn't be that hard, there's a pretty low bar for heroes at the moment."

The commander spluttered. "That would be—"

"Oh, I'm not done," I interrupted. "Secondly, I want pardons for all my so-called accomplices. Even my parents," I added reluctantly, "on the condition that they commit no more crimes. We can't have it look like you are just handing out impunity.

"Thirdly, I want a full investigation into the Blythwoods' corruption. Not some half-hearted, 'They were one of us, so we'll let their reputation rest in peace,' rubbish. And I'm not going to make it a condition, but I highly recommend you pass a lot of laws very quickly to tackle pollution, because in my personal opinion, so long as Mundmere Lake is polluted, the Dirt Man is going to keep coming back. The sooner you deal with it, the faster you'll be rid of me."

I smiled at them. They stared at me.

"Those are some steep terms," the chief inspector said sharply.

"I could make them steeper," I offered.

"You seem to be forgetting that we have the power to make your life very uncomfortable," he retorted coldly.

"And you are forgetting that my function makes me immune to the British government's go-to method of enforced cooperation," I replied, matching his tone. "Go ahead, try to coerce me. See how that works out for you."

❖ ❖ ❖

I stood outside Scotland Yard, in the basement of which I had enjoyed such wonderful hospitality. I closed my eyes and tilted my head to the sky. It was nice to feel the sun, no matter how cold the air was. I shoved my hands deep into the pockets of the coat the chief inspector had been kind enough to give me. It was too big and smelt like someone had been murdered in it. I did not know what had happened to the Miss Take costume, but the world would be better off without it.

With a great flapping of wings, a pigeon swooped down from a window ledge and landed on my shoulder.

"Hello to you, demon bird," I said. "I see you survived your first knife fight."

He pecked me.

"No, I don't have any porridge."

He took off from my shoulder and vanished.

"I see how it is," I muttered to myself. It would appear Victor only liked me when I was buying him things. I supposed that was what came from being the breadwinner in the relationship.

An assassin dropped down beside me. I clutched my heart as it stuttered painfully. How was I supposed to convalesce with all these assassins in my life?

"Which one are you?" I asked.

"You would think by now you would be able to recognise me," Morgan said.

"Cut me some slack, I nearly died."

Morgan pulled back her hood far enough for me to see her eyebrows were furrowed disapprovingly. I was happy to see any part of her face.

"Hi," I said stupidly.

"Hello," she replied.

I could not think of anything further to say. I realised I didn't mind. This was enough. Wrapping the coat around me tighter, I began a leisurely stroll down the street. Morgan kept pace beside me. Passersby did a double take when they got close enough to identify me. Whispers of, "Is that Miss Take?" followed us like a bitter wind.

"Are you even allowed to talk to me?" I asked.

"Technically, no. You've been barred from the school."

"What does that mean?"

"If I take any contracts from you or engage with you socially, I will have my seal revoked. They called us all together and told us how disappointed they were that we got involved in exposing the Blythwoods. They pretended they knew which of us had participated in your coup, but it was all a façade. If they knew, the penalties would have been more severe."

"Then isn't this conversation forbidden?"

"I found a loophole," she said smugly.

"Do tell."

"You cannot hire me, but I can hire you as a pain reliever. I can converse with you in a professional sense."

"Are you in pain?"

"Very much so," she said seriously. "It is quite incessant."

"I see. It sounds serious. Of course, I will need regular contact for my relief to be effective."

"I'm not sure I can afford you."

"I have mates' rates," I assured her.

"That's funny, because Dan told me you charged him full price when you took his pain after he had fallen off a ladder even though you were the one who was supposed to be holding the ladder."

"I don't know what I did that made him think I was reliable enough to hold a ladder."

"You have a trustworthy face. I see you managed to charm your way out of trouble with the police."

"There wasn't much charm involved. It was mostly coercion." I turned right towards Westminster Abbey. "I'm not sure it was worth it. I don't want to have to take Dirt Man's pain again. That really sucked."

"Yes. Your thoughts stopped." Morgan was upset. I was upset about it too, but I did not want to examine my feelings too closely. The trauma was a problem for future me.

Morgan did not agree with this assessment. "What happened after the police took you away from Mundmere?"

I shrugged. "I don't know, I was in a coma."

"Should you even be walking around right now?"

I shrugged again. I could feel Morgan giving me her death stare.

"Any long-lasting effects?"

"Nothing I can't handle," I replied, thinking about the doctor's advice.

"You were told to avoid stressful situations?" she asked in disbelief. "Have they met you?"

"Get out of my head, Morgan. My medical records are private." There was no real venom in my voice. I had given up on my privacy by this point. "Look, if they thought I was about to die, they would have kept me in. I am valuable to them. At least for now."

"Why only for now?"

"I'm free for as long as the Dirt Man stalks the streets, but one day, they'll clean up Mundmere. And when they do, there will be no more Dirt Man, and they will have no more reason to entertain my demands."

"Bold of you to assume they'll clean up Mundmere."

"It's in their interests."

"It's out of their pockets," she countered.

I nodded. "True. Maybe I'm safe after all. The world may be destroyed, but I won't go to prison. It's not a very comforting thought, actually."

It was hard to think that anything would ever change. Great clouds of black smoke rose into the cold, blue sky from the hulking chimneys that decorated the skyline like candles on a birthday cake. It would take a lot to suck the smoke from the sky and scrape the filth out of the sea. All evidence pointed against it, but who knew? Maybe they would surprise us all and do the right thing for once.

I realised I had just had an optimistic thought. Gross.

Darcy is rubbing off on you, Morgan said.

I grimaced. "Please take that back. If I lose my pessimism, I won't recognise myself."

"Roll up, roll up. Hear all about it!" screamed a boy selling newspapers. "Eyewitness says Miss Take has started throwing up dirt!"

I stopped as we passed him. "What the hell? I'm right here."

The boy gawked at me, then he adjusted his hat and smiled sheepishly. "Sorry, miss, I'm just trying to sell papers."

"Fair enough," I said wearily. "Carry on."

"Miss Take is growing horns and a tail!" he screeched as we walked on.

Unbelievable. The government's propaganda division was going to be working overtime trying to turn me into some kind of godsend.

Waiting for a carriage to pass before crossing the street, I realised I had no idea where I was going. I didn't have any money, and though the charges against me were being dropped, it would take a while for that to filter into common knowledge. It would be some time before I could walk into any upmarket establishment without a well-meaning patron calling the police on me.

"We should go and see the others," Morgan said. "They have been worried about you. Darcy and Quentin are mad at you for lying to them, of course, but they would still like to know that you are alive."

I groaned. Just what I needed, to be smothered in sympathy. Was it too late to go back and ask for an execution?

Morgan shook her head at me, but her eyes were crinkling at the edges.

"I suppose," she said slowly, "that we could pretend you are still being imprisoned and go get a drink instead. It probably goes against your medical advice, but today feels like a good day for making bad choices."

I grinned. "Morgan, you just read my mind."

About the Author

Faye Murphy has a degree in English literature and history, and a master's in international heritage. She lives in Surrey, England, where her pet pigs exploit her preoccupation with writing by digging up the lawn.